DEATH IN POTTER'S WOODS

Death in Potter's Woods

A Witherston Murder Mystery

BETTY JEAN CRAIGE

LUMINARE PRESS
WWW.LUMINAREPRESS.COM

Death in Potter's Woods: A Witherston Murder Mystery
Copyright © 2021 by Betty Jean Craige

Printed in the United States of America

Luminare Press
442 Charnelton St.
Eugene, OR 97401
www.luminarepress.com

LCCN: 2021920746
ISBN: 978-1-64388-835-4

Acknowledgments

In mid-March of 2020, in the early weeks of the COVID-19 pandemic, the wise mayor and the wise Commissioners of Athens, Georgia, issued a shelter-in-place order. I applauded their difficult decision and then got down in the dumps. I stayed down in the dumps until I heard the Reverend Al Sharpton remark, "When I'd get hauled off to jail, I'd tell myself, Don't serve time; let time serve you." Wow, I said, that's the best advice from a preacher I ever heard! My brother said, "That's the only advice from a preacher you ever heard." Anyway, that very evening I began working on this mystery. Thank you, Rev.

I would like to thank my dear friends Susan Tate and Margaret Anderson for their critical reading of the manuscript now titled *Death in Potter's Woods*. Susan and Margaret have read all the fiction I've written and have advised me well. For their encouragement and their loyal friendship over many years, I owe them more than I can say.

I would not have chosen to write mysteries without the influence of my Mystery Lunch Group, which includes Margaret, Linda Schramm, Nelle Shehane, and Barbara Timmons.

I thank my oldest best friend, Sue Moore Manning, whose artistic talent I've admired since first grade, for the delightful drawing she contributed to *Death in Potter's Woods*. Thank you, Sue!

I thank Cosmo, my smart, talkative, mischievous, funny African Grey parrot, for amusing me endlessly during the pandemic.

And I thank Julia Butterfly Hill, author of *The Legacy of Luna*, and Suzanne Simard, author of *Finding the Mother Tree*, for inspiring me with their books.

As always, I am grateful to the late Terry Kay and the late Judith Ortiz Cofer for urging me to write fiction.

The year 2020 was a turning point for humans everywhere. We kept our distance from each other, which eliminated our hugs. We wore masks, which hid our smiles. We feared crowds, which halted our travel. We found new meaning in the phrase "Aging in place." And we realized that we could never predict the future. So let us seize the day and remember Al Sharpton's counsel: "Don't serve time; let time serve you."

Witherston, Georgia

LOCATION: Lumpkin County, Georgia, USA. The town of Witherston, founded in 1860, is located in the southern Appalachian mountains 20 miles north of Dahlonega in Saloli Valley. The incorporated area of 39.9 square miles includes Tayanita Village, a community of fifteen-to-twenty young men and women whose Cherokee ancestors occupied north Georgia, southern Tennessee, and western North Carolina for a thousand years.

POPULATION: 3,916 (2018)

WITHERSTON CITY OFFICIALS as of January 1, 2019: Rhonda Rather, mayor; Neel Kingfisher, chair of the Town Council; Trevor Bennington, Jr., Tabby Grammer, Lydia Gray, Ruth Griggs, and Blanca Zamora, members of the Town Council

TAYANITA VILLAGE OFFICIALS as of July 1, 2018: John Hicks, chief; Amadahy Henderson, treasurer; Sequoyah Waters, historian

WITHERSTON POLICE DEPARTMENT: Mev Arroyo, chief; John Hicks, detective; Pete Koslowsky, officer.

WITHERSTON VOLUNTEER FIRE DEPARTMENT: Bobby Bracker, chief

ONLINEWITHERSTON.COM: Catherine Soto-Perry, publisher; Amadahy Henderson, editor; Dr. Charlotte Byrd, columnist; Jorge Arroyo, columnist and cartoonist.

SCHOOLS: Witherston Elementary School; Witherston Middle School; Witherston High School

CHURCHES: Witherston Baptist Church; Witherston Methodist Church; Frederick Douglass Baptist Church

Every contact leaves a trace.
—Edmond Locard
(1877–1966)

PROLOGUE

On Friday, December twentieth, 2019, Robin Hood reread an item in the *Blue Ridge Quarterly*.

> *Witherston, situated in the southern Appalachian mountains of north Georgia, is the fifth richest small town in the United States, according to IRS records.*
>
> *Witherston received its name from the gold-digger Hearty Withers. Hearty Withers, born in 1798, made a fortune in the 1828 Dahlonega Gold Rush, won 40 acres in the 1832 Georgia Land Lottery, and established a settlement he called "Witherstown" on the ruins of the Cherokee village Tayanita.*
>
> *Hearty Withers's great-great grandson, Francis Hearty Withers, inherited his wealth and increased it exponentially.*
>
> *Francis Hearty Withers bequeathed $1 billion to be divided evenly among the residents of Witherston—approximately $250,000 to every man, woman, and child—upon his death in 2015.*
>
> *Witherston is the home of the acclaimed writer Tabitha Grammer.*

"Now is the time to make Francis Hearty Withers's beneficiaries pay for Hearty Withers's theft of gold and land,"

Robin Hood said aloud. "This paragraph will do it."

By midnight on Wednesday, December 25, exactly 3,000 of Francis Hearty Withers's beneficiaries— that's 75 percent of Witherston's population—must each contribute $5,000 of their inheritance to the Indigenous Peoples Reparations Initiative, or Mayor Rhonda Rather will die, along with other beneficiaries who do not contribute. I do not jest. I am no stranger to murder.

Robin Hood hesitated. "Will that last sentence advance my cause? It's ambiguous enough. But it could hurt me if I'm caught."

Robin Hood deleted the reference to murder and emailed the letter to OnlineWitherston.

BETTY JEAN CRAIGE

CHAPTER ONE
Friday, December 20, 2019

"Tonight I present the Key to the City to our own Tabby Grammer, author of the best-selling murder mysteries *Interred in the Low Country*, *Revenge of the Brave*, and *OnlineCrime*, the children's book *Gaia Says*, and the new non-fiction book *Paving Gaia*."

The guests who filled Witherston's Pinetops Hall applauded.

"Thank you, Mayor Rather, for the honor you and your city have bestowed on me," Tabby Grammer said, accepting a glass box with a large brass skeleton key stamped KEY TO WITHERSTON from the stylish politician with curly platinum hair and glossy red lipstick and nails.

Mayor Rhonda Rather raised her glass as a tribute. Fifty-six-year-old Rhonda Rather wore a red velvet tunic over black knit pants with high-heeled boots and a royal blue Christmas-tree silk scarf. She carried a red Brahmin tote bag. As always, she held everybody's attention. Rhonda had succeeded her husband Rich in Witherston's 2018 mayoral election and had replaced most of his policies with her own progressive ones. Rich died of a heart attack a month after she took office.

"You're my favorite writer, Tabby!" she said as she lifted her beloved Coco Chanel off her chair on the dais, sat down, and settled the nine-pound Pomeranian on her lap.

Tabby Grammer moved to the podium. She wore Birkenstock boots, tight jeans, and a chartreuse sweatshirt with SAVE GAIA embroidered in navy on the back. Her black hair was piled high on her head. Her red nail polish matched her lipstick.

"And thank you, Neel, for the flattering introduction," Tabby said.

Dr. Neel Kingfisher chaired the Witherston Town Council. After retiring from a medical career, he devoted himself to his garden, his peacocks, his books, his collection of local art, and his wife Gretchen Green. He also took an active role in Witherston's civic life.

Neel gave Tabby a thumbs up. "Talk to us, Tabby."

The audience clapped.

"I'm texting Annie," Jaime Arroyo whispered to his identical twin Jorge. "I want see how she's doing up in Big Yellow." Annie Jerden, Jaime's former girlfriend, had just moved into the county's tallest tree to protest developer Thomas Tankard's planned clear-cutting of Potter's Woods.

"You still love Annie, don't you?" Jorge whispered back.

Jaime texted Annie. Annie texted back. They would see each other in Big Yellow the next day at two o'clock. Jaime sent her a thumbs-up and a heart emoji.

Jaime and Jorge sat together on the second row with their father Paco Arroyo, a high school biology teacher, and their mother Mev Arroyo, chief of the Witherston Police Department.

Inside Pinetops Hall a hundred curious people awaited Tabby Grammer's speech.

"I am happy to talk about *Paving Gaia*," Tabby Grammer began. "After writing three books of fiction in which humans murdered humans, I decided to write the non-fiction book

Paving Gaia about humans murdering non-humans, or more specifically, about humans murdering Earth.

"I had initially titled the book 'Paving Paradise,' as a nod to Joni Mitchell's lines 'They paved paradise / and put up a parking lot.' Joni Mitchell wrote the song 'Big Yellow Taxi' in Honolulu when she saw gorgeous green mountains in the distance and pavement extending almost that far out. I changed the title to 'Paving Gaia' because I didn't like the biblical concept of 'paradise.' I don't believe that Earth was created for us humans.

"The day *Paving Gaia* was released, three weeks ago," Tabby continued, "I learned that an old-growth forest several miles north of downtown Witherston was about to be razed. Now I see how relevant the book is to our community. Mr. Thomas Tankard will pave Gaia and put up a subdivision. I ask, what are we going to do about it?"

"Wait, Mrs. Grammer," a lady on the front row called out. "You've lived in Witherston for only three years, so you're not part of 'we.' Do you really think we are going to listen to you?"

"You're right, I've lived here for only a short while, but I can imagine what's about to happen to Witherston. Mr. Tankard will log Potter's Woods and bulldoze the undergrowth to make a clearing for a hundred houses. The owners of the new houses will want trees and bushes, so they'll buy young specimens from a nursery. They'll plant grass, which they'll have to mow. They'll put up squirrel-proof bird feeders to attract the birds and keep out the squirrels, and they'll fence in their gardens to keep out the deer. They'll shoot the occasional coyote."

"The deer were there first," Jorge interrupted. "So was the coyote."

"That's my point, Jorge. So was the forest."

A well-dressed man with sandy hair stood up. "I am Thomas Tankard," he said. "I built the houses many of you all live in. And I own Potter's Woods."

"Hello, Mr. Tankard," Tabby Grammer said. "I have nothing against you personally. I simply oppose the logging of old-growth forests that once gone will be gone forever."

"Do you not believe in private property?"

"I do. But I also believe in public property, Mr. Tankard, such as air and water and old-growth forests, which the community needs for the health of its members. Such resources should not belong to a single individual."

"True," someone shouted from the back. "Nobody gets to own a river. Not even rich people like you, Mr. Tankard."

"Will you read a passage from your book, Mrs. Grammer?" Neel asked.

"I'll read the preface." Tabby opened her book.

We humans have taken three thousand years to pave Earth, but we did it.

In Genesis 1:28, God ordered humans to "Be fruitful, and multiply, and replenish the earth, and subdue it: and have dominion over the fish of the sea, and over the fowl of the air, and over every living thing that moveth upon the earth."

And that's what we did. We multiplied so well that we now number eight billion people. We subdued the earth by replacing wilderness with cities, displacing the animals and plants that once lived there. We took control of the land, the sea, and the air. We took dominion over every living thing on Earth.

BETTY JEAN CRAIGE

We turned the living stuff of Earth into commodities for us humans.

In Paving Gaia I tell the history of Earth from Earth's viewpoint, that is, Gaia's viewpoint. In Greek mythology, Gaia is the Earth goddess and the mother of all nature. In my book, Gaia is Earth.

I am motivated by the belief that Gaia's long-term health should take priority over humans' immediate desires.

"Thank you," Tabby said as she closed her book. "Do you all have any questions?"

"I like your personification of Earth as Gaia. Would you call yourself a Gaia-centrist?"

"Yes, Neel. I'm a Gaia-centric environmentalist who tries to see human activity from Gaia's viewpoint."

"After reading your book I've come to think of myself as a Gaia-centrist. Gretchen and I have been vegetarians for years, to reduce our impact on the earth," Neel said.

"I am a vegetarian too, Neel. I want my impact on Earth to be minimal."

"Sounds like you want our impact to be minimal too," Ruth Griggs said. "Well, you're not going to come to Witherston from Savannah and tell us what to do with our lives or what to do with our land." Ruth Griggs, a three-term Council member, represented Witherston's conservatives.

"Right, Ruth!"

"You tell her, Ruth!"

"Be quiet, Ruth," Blanca Zamora said. Blanca owned Zamora Winery and also served on the Town Council. She and Ruth opposed each other on almost every issue that came before the board.

"Is it true you keep a goat?" Pastor Paul Clement asked.

"Yes, that is true. Allie Baba is my pet. She lives in the field behind my house."

"Allie Baba is a Muslim name," Pastor Clement said.

"Allie Baba is not religious," Tabby said. "Neither am I. Neither is my kitten Smoky. We are all three atheists."

"Are you married?"

"No, I am divorced. Is that relevant?"

"I just wondered," Ruth said.

"Will you please explain Gaia-centric environmentalism to our audience, Tabby," Lottie Byrd asked. Dr. Charlotte Byrd, a retired journalist affectionately known as "Lottie," knew that Tabby's environmentalism was much like hers. Lottie had supported environmental causes for over forty years—as a student at the University of Georgia in the seventies and thereafter as a history professor at Hickory Mountain College. When she retired she moved to Witherston next door to her niece Mev Arroyo, wrote a book about the Cherokees titled *Moccasins in the Mountains*, and published an online column titled "North Georgia in History."

"Of course, Lottie," Tabby said. "A Gaia-centric environmentalist judges human actions by their effect on the planet, rather than by their benefit to us humans. A Gaia-centric environmentalist says 'Gaia first.'"

"Gaia-centrists believe that we humans have no right to subordinate the lives of other living beings to our own lives," Rhonda spoke out from her seat on the stage.

"In a capsule it means that Earth does not belong to us," Tabby said. "We belong to Earth."

"Whoa," twenty-year-old Doug Hanley stood up. "So you're an atheist, a vegetarian, and a so-called Gaia-centric environmentalist. I'll bet you're some sort of egalitarian too.

Would you sacrifice your own life for the life of Gaia? I'm telling you, I won't sacrifice mine."

"Hey, Doug," Jorge said. "Give Mrs. Grammer some respect. She's written a whole book on Gaia that most of us haven't read."

Doug sat down.

Jorge knew Doug from the service station where Doug worked. Doug was a passionate reader and had always engaged Jorge and Jaime in discussions of books. Instead of going to college Doug had emptied his savings account to buy a Lamborghini.

Sequoyah Waters raised his hand. "Would you call the Cherokees Gaia-centric?"

"Yes, Seq. The Cherokees' first commandment is 'Treat the Earth and all that dwell thereon with respect.' The European settlers and their descendants ignored their wisdom."

Tabby knew that Seq Waters had taken his Cherokee name from Chief Sequoyah when he moved to Tayanita Village.

Seq continued. "Did you know that the Cherokees had no concept of private property? The European settlers not only stole the Cherokees' land, but they also replaced the Cherokees' Gaia-centric ethics with their capitalist concept of private property."

"I do know that, Seq. That's how the European settlers were able to take the land. The Cherokees didn't know that land could be bought and sold."

"We are occupying Cherokee land right here in Pinetops Hall," Seq said.

"Sit down, Seq," Neel said. "Let's not get into this now."

"Can we talk sometime, Mrs. Grammer?" Seq asked.

"It would be my pleasure, Seq," she said. "Call me. We'll have dinner."

The door to the left of the stage opened and Amadahy Henderson, editor of OnlineWitherston, approached the mayor and handed her a note. Rhonda read it and turned pale.

Tabby Grammer looked over. "Is anything wrong?" she asked.

"You tell them," Rhonda said to Amadahy. "Go ahead, take the mic."

Tabby handed the mic to Amadahy.

"I must report a threat to Mayor Rather's life," Amadahy said. "You all will soon read a letter to the editor in OnlineWitherston signed by, quote, Robin Hood. Robin Hood demands that three thousand beneficiaries of Francis Hearty Withers's fortune donate five thousand dollars each to the Indigenous Peoples Reparations Initiative by midnight, December twenty-fifth. That's Wednesday. Otherwise, Mayor Rather will lose her life."

"Oh, no!" Tabby exclaimed.

"And so will another beneficiary, someone who does not donate," Amadahy added.

"Can you trace it?" Jorge asked.

"It was emailed to us anonymously," Amadahy said.

"It's extortion!" Ruth Griggs exclaimed.

"This Robin Hood writes that we owe our bequest to the Cherokees, that our wealth originated in Hearty Withers's theft of Cherokee gold and land," Amadahy said.

"Is that commune Tayanita Village behind this?" Ruth asked. "You Indians all got your share of Withers's money. You spent it on yurts."

Amadahy Henderson, of Cherokee descent, lived at Tayanita Village with her husband and three-year-old daughter. A few years ago they had founded Tayanita Village as a commune modeled after an eighteenth-century Cherokee settlement. The villagers, who included Sequoya Waters, now numbered sixteen.

"Could you please be kind, Mrs. Griggs. In Tayanita Village we try to be kind to one another," Amadahy said.

"Robin Hood is not getting a cent from me," Ruth replied.

"Is Rhonda's life not worth five thousand dollars to you, Mrs. Griggs?" Lottie raised her voice to accommodate Ruth's deafness. "Or have you spent all your money?"

"Mind your own business, Dr. Byrd."

"*Cállate*, Ruth," Blanca Zamora muttered audibly.

"Maybe this is a joke to scare us into giving our money away," someone said.

"The Federal Bureau of Investigation does not take this as a joke," Amadahy said. "I contacted the FBI. The FBI will help the Witherston Police find Robin Hood. Special Agent Debra Danzer may interview some of you."

"Does Agent Danzer think Robin Hood is one of us?"

"Not necessarily," Amadahy said. "But possibly."

"Let's hear from the mayor!"

Mayor Rhonda Rather stood up and took the mic.

"I don't take Robin Hood's threat as a joke. Robin Hood obviously wants me out of office," she said. "And I've been in office less than a year."

Rhonda could not help playing the comic.

A man on the fourth row waved his cane. "Mayor Rather, I'd like to speak, if I may," he said. Trevor Bennington, Jr., a stockbroker, a member of the Town Council and a defeated candidate for mayor, walked carefully down the aisle and onto the stage. He took the mic.

"Before you liberals capitulate to this extortionist, let me remind you that Robin Hood of Sherwood Forest was an outlaw. So is this Robin Hood. Only this Robin Hood is craftier. If we give him our money, he will come back next year for more. Or somebody else will. I urge you all—every one of you—to refuse his demand."

Sam Farthy, owner of Farthy Construction Company, stood up. "I agree. Robin Hood can't tell us what to do with our money."

"Robin Hood of Sherwood Forest was an outlaw, but a good outlaw," Lottie said. "Maybe our extortionist took the name Robin Hood because he's righting a wrong."

"If you're siding with this Robin Hood, then you're as much an extortionist as he is," Sam Farthy said.

"Francis Hearty Withers left us all a lot of money," Lottie said. "Why won't you give a small percentage of yours to indigenous peoples?"

"Because I'm law-abiding."

"Tabby, do you favor reparations to indigenous peoples?" Rhonda asked.

"I do," Tabby Grammer said, "in the form of free education. And I refer to indigenous peoples as Native Americans."

"I favor reparations for Native Americans too," Rhonda said.

"How about reparations for the descendants of slaves?" Ruth asked.

"May I be heard, please," Trevor Bennington said. "The police can protect Mayor Rather until the FBI captures Robin Hood. Agreed, Chief Arroyo?"

"Of course, Trevor. That's what we do. Protect our citizens from harm," Mev said.

Ruth Griggs raised her hand. "Mrs. Grammer, will you give five thousand dollars?"

"Of course."

"Are you Cherokee? You look Cherokee," a woman asked.

"I take that as a compliment. I am part Cherokee."

"Mrs. Grammer, are you Robin Hood?" Sam Farthy asked.

"I refuse to answer that silly question."

"She is! She is!" another responded.

Seq stood up again and faced the audience. "Whether Mrs. Grammer or somebody else is Robin Hood is irrelevant. Robin Hood represents justice. I ask you beneficiaries of Francis Hearty Withers's fortune, don't you feel guilty that you inherited dirty money?"

"Do you favor reparations too, Mr. Sequoyah half-breed?" Sam asked.

"Yes, sir, I do. I favor reparations for half-breeds like me because your white ancestors raped my Cherokee ancestors and you owe me more than an ethnic slur."

Neel took the mic. "Sit down, Sam. Sit down Seq. Hey, folks. I think it's time we adjourned for tonight. But I ask the Town Council to join me in the dining room to discuss Robin Hood's letter."

"I suggest you excuse Mrs. Grammer from this meeting," Ruth said. "She's made her position known."

Tabby had been elected to the Council the previous November.

"Thank you, Ruth," Tabby said.

"That's fine," Neel said. "Now let us all give a hand to Tabby Grammer for what she has done for our community. Thank you, Tabby. We'll get you to sign our copies of *Paving Gaia* another time."

Lottie, Jorge, and Jaime gave her a standing ovation, inspiring half the audience to do the same. Seq stood as well.

The other half remained seated.

"I have one unrelated announcement to make before you leave," Rhonda said. "Neel Kingfisher needs volunteers tomorrow to start converting the old Gertrude Withers School building into a Witherston Museum of Material Culture. I have appointed Dr. Kingfisher as project manager and Ms. Grammer as curator."

Rhonda looked directly at Jorge and Jaime.

"Jorge and I can do it," Jaime said.

"Be there at ten o'clock tomorrow," Neel said.

Descending the steps of the stage, Tabby bumped into Lydia Gray, owner of Gray's Farm.

"May I come see you, Tabby, before the Board meeting? I'll call ahead of time."

"Certainly, Lydia. I always enjoy getting together."

Then Tabby saw Lottie.

"Hey, Lottie. Thanks for helping out," Tabby said.

"I enjoyed the evening, Tabby. Would you like to join us for a drink at my place? I'll give you a lift."

CHAPTER TWO

Friday, December 20, 2019

OnlineWitherston.com

NEWS BULLETIN
ROBIN HOOD THREATENS WITHERSTON

This evening at 7:35 pm OnlineWitherston received a letter to the editor signed "Robin Hood." After consultation with our publisher and with the Federal Bureau of Investigation, I have decided to publish the letter in full. The FBI asks anybody with knowledge of "Robin Hood" to contact either local police, the FBI, or WitherstonOnline immediately.

—Amadahy Henderson, Editor

———•—

LETTERS TO THE EDITOR

To the Editor:

Historians have exposed the crime underpinning America's prosperity: the theft of land, gold, and minerals from the original inhabitants of this continent.

The descendants of Hearty Withers benefitted directly from such theft. Hearty Withers mined successfully for gold in 1828—gold that belonged to the Cherokees—and passed his fortune on to his heirs. His great-great-great grandson, Francis Hearty Withers, III, divided it among the residents of Witherston.

This Christmas Witherston will rectify the injustice done to the Cherokees.

By midnight on Wednesday, December 25, exactly 3,000 of Francis Hearty Withers's beneficiaries—that's 75 percent of Witherston's population— must each contribute $5,000 to the Indigenous Peoples Reparations Initiative, or Mayor Rhonda Rather will die, along with other beneficiaries who do not contribute. I do not jest.

The contribution may be made in either of two ways:

1) Transfer $5,000 to the bank account of "Online-Witherston" in the Bill-Pay category of Newspapers, Magazines, and Subscriptions, with an email to Amadahy Henderson, Editor; OR

2) Send a check for $5,000 to Amadahy Henderson, Editor, made out to "OnlineWitherston" with the words "For Reparations" in the "For" line.

Amadahy Henderson, if she values the mayor's life and the life of any other resident of Witherston, will send the money to the Indigenous Peoples Reparations Initiative (c/o Kallik Kootoo, P.O. Box 76992, Juneau, Alaska 99803).

OnlineWitherston will publish daily a list of contributors under the headline "Contributors to Indigenous Peoples Reparations Initiative," so that everybody will know who contributes.

Betty Jean Craige

The $15 million Witherston will raise for IPRI will not adequately reimburse the indigenous peoples for their loss of gold and land to white settlers with guns, but it will be a start. It may be a model.

—*Robin Hood*

CHAPTER THREE

Friday, December 20, 2019

The members of the Council, minus Tabby Grammer, sat down at a large oblong table in the Witherston Inn dining room. They included Lydia Gray, Blanca Zamora, Trevor Bennington, Jr., and Ruth Griggs, with Mayor Rhonda Rather as an *ex officio* non-voting member.

"Thank you, Blanca, for treating us to this excellent wine," Neel said as he called the meeting to order.

Blanca Zamora had ordered a couple of bottles of her winery's best red blend. "Just remember the label," she said.

"Thank you, Blanca."

"Thanks, Blanca."

Mayor Rather took two seats, one for herself and the other for Coco Chanel. "I will give Robin Hood ten thousand dollars—five from my late husband Rich and five from me," she said. "I hope you all will contribute too. After all, five thousand dollars is a small percentage of your inheritance."

"It's two percent," Blanca said.

"So you'd reward Robin Hood with ten thousand dollars for threatening your life," Trevor said. "I should have guessed as much."

"She's doing it to save her life," Ruth said.

"I'm not giving the ten thousand dollars to Robin Hood, Trevor," Rhonda said. "I'm giving the ten thousand dollars to the Indigenous Peoples Reparations Initiative. There's a big difference."

"Quiet please. I'd like to read Robin Hood's letter to you all," Neel said, looking at his laptop.

Neel read the entire letter aloud. After some seconds of silence he asked, "Should the Board reply to Robin Hood's email?"

"I say Robin Hood's email doesn't merit a reply," Trevor said. "If we reply we consent to discussing the matter with him."

"Or her. Robin Hood could be a woman," Blanca said. "Women are just as capable as men of committing crimes."

"Let me continue, Blanca. Instead of replying, I would like for the board to order the citizens of Witherston to ignore the email. I'd be happy to write something," Trevor said.

"Whoa, Trevor. What happens to me?" Rhonda asked.

"We have to be theoretical here, Madame Mayor," Trevor said.

"I think I should leave. May I, Neel?"

"Certainly, Rhonda."

"Bye, folks. I'll buy you each a drink if you'll save my life. Otherwise I won't." With that, Rhonda put Coco Chanel into her capacious tote bag and departed.

"Rhonda may take Robin Hood's threat lightly, but I don't," Neel said. "If the board does anything officially, her life is our responsibility."

"I think that the board should not do anything," Blanca said. "It's not our business to tell people what to do."

"We were elected to the board to tell people what to do," Trevor said.

"You lost the election for mayor because people didn't want you to tell them what to do, Mr. Bennington," Blanca said. "Rhonda doesn't tell anybody what to do. I say, leave it up to everybody to do what they think is right."

"I refuse to pay five thousand dollars of my own money to an extortionist," Ruth Griggs said. "But I wouldn't mind if the municipality of Witherston saved the mayor's life."

"How would that work, Ruth?" Neel said.

"Witherston could provide fifteen million dollars from its treasury to send to those indigenous people. That's what I propose."

"We can't decide tonight, because Tabby Grammer is not here, but we can put your proposal on our December twenty-fifth agenda."

"Please do," Ruth said.

"What's the issue here, Neel?" Trevor asked. "Reparations or extortion? I think we're talking about extortion, and I am vehemently opposed to paying off an extortionist."

"If you vote for my proposal, Trevor, then you don't have to pay off an extortionist yourself," Ruth said. "The municipality of Witherston pays, and nobody loses any money."

"Doesn't anybody here see the logic of Robin Hood's demands? Robin Hood is trying to right a wrong," Neel said.

"Unlawfully. Extortion is a felony," Trevor said.

"But Robin Hood has a point, Trevor. Our windfall comes from a crime against the Cherokees," Neel said.

"I didn't commit the crime," Trevor said. "So why should I pay for it?"

"Where did you get your money, Mr. Trevor Bennington junior? I think you got it from your rich father Mr. Trevor Bennington senior."

"That's not the point, Blanca," Trevor said.

"That is the point of reparations, isn't it, Trevor," Neel said. "You oppose reparations because you don't believe that historical injustices should be rectified."

"Yes, Neel. I don't believe that individuals living now should be punished for the sins of their fathers. We can't redo history. That's my position. Evidently, it's not yours."

"I have not decided my position, Trevor. But I know that that historical events can cast long shadows of injustice," Neel said.

———•———

LOTTIE OPENED HER UNLOCKED BACK DOOR AND USH-ered Tabby Grammer into her home.

"Have a seat while I get us some wine," Lottie said to her fellow writer. "I assume you'll have a glass of Rioja?"

"I've never turned down an offer."

"Neither have we, Aunt Lottie!" Jorge called out.

"Hey, Aunt Lottie," Jaime said. "Thanks for inviting us."

Hamlet, their Great Dane, followed them into the living room.

"Hello, Mrs. Grammer," Jorge said. "We're Gaia-centrists too. We're going to read your books."

An African Grey parrot flew from the top of the Christmas tree onto Tabby's right shoulder.

"Well, hello!" Tabby exclaimed.

"Meet Doolittle," Lottie said.

Doolittle flew onto Lottie's outstretched hand.

The door opened again.

"Hey there, everybody!"

"Hey Pop, hey Mom."

Paco Arroyo carried in a plate with sliced salami. Mev followed with Roquefort cheese and crackers.

Lottie opened two bottles of Rioja and poured glasses for all.

"Now for a toast," she said. "Here's to my favorite mystery writer, friend of the Cherokees, protector of nature, Gaia-centrist, and recipient of the Key to the City. Congratulations, Tabby!"

"And here's to Lottie," Tabby replied, "my favorite historian, wine connoisseur, gourmet cook, animal rights advocate, environmentalist, and indefatigable supporter of progressive causes!"

"Attention, everyone," Jorge said, looking at the screen of his phone. He read aloud the letter to the editor from Robin Hood.

"Oh, Lord!" Tabby exclaimed. "Robin Hood is threatening not just Rhonda but every single one of Withers's beneficiaries!"

"He's scaring the beneficiaries who don't contribute," Jorge said.

"How do you know Robin Hood is a he?" Lottie said.

"I guess Robin Hood could be Mrs. Grammer." Jorge said.

"Not likely," Tabby said.

"Here's the key sentence in Robin Hood's letter," Jaime said, reading over Jorge's shoulder.

By midnight on Wednesday, December 25, exactly 3,000 of Francis Hearty Withers's beneficiaries— that's 75 percent of Witherston's population—must each contribute $5,000 to the Indigenous Peoples Reparations Initiative, or Mayor Rhonda Rather will die, along with other beneficiaries who do not contribute. I do not jest.

"Along with other beneficiaries who do not contribute," Jorge repeated. "That's the motivator."

"Rhonda got only fifty-one percent of the votes," Lottie said. "She doesn't have three thousand supporters."

"Robin Hood knows that," Jaime said. "He's torturing the forty-nine percent who voted for Trevor Bennington."

"He's torturing everyone who doesn't want to part with five thousand dollars," Jorge said.

"Robin Hood doesn't say when his or her victims will die. Everybody dies at some time or other. Maybe this is not a threat."

"It was meant as a threat, Lottie," Paco said.

"Robin Hood is playing a game with us," Jorge said. "Assume you're not a fan of Rhonda's and you don't want to contribute five thousand dollars to save her life. So why would you contribute?"

"Whoa, Jorge," Jaime said. "Lots of people who voted against Rhonda would not want her to get murdered."

"I know, I know," Jorge said. "But this is a game. Say you don't particularly care about Rhonda's life, but you care about your own. Say you're a selfish creep who doesn't want to give up five thousand dollars. So you wait to see how many of your fellow citizens will pay in the next few days, and on the morning of December twenty-fifth, if the money doesn't amount to fifteen million dollars, you decide whether to risk your life."

"Or Rhonda's," Lottie said. "If the the money doesn't amount to fifteen million dollars by midnight Wednesday, Rhonda loses her life and one of the non-donors loses his. Or hers. But nobody knows who, or when."

"It's a beautiful game," Jorge says. "If by midnight Wednesday there's not fifteen million dollars, then all the non-contributing beneficiaries of Withers will suffer torment until one of them dies."

"Not to mention Rhonda," Mev said.

"You all, we're focusing on the game," Lottie said. "I think we should focus on Robin Hood's moral argument." She leaned over Jorge's shoulder and read aloud:

Here's the logic: Witherston's wealth was derived from a crime against the Cherokee nation. The residents of Witherston owe compensation for that crime.

The $15 million Witherston will raise for IPRI will not adequately reimburse the indigenous peoples for their loss of gold and land to white settlers with guns, but it will be a start. It may be a model.

"I find it hard to argue against Robin Hood," Lottie concluded.

"Ditto," Tabby said.

"You're right, Aunt Lottie," Jaime said. "We're all beneficiaries of that crime."

"So are all the descendants of the European settlers," Jorge said.

"But we here in Witherston benefitted particularly from that theft of gold and land," Lottie said. "We are descendants of white settlers who stole gold and land from the original inhabitants of North America, and we did not reimburse them. The white settlers accumulated their riches at the expense of the indigenous peoples."

"Robin Hood is trying to make things right," Paco said.

"Robin Hood, Robin Hood, riding through the glen, Robin Hood, Robin Hood, with his band of men," Jorge sang.

Jaime finished the verse. "Feared by the bad, loved by the good, Robin Hood! Robin Hood! Robin Hood!"

"Boys, where did you all learn that old television song?" Lottie asked.

BETTY JEAN CRAIGE

"We sang it in elementary school, in a play," Jorge said.

"We learned its moral message," Jaime said. "It's good to rob the rich."

"With bow and arrows," Jorge said. "And I have a bow and arrows."

"Please don't act on that, sons," Mev said.

"I'm sending in my five thousand dollars tonight," Lottie said. "I recognize the criminality of Robin Hood's letter, but I don't want to endanger Rhonda. We don't have a choice."

"I'm with you, Lottie," Paco said.

"So am I," Tabby said.

"I agree," Jaime said. "I'll just think of it as reparations to the Indigenous Peoples."

"Me too," Jorge said. "But I don't want to judge Robin Hood as a criminal, at least not yet."

"I'll email our friends and suggest that they do it too," Jaime said.

"Tell them to consider it reparations," Jorge said.

"We need another glass of wine. Paco, you pour," Lottie said. "And could someone please pass the cheese? Doolittle won't leave my hand."

"I guess my Gaia-centrism did not please everybody," Tabby said. "Some of our fellow citizens got heated up."

"You didn't correct Doug Hanley when he called you an egalitarian," Lottie said. "That may have riled some folks."

"Why would they be riled?"

"Egalitarianism threatens people who are afraid to lose what they've got," Jorge said. "Any form of egalitarianism threatens them—gender egalitarianism, racial egalitarianism, social egalitarianism, economic egalitarianism."

"I'm all of that."

"Right. So you threaten people like fat Sam Farthy and greedy Trevor Bennington, who have more than their share of money and power."

"They're afraid of you, Mrs. Grammer," Jaime said.

"I think Earth's bounty ought to be shared," Tabby said.

"Do you know John Lennon's song 'Imagine'?" Jaime asked her.

"Of course."

"John Lennon imagined 'no heaven,' 'no hell,' 'no countries,' 'no religion,' 'no possessions.' He imagined 'a brotherhood of man.' He imagined 'all the people sharing all the world.'"

"That song could be a 'Gaia-centrist's' anthem," Tabby said. "I wish I had known John Lennon."

"Me, too," Jaime said.

Tabby stood up. "Time for me to leave," she said. "Good night, everybody."

"Good-bye, Mrs. Grammer."

"Good-bye, Tabby."

"May I drive you home?" Jaime asked.

"Yes, Jaime." Tabby said. "Thank you."

Tabby donned her puffer jacket and outback hat, blew kisses to everybody, and walked out on Jaime's arm. Jaime opened the door of his black Corolla for her.

"You and Jorge seem very close," Tabby said as they headed toward her house.

"We are. Jorge is my intellectual buddy and my best friend for life. We're turning nineteen tomorrow."

"You all are so fortunate to have each other."

"We know that. We're never lonely."

"You never feel an emptiness inside? You never have an aching feeling that you need something but you don't know what? That's the way I used to feel."

"No. I guess I don't." Jaime hesitated. "Are you asking if I want a girlfriend? I do want a girlfriend. I already know the person I want."

"Well, good luck there."

Jaime drove up Tabby's driveway, parked, and jumped out of the car to walk her to her door.

"What a gentleman you are, Jaime! Thanks so much for the ride. And happy birthday to you and Jorge."

"Would you like to come to our birthday party tomorrow, Mrs. Grammer? Six thirty at Aunt Lottie's house."

"I'd love to. Thank you, Jaime."

———•———

ANNIE JERDEN, TERESA FUENTES, AND PATTY HICKS finished their dinner of sandwiches and kombucha and listened quietly to the forest sounds. They sat cross-legged on the blanketed floor of Annie's make-shift tree house in Big Yellow. The heater kept them warm, and the lantern illuminated the pup tent's interior.

After a while Annie spoke. "Have you all read *The Legacy of Luna*? The author is Julia Butterfly Hill, who lived in a giant redwood named Luna for two years to save an ancient forest."

"Wow."

"Wow is right, Patty. Julia Butterfly Hill became a famous environmental activist. She changed our thinking about ancient forests. Or at least some folks' thinking."

"Did she inspire you to camp in Big Yellow, Annie?"

"Yes. I wanted to save Potter's Woods, and her book inspired me to protest by living up here. Her book also taught me that if you want to change the world you must be willing to change your life. Changing the world can't be done from a distance."

"How do you want to change the world?" Teresa asked.

"I want to change Witherston first. I'll stay up here till the chainsaw people of our town, like Thomas Tankard, admit that their health depends on trees."

"You'll stay up here till you save Potter's Woods, Annie?"

"Sure. If I like winter, I'll love summer. I'll befriend owls and raccoons."

"And bobcats and possums," Patty added.

"How will you change the world?" Teresa asked.

"I'll make trouble for chainsaw people all over our planet."

"My parents are chainsaw people," Teresa said.

"Don't feel bad. So are mine. Chainsaw people just need to be educated," Annie said.

"Some chainsaw people are not educable," Patty Hicks said. "Thomas Tankard and Sam Farthy and Arthur Hanley and Trevor Bennington make truckloads of money by turning trees into houses."

"What's the opposite of chainsaw people?"

"Tree people, Teresa," Annie said. "Tree people believe that we're connected with each other and with the earth and that when we harm the earth we harm ourselves and future generations."

"John and I are tree people," Patty said. "So are all the Tayanita Villagers."

"My boyfriend and I are tree people," Teresa said.

"It's late. I have to go home," Patty said.

"You must be so happy, Patty! You're going to have a baby."

"I am happy."

"I have to go home too," Teresa said. "Annie, do you feel safe up here all alone tonight?"

"Who is going to harm me? Not owls or raccoons."

"How about people?"

"You're right. People could harm me. Chainsaw people don't like me."

After watching Teresa and Patty climb down the ladder, Annie composed another letter to OnlineWitherston and emailed it.

Then she picked up her mandolin and very softly sang "Go Tell It on the Mountain."

At eleven she got a call from Jaime on FaceTime.

"Hello, Jaime," she said, as Jaime's face came into view. "So nice to see you."

"How are you doing, Annie?"

"All is cool. Teresa and Patty just left."

"I wrote a letter to the editor about Big Yellow."

"And I wrote one about what trees do for us."

"Are you sure you can't come to our joint birthday party tomorrow night?"

"I'm sure, Jaime. Anyway, Seq is coming up then."

"Oh. Okay. Well, I'll see you at two tomorrow, Annie."

Jaime disconnected.

———•———

RHONDA FIXED HERSELF A HONEY-BOURBON TODDY AND sat down at her computer to write an email to Tabby Grammer.

GO GAIA
Dear Tabby,

 I email you tonight to thank you for your splendid presentation. Let me assure you that I will do all I can to save Potter's Woods.

 Also, don't worry about me. I doubt that my fellow citizens will raise $15 million, but I also doubt that Robin Hood will carry through on his threat.

And just between you and me, I'd be on Robin Hood's side if he hadn't had the discourtesy to threaten to kill me.

At least Robin Hood threatened me because I'm mayor and not because he or she doesn't like me. Who couldn't like me? Well, maybe the folks who don't want solar panels on their roof or bicycle paths on their streets.

If I should be killed, that's okay. I'm 56 years old. I'd soon be losing my looks anyway.

Maybe I should tell him.

Sincerely,

Rhonda

Rhonda pressed SEND, fixed herself another honey-bourbon toddy, and composed an email to Mev.

FIFTY WAYS TO KILL A MAYOR

Dear Mev,

Please don't worry about me. I'm not worried. I don't think that Robin Hood would have the nerve to take my life. He wouldn't like jail. But if he does take my life, there are fifty ways to kill a mayor.

Stab me in my heart, Bart.

Stab me in my back, Jack.

Stab me in my head, Jed,

Shoot me in the brain, Wayne.

Give me a pill, Phil.

Poison my bourbon, Herman.

I can't think of another forty-four.

Oh, yes. Hit me with a bat, Matt.

Mev, you are charged with keeping me from

being killed. OMG. Like the Secret Service is charged with keeping the president from being killed. I send you my condolences.

Did you know that when the president travels his Secret Service agent follows him with a bag of his blood?

By the way, may I have that cute, young, smart Officer Pete Koslowsky as my security detail? He can follow me with a bottle of bourbon.

I just thought of another way to kill a mayor: Feed me to the bear, Pierre.

There's a bear behind my house. Really. I can see her through the window.

Anyway, you have a big job keeping me above ground, Chief Arroyo.

Sleep well.

Rhonda

Rhonda pressed send, turned out the lights, and took Coco Chanel to bed.

———•—•———

MEV ARROYO FIXED HERSELF A BRANDY AND PULLED her chair close to the fireplace. She finally had the quiet time to read.

What a long day.

Hamlet slept at her feet. Paco was in the shower. Jorge and Jaime were in their bedroom. She could hear Jaime playing the guitar softly. Was he playing "Imagine"? Again?

She checked her email and opened the one from Rhonda. What was Rhonda drinking? She had to laugh. Fifty ways to kill a mayor!

Now she had responsibility for Rhonda's life. That would be a challenge.

Mev emailed Detective John Hicks to set up a meeting the next morning. She asked John to learn what he could about the Indigenous Peoples Reparations Initiative.

Then she put her feet up on the ottoman and picked up *Revenge of the Brave*. As she was about to close the book she reread the last paragraph:

> *The perceived injustices of long ago are remembered and passed down as truth from generation to generation—at holiday dinners, in worship services, at weddings and funerals, and in legends, song, art, theater, and dance—until they re-emerge in the present among those who have the power to rectify them. The past inhabits the present.*

"Now that's an argument for reparations," Mev said to herself.

———— • ————

PILIP PITKA, FORMERLY TIMOTHY PHILIP POTTER, SET down the dancing bear he was carving out of soapstone, swallowed the last of his brandy-spiked coffee, stoked the fire, and opened his tablet to OnlineWitherston.

Snow was falling heavily on the southern coast of the Seward Peninsula, and by six o'clock the temperature had dropped to five degrees below zero. Pil could hear the waves pound the beach, but he could not see them. At this time of year Nome's arctic darkness lasted from three thirty in the afternoon until noon the next day.

In both summer and winter Pil monitored the activities of Witherston. He had done so for two years, ever since he had lost Potter's Woods. Online, Pil had become acquainted with every Witherston resident whose name appeared in the news source. He knew Jorge Arroyo from Jorge's occasional cartoons. He knew Jaime Arroyo from Jaime's letters to the editor. He knew Charlotte Byrd from her column. He knew the inhabitants of Tayanita Village, particularly John Hicks and Sequoyah Waters, from their public actions on behalf of their Cherokee ancestors. He stayed up-to-date on police investigations, legal transactions, fires, floods, political campaigns, and marriages, births, and deaths. He possessed everybody's email address and many of their images.

Pil was a lurker.

Pil read Robin Hood's letter to the editor. Brilliant, he thought. How would Witherston react?

CHAPTER FOUR

Saturday, December 21, 2019

OnlineWitherston.com

NEWS

ANNIE JERDEN PROTESTS DEVELOPMENT OF POTTER'S WOODS

Yesterday Witherston native Annie Jerden ascended Witherston's "Big Yellow" poplar tree to protest the scheduled logging of Potter's Woods by Tankard Developers. She says she will live in Big Yellow's branches until Potter's Woods, an old-growth forest, is "safe from the chainsaw."

With the help of Sequoyah Waters, who built a rope ladder and a 6' x 8' wood platform 60 feet off the ground, Annie established her campsite. She and Seq brought up a pup tent, an extended-life lantern, a battery-powered heater, and a backpack containing warm clothing, a blanket, water, breakfast bars, a cell phone, a journal, a book, and her mandolin.

"Enough equipment for her to stay a while," Seq Waters said.

On the tree trunk Seq nailed a sign that says I AM 300 YEARS OLD. DON'T KILL ME.

Annie Jerden takes bathroom breaks and showers at Bear Lodge across Witherston Highway. She charges her phone there too.

Her support team, composed of Seq, Teresa Fuentes, and Patty Hicks, brings her food.

Big Yellow is a 175-foot tall Yellow poplar tree that may be more than three centuries old. It stands 50 yards away from the north-west edge of Potter's Woods, near the old Gertrude Withers School. Big Yellow got its name from its yellow blossoms in the spring and its yellow leaves in the fall. Its branches are bare now, at winter solstice.

Asked who or what had prompted her to take this action, Annie replied, "Julia Butterfly Hill."

Julia Butterfly Hill, author of "The Legacy of Luna," lived in a California Redwood for two years (1997-1999) to prevent its destruction by the Pacific Lumber Company.

Annie is a student at the University of North Georgia in Dahlonega. She will have to descend from Big Yellow on January 7, when classes resume.

—Amadahy Henderson, Editor

ANNOUNCEMENTS
Town Council Meeting

The Witherston Town Council will meet as usual on the fourth Wednesday of the month, that is, December 25, at 6:00 pm in the Mayor's Conference Room of City Hall.

The following proposals have been submitted.

PROPOSED (by Tabby Grammer): That the Witherston Town Council allocate $1 million from municipal revenues to buy back Potter's Woods from Thomas Tankard because of its value to the community as an old-growth forest.

PROPOSED (by Ruth Griggs): That the Witherston Town Council allocate $15 million from municipal revenues to meet the demand of Robin Hood.

Anybody wishing to submit an additional item of business must email it to me by Tuesday at 6:00 pm.

—Neel Kingfisher, Chair of the Town Council

———•———

Contributors to Indigenous Peoples Reparations Initiative

Fifteen citizens of Witherston each transferred $5,000 overnight to the bank account of OnlineWitherston for the Indigenous Peoples Reparations Initiative.

The list of "Contributors" is available at: www: OnlineWitherston.com/contributors

—Amadahy Henderson, Editor

———•———

NORTH GEORGIA IN HISTORY
By Charlotte Byrd

Since Potter's Woods may soon be taken down by loggers, I will devote my column in the next few days to its history. This is the story of the Potters and the Withers I've pieced together from newspapers, courthouse records, and Eula Potter's diary, kept in the University of Georgia Hargrett Library.

In 1829, penniless Hearty Withers joined other down-and-out men to pan for gold in the mountain streams here in Lumpkin country. Picture him: 31 years old, bearded, dirty, smelly, trousers rolled up, sifting sand in the cold rushing waters. He got lucky. He found gold, lots of it, and he became rich.

Before long Hearty Withers got lucky again. In the 1832 Georgia Land Lottery he won 40 acres of the Cherokees' homeland on Saloli Stream. In the same lottery Patrick Potter won the adjacent 40 acres of land.

Hearty turned his woods into fields and pastures and increased his wealth. Patrick did not, for his plot was landlocked and unfit for farming.

A year later, Hearty Withers and a few other settlers took over a Cherokee village called Tayanita, burned the Cherokee dwellings to make room for their log houses, and renamed the village Witherstown.

Patrick Potter moved to Dahlonega in search of gold, but failed in that endeavor. In 1839 he married Hearty Withers's younger sister Eula, built a house in Dahlonega, and produced a son, Mark Potter.

The story of the Potters and the Withers goes on.

In 1862, Mark Potter and Hearty Withers's son Harry were drafted to serve the Confederate cause in the War Between the States. Mark went willingly. Harry hired a young Cherokee, John Sando, to take his place, invested his wealth in the Mayfield Arms Company, and became extremely rich.

In the Battle of Atlanta on July 22, 1864, according to Eula Potter's diary, John Sando died and Mark lost his right leg, both of them shot by Mayfield muskets.

Eula wrote, "I shall forever hate my brother for making the gun that took my dear son's leg and his Cherokee friend's life. Never again will I speak to him."

In the Dahlonega courthouse I found the source of the famed quarrel between the Potters and the Withers.

In April of 1866, when Hearty Withers's son Harry decided to build the Gertrude Withers School for Children, a survey showed that the boundaries of the plots acquired in the 1832 Georgia Land Lottery had been drawn in such a way as to give 41 acres to Hearty Withers and 39 acres to Patrick Potter.

Both men laid claim to the acreage Hearty Withers had designated for the Gertrude Withers School.

Patrick Potter sued Withers but lost his case on the grounds that Patrick lived in Dahlonega and was not occupying the land. The judge was a man named Ben Withers.

Since Patrick lived in Dahlonega and seldom visited Witherston, Harry and Gertrude proceeded to build the Gertrude Withers School on the disputed acre. To reach the school they cut a half-mile access road through Patrick Potter's undisputed property. The school opened in mid-September.

On December 18, 1866, Eula Potter reported Patrick missing. In her diary Eula wrote, "I will send Mark to search for his father, but I know in my heart that Patrick is dead."

On the night of December 23, according to the December 28 issue of the Witherston Weekly, Harry Withers was shot and killed in the alley behind Finney's Saloon in Witherston. The assailant was not officially identified but was rumored to be Mark Potter.

Patrick Potter was never found. When he was officially declared dead in 1873, Mark Potter inherited Potter's Woods.

———•———

LETTERS TO THE EDITOR

To the Editor:

Last night at Pinetops Hall author Tabby Grammer called herself a "Gaia-centrist." That means she favors the earth over civilization. If civilization is her enemy, she is our enemy.

Right, Mrs. Grammer?

—Doug Hanley

To the Editor:

On December 18, Thomas Tankard was granted a permit to log Potter's Woods and to construct 100 houses on the land.

On January 6, if we do not stop him, Mr. Tankard will chainsaw Potter's Woods, sell the timber, and use the proceeds to finance the subdivision. And—after the woods are all gone!—he will call the subdivision "Potter's Woods Retirement Community."

Mr. Tankard must not know that we humans need forests for our survival. Forests, especially such old-growth forests as Potter's Woods, are "earth's lungs." Trees take carbon dioxide out of the air and put oxygen back into it.

I will camp in the branches of Big Yellow until the Witherston Town Council blocks the development.

How did Thomas Tankard come to own Potter's Woods anyway?

—Annie Jerden

From the Editor:

Here is what I have learned.

In 2017, the Witherston tax assessor discovered that no taxes had ever been paid on the property known as Potter's Woods.

Patrick Potter acquired the acreage in 1832. He owed minimal property taxes because the wooded land had no access to water and therefore could not be farmed. There is no record that Patrick Potter paid the taxes.

In 1835, the Georgia General Assembly did away with property taxes. By 1840, when the General Assembly reinstated property taxes, Patrick Potter was living in Savannah. There is no record that he paid taxes on Potter's Woods. Nor is there any record that his son Mark paid taxes on Potter's Woods either.

Patrick Potter's grandson Nathaniel, great-grandson Chauncey, and great-great-grandson Timothy all lived in Fairbanks, Alaska, which did not become a state until 1959. There is no record that any one of them paid taxes on Potter's Woods.

By 2017, the compounded back taxes amounted to about $1.2 million, more than the property was assessed to be worth.

Witherston's tax assessor attempted unsuccessfully to contact Timothy Potter during the summer of 2017, on June 1, July 6, and August 3. Timothy Potter seemed to have disappeared. In September of 2017 the mayor foreclosed on the property and transferred ownership to the municipality of Witherston.

In October of 2017, Thomas Tankard, who was a friend of the mayor, offered to buy Potter's

Woods from Witherston for $1 million, and the Town Council approved the sale.

Timothy Potter's whereabouts remain a mystery.

—Amadahy Henderson

To the Editor:

Annie Jerden is trying to save a small, a very, very, very small piece of the Cherokees' homeland.

—Sequoyah Waters

To the Editor:

Big Yellow stood here when English and Scottish settlers claimed Cherokee land for their own and ended the thousand-year-old Cherokee civilization. Big Yellow stood here during the Georgia Gold Rush, the Trail of Tears, the Civil War, and the Great Depression.

The sun's energy nourished Big Yellow for three hundred years. Are we to let a chainsaw take down Big Yellow in three hours?

—Jaime Arroyo

To the Editor:

As a nod to Ms. Annie Jerden's passion for trees, I will save Big Yellow and will build the assisted-living homes around that tall poplar.

—Thomas Tankard

To the Editor:

How did it happen that Mayor Rather gave Witherston's first "key to the city" to a woman who writes stories that are not true? She makes Georgia look like *a breeding ground for murderers. Her books are as bad as "Deliverance."*

What's a key to the city, anyway?

—*Ruth Griggs*

From the Editor:
Last September the Town Council established the "Key to the City" to honor outstanding citizens and selected award-winning mystery writer Tabby Grammer as the first recipient.

The tradition of honoring individuals with a key to the city originated in the European Middle Ages when walled cities granted trusted visitors the freedom to come and go as they pleased.

—*Amadahy Henderson, Editor*

CHAPTER FIVE

Saturday, December 21, 2019

J aime and Jorge arrived at the Gertrude Withers School a little before ten. Hamlet leapt out of the car and raced ahead to the white picket fence.

"Resus cresus," Jorge exclaimed, opening the gate. "We've come to an ancient cemetery!"

In the old school yard they made their way through pottery shards and concrete body parts—legs, arms, partial busts, torsos, feet—rooted in the ground and half-covered with dead leaves and branches.

"It's yard art," Jaime said.

"Hey, Neel," Jorge shouted. "We're here!"

"This porch is about to collapse," Jaime said.

The wooden planks, once painted white, splintered beneath their feet.

Neel Kingfisher stood by the open door with his Nikon. Trained as an artist, Neel had become a skilled photographer.

"Hey, Neel," Jaime said.

"Come inside, guys. Watch out for nails." Neel gave Hamlet a pat on the head.

"This place reeks of gasoline," Jaime said.

"You're smelling kerosene, Jaime," Neel said. "This was an art studio, that is, after it was Hank Ridge's Feed and Seed store and before that the Gertrude Withers School. Scorch Ridge, a sculptor and a painter, and Scorch's wife Abby, a potter, inherited the building and worked there until Scorch died in 2017 and Abby left town. The Ridges left cans of paint, turpentine, kerosene, and varnish."

"Abby Ridge should have cleaned up," Jaime said.

"I like the skylight," Jorge said. "It brings in sunshine. Good for painting."

"Scorch and Abby probably installed it when they transformed the store into their studio," Neel said.

The well-lighted space was possibly thirty feet by thirty feet, with a small kitchen and pantry on the west wall and a small bathroom on the north wall. On the east wall was a heavy oak door. Neel opened the door and aimed his flashlight down a dark stairwell.

Hamlet raced down the steps.

"Follow me," Neel said. "And hang on to the rail. I want to show you all something."

In the basement, Neel led them to a cabinet, which he opened. He brought out four watercolor paintings of birds. A Red-tailed hawk, a Barred owl, a Mallard duck, and a Carolina parakeet.

"These were not done by Scorch," Neel said. "They were done by an amateur, in the nineteenth century.

"They're really good," Jorge said. He took pictures.

"The Carolina parakeet is now extinct," Neel said. "It's a true parrot. Look at the shape of the beak."

"Here's a treasure chest," Jaime exclaimed. Jaime tried to pick it up. "And it's heavy!"

"It's locked," Jorge said.

Hamlet was sniffing behind the stairs. He started digging.

"Holy shirt!" Jorge said. "There's a skeleton here!"

At eleven o'clock Saturday morning, Detective John Hicks entered Chief Mev Arroyo's office with two cups of coffee.

"Aren't you thoughtful, John! Thank you," Mev said, accepting a cup. "Let's talk about protection for Mayor Rather."

"I suggest assigning Pete to the case. He'll be a good bodyguard, and Mayor Rather and he like each other. Also, Pete likes the mayor's dog Coco Chanel."

"Good idea. I'll contact Pete."

"Now for the interesting stuff. Here's my report on the Indigenous Peoples Reparations Initiative." John laid a computer print-out on her desk. "First, IPRI, as it's called, is not a non-profit. It is a political organization."

"So contributors can't deduct their five thousand dollars," Mev observed.

"Right, I guess. Second, its director Kallik Kootoo is Inuit. His office is in Juneau. Third, IPRI provides small grants to reparations advocacy groups all over the United States but mostly in Alaska and the Pacific northwest. None for Cherokees. Fourth, fifteen million dollars would greatly— and I mean greatly—exceed the funding it has acquired since its formation in 1987."

"What was its budget last year, in 2018. Did you find out?" Mev asked.

"In 2018, IPRI distributed five thousand dollars. IPRI has an endowment of a hundred and five thousand dollars. So it can distribute five thousand a year, more or less. I can't find the source of the endowment."

"Do you have contact information for Kallik Kootoo?"

"Yes. Here it is." He wrote it on a post-it note. "Would you like me to go to Alaska and snoop around?"

"I don't see the need."

"I do. I'd like to visit Juneau to find out what I can about IPRI. IPRI could be a front."

"Would you take Patty?"

"Yes. I'd pay for her ticket."

"Okay, go. For four days. Email me daily."

"Would you like for me to snoop around in Fairbanks for Timothy Potter."

"You know that our tax assessor searched for Timothy Potter in 2017 and couldn't find him."

"I'll do better. And if I find him I'll let him know what's happening to Potter's Woods."

"Okay, go."

"Thank you, Chief! Merry Christmas! We'll be back Thursday night."

Mev sent an email to Kallik Kootoo.

REQUEST FOR INFORMATION
Dear Mr. Kootoo:

   I contact you in reference to a letter written by a "Robin Hood" that was emailed anonymously to our local news source on Friday, December 20. The letter is attached.

   As you see, Robin Hood's stated intention is to raise $15 million for the Indigenous Peoples Reparations Initiative.

   I have some questions for you.

   Are you aware of this letter? If so, do you know who wrote it? If you do not have direct knowledge, can you tell me who may have had reason to write it?

What is the source of funding for the Indigenous Peoples Reparations Initiative?

What is the IPRI street address and telephone number?

I would be grateful for any information you can share with me.

Thank you.

Chief Mev Arroyo, Witherston Police Department

———•—

Trevor Bennington, Jr., his son Trey Bennington, Thomas Tankard, Mitch Melton, Arthur Hanley, and Sam Farthy sat down at the Bennington Brokerage conference table. Trey had brought doughnuts and coffee.

After an extended adolescence that included juvenile detention, Trey now worked for his father at Bennington Brokerage.

"So why have you brought our team together this Saturday morning, Trevor? I have a hunch this meeting has something to do with last night's event," Thomas Tankard asked.

"Now that you've received the construction permit for the retirement community, Tabby Grammer and other tree nuts are getting active," Trevor said. "We're worried."

"I've already accepted down payments from nineteen future residents, including Lydia Gray," Arthur said, and commitments from twelve more. I don't want to return those down payments or renege on any promises."

"I have a half-million dollars riding on this contract," Sam Farthy said.

"We all have that, and more," Tom said. "We each own twenty-five percent of the project."

"What about me?" Trey asked. "You keep forgetting about me."

"Just a minute, son. Don't interrupt."

"We have trouble ahead," Arthur said. "Tabby Grammer and Annie Jerden are turning more and more people against you, Tom. I foresee a battle at the Council meeting."

"Tabby Grammer has already submitted a proposal to buy back our property," Sam said.

"But Witherston needs retirement cottages. The old folks want social clubs, bridge games, a daily meal together in the cafeteria, health care, and medical facilities," Tom said. "They will wage a campaign to save Potter's Woods Retirement Community."

"Tabby Grammer will fight them. She likes trees more than people," Arthur said. "And she's got power."

"Annie Jerden is refusing to get down from a giant Yellow poplar in Potter's Woods until the Board blocks the development," Trey said.

"So we have two problems. They are Tabby Grammer, who is on the Board, and Annie Jerden, who is up a tree," Arthur said.

"Tabby Grammer stands between us and a fortune," Sam Farthy said. "But I'll handle her."

"I'll handle Annie," Trey said.

"Son, if you can help make this project happen, I'll give you ten thousand dollars now and a piece of the action later."

"Got it," Trey said.

"On another topic," Tom said. "What are you all doing about Robin Hood? I'm inclined to pay my five thousand and not worry about it."

"I'm not paying," Sam said. "I'm waiting for three thousand others to pay, and then I won't have to."

"Same here," Arthur said. "I'll belong to the twenty-five percent who don't pay."

"And risk your life?" Tom said. "Arthur, you're too prominent to go unnoticed by Robin Hood."

"The FBI will catch Robin Hood by Christmas Day," Sam said. "I think Robin Hood is a woman, namely Tabby Grammer."

———•———

At one forty-five, Jaime left his car in the Bear Lodge parking lot, crossed the Witherston Highway, and proceeded up the deer trail toward Big Yellow. Before he'd traveled ten yards he realized that somebody was ahead of him. He could hear human footsteps on the dry leaves.

He stopped, waited a minute, and then continued walking quietly along the path to the clearing. He looked up. Trey Bennington was slowly and silently climbing the ladder to Annie's arboreal campsite. The tent flap remained closed.

"Hey, Trey," Jaime shouted. "What are you doing here?"

Trey appeared startled. He looked down at Jaime.

Annie opened the tent flap and stepped onto one of the branches.

"What's happening? Trey Bennington, what are you doing here?"

Trey looked up at Annie. "I just wanted to pay you a visit, Annie. I have a deal for you."

"Get off my ladder."

"Alright. I'll go down."

"I'm coming down too," Annie said.

When both Trey and Annie were on the ground, Jaime said, "I'm not leaving, Trey. You can offer Annie your deal in front of me."

Trey turned to Annie. "My father will give you some shares of the Potter's Woods Retirement Community if you stop blocking construction."

"I'm not interested. Why would you think I'd choose money over principle, Trey? Because you would? Why would you think I'd choose you over a tree?"

"Okay, Annie. Okay, okay. I get your point."

"Leave, or I will tell your father what I know about you."

Trey left.

"Jesus, Annie. That was unnerving. What do you know about Trey?"

"Nothing." Annie laughed. "Nothing concrete, that is. I've just heard rumors about him and Doug selling drugs."

"I'm putting bells on the ladder, so if you get an unexpected visitor you can hear him. I've got jingle bells in my car which I'd bought for our Christmas tree. I'll get them."

After rigging the jingle-bell alarm system, Jaime joined Annie in her tree house.

"You've turned Trey into an enemy, Annie. He'll try to hurt you now."

"He wouldn't dare. He doesn't know what I could tell his father."

"Right. That's what I mean."

"Anyway, he can't offer anything that would make me come out of this tree, Jaime."

"What if the Board doesn't buy back Potter's Woods? Are you planning to go down with the tree?"

"Yes. I would like to tell my children someday that I took the side of the tree rather than the side of the chainsaw."

"I guess I would too, Annie."

"Have you ever thought that when we're young we're creating the account of ourselves that we'll tell our children?

We're actually creating ourselves, the people we'll be proud to be when we're forty years old, or sixty, or eighty. I want to say to my children, when I have them, that when I was nineteen I acted to save the planet for them, even though I had to disobey my parents, who were on the side of the chainsaw."

"Is that hard, Annie? I mean, is it hard not to have the support of your parents?"

"I wish they liked me better, but I have to follow my conscience. When I was little my parents told me to be a leader. Then when I started thinking for myself they asked me, 'Whom are you following?' I told them I wasn't following anybody, that I was a leader."

"You are a leader, Annie. You've always been a leader."

"I don't want to tell my children in ten or twenty years that I obeyed my parents even though I thought they were wrong."

"You are looking forward, Annie."

"I am. I want my children to know I followed my conscience, even when it was hard, even when I was lonely. And I hope my children won't have to choose between me and what they believe is right."

"Do you feel lonely this Christmas?"

"No, not really. I feel exhilarated. I know what I want to do in life. I want to encourage others to save our trees from the chainsaw."

"Do you see just two sides?"

"I do, Jaime. Trees versus chainsaws."

CHAPTER SIX

Saturday, December 21, 2019

P ilip Pitka did not suffer from loneliness. He satisfied his desire for connection with other human beings through OnlineWitherston.

Today Pil discovered that the developer Thomas Tankard had acquired a permit to transform Potter's Woods into a retirement community, that Annie Jerden had moved into the branches of a Yellow poplar to protest Tankard's destruction of the old-growth forest, and that the Town Council might buy back Potter's Woods. He found out that fifteen of Francis Hearty Withers's beneficiaries had already contributed their five thousand dollars to the Indigenous Peoples Reparations Initiative.

He continued reading. He cheered Sequoyah Waters's letter to the editor. Through his anonymity app he sent Sequoyah Waters an email.

HELLO

To Sequoyah Waters:

 I read your letter to the editor in OnlineWitherston.
 Since the whites' appropriation of Native land accompanied their conquest of Native people,

Potter's Woods represents the remnants of Cherokee civilization.
    Could you argue that Potter's Woods should be returned to the Cherokees?
    Most sincerely,
    A Native American

Pil read Charlotte Byrd's column. Yes. That was the story his father had told him, the reason Potter's Woods was thirty-nine acres and not forty. He continued reading.

> *In 1862, Mark Potter and Hearty Withers's son Harry were drafted to serve the Confederate cause in the War Between the States. Mark went willingly. Harry hired a young Cherokee, John Sando, to take his place, invested his wealth in the Mayfield Arms Company, and became extremely rich.*
>
> *In the Battle of Atlanta on July 22, 1864, according to Eula Potter's diary, John Sando died and Mark lost his right leg, both of them shot by Mayfield muskets.*

Pil's familiar anger overtook him. He helped himself to another beer and mused about the unending consequences of single events.

Because Hearty Withers had found gold in 1829, young Harry Withers dodged the war, invested his money in guns, and increased his wealth exponentially. And because Patrick Potter had not found gold, young Mark Potter went to war and lost his leg.

John Sando lost his life.

Harry Withers had purchased the Cherokee's death. Wasn't that emblematic?

Harry Withers became an upstanding citizen and passed down his wealth, his genes, and his name to succeeding generations of upstanding citizens of Witherston.

Pil thought about the last line of Charlotte Byrd's book *Moccasins in the Mountains*: "When victors render their victims invisible, the victors' crimes become difficult to trace."

Difficult to trace, but still traceable.

Where did Hearty Withers's wealth come from? The Cherokees, who were John Sando's people. Where did John Sando's given name come from? The whites, who were Withers's people. Before the whites arrived, no Cherokee was named "John." The only thing the whites gave the Cherokees were names and diseases.

The accidents of the past engendered the possibilities of the future. What if Hearty Withers had not found gold? Then John Sando might have lived to have children, and grandchildren, and great-grandchildren. What if Patrick Potter had found gold? The lives of all the Potters thereafter would have been different. His grandfather Nathaniel might not have gone to Fairbanks. He, Pil, might not be living in Nome.

For Pil, the tale epitomized the fate of the Native Americans, the First Nations, the Alaska Natives, the Native Hawaiians—all the indigenous peoples whom the whites had conquered. The story of conquest was the same everywhere. In Alaska, in Hawaii, in Georgia, and over the entire continent.

Pil had taught that story to a thousand students during his tenure as a high school teacher in Fairbanks. He had led many demonstrations on behalf of the Native Movement, and he might still be active if he hadn't decided to disappear.

Pil had disappeared twice. He had had several identities. He still thought of himself as Pilip Pitka, but he enjoyed the freedom that came from discarding one identity for another. It allowed him to escape the burden of other people's knowledge of him as well as the consequences of his deeds. With each identity he had started over with a different persona, though with the same rage against injustice.

He leased a log cabin that had once belonged to his grandfather. Pil had made it comfortable, even in winter. He had hung his mother's quilts on one wall and his grandmother's paintings on another. He had placed a bearskin rug in front of the hearth and a caribou pelt on his bed. From the front door, facing the Bering Sea, he could see the seven-foot-tall white granite polar bear his grandfather had carved on the cliff. He, Pilip Pitka, now calling himself Oki Yukon, belonged here among the Inuits.

Pil remembered his mother, Akna Pitka, a beautiful Inuit woman whom his father had impregnated when she was a nineteen-year-old waitress in Fairbanks. She had had to marry him. After the divorce she returned to Nome to be with her extended family. Thanks to the summers Pil had spent with her here in Nome, he spoke Inuktitut. He learned the art of carving from his mother's father, the art of painting from his mother's mother, and the history of Alaska from their Inuit friends.

Pil spent Nome's long summer days hunting moose, caribou, and bear, or gathering sea glass and driftwood on the beach. He spent the long winter nights reading, watching movies, listening to Alaskan music, and carving bears, walruses, seals, and otters, as he had learned to do from his grandfather.

He sent his sculptures to a Fairbanks gallery for sale and became known there as the reclusive Oki Yukon from Nome.

Occasionally he wondered whether he should have moved to Juneau when he left Fairbanks, but Nome was his mother's birthplace, his grandparents' birthplace, and the home of five generations of their ancestors, almost all of them artists like himself.

Pil read the editor's reply to Annie Jerden's letter. "Timothy Potter's whereabouts remain a mystery."

"Good," Pil said to himself, and picked up his chisel.

———•·•———

It was four forty-five in Witherston. Tabby Grammer had sat at her computer for over an hour. Sam Farthy would arrive soon. She reread a sentence: "I propose that free higher education—in public institutions, for four years—be made available to all Americans under the banner of 'reparations.'"

That will do, she decided.

Smoky rubbed against her legs, meowing loudly.

"Okay, Smoky. Dinnertime!"

She emailed the column to her contact at the *National Post-Herald*, left her computer, and followed Smoky into the kitchen.

The doorbell rang.

"He's early," Tabby said to herself as she spotted a maroon Cadillac parked in front.

She opened the door for Sam Farthy, cigarette between his lips, briefcase in his hand. Stout Sam Farthy was unaware that he was not attractive.

"How are you, Mrs. Grammer. You look pretty this afternoon."

"Well, Mr. Farthy. To what do I owe the honor of your social call on a Saturday evening? May I take your jacket?"

Tabby hung Sam's expensive tan leather jacket on the hook by the door.

"Actually, it's not a social call, Mrs. Grammer. It's a business call."

"Come in. Would you mind putting out your cigarette?"

"Do you have an ashtray?"

Tabby extracted a glass dish from her desk drawer, dumped the paper clips, and handed it to him.

"I guess you vegetarians don't smoke either. Do you drink?"

"Of course. Would you like a drink?"

"If you have scotch. Thank you. On ice."

"As you wish. I was just fixing dinner for my cat, so please excuse me for a minute and make yourself at home."

Smoky kept meowing until Tabby opened the can, spooned the Fancy Feast salmon *paté* into his bowl, and set his water dish on the floor. She poured two glasses of Johnny Walker Black and dropped two cubes of ice in each.

When she returned to the living room Sam was putting his cell phone back into his pocket.

Sam raised his glass and said, "Here's to Witherston's prosperity."

Tabby raised hers and said, "Here's to Witherston's health."

"Tell me about your house."

"I found a nineteenth-century log cabin for sale near Potter's Creek outside of Blairsville. I liked it, so I had it hauled to this lot. A couple of construction workers who were friends of mine managed the project. I put in a bathroom and redid the kitchen and bedroom. It has a loft for storage. What do you think?"

"It's unique," Sam said. Sam looked around at the Native American paintings on her walls and the Cherokee artifacts in the lighted glass cabinets and curio cases.

"You collect Native American paraphernalia?" Sam asked.

"I collect Native American art, if that's what you mean. Now what brings you here tonight?"

"I want you to stop your campaign to preserve Potter's Woods. More specifically, to withdraw your proposal before the Town Council."

"Why should I do that?"

"The first reason is that the development of Potter's Woods will bring revenue to Witherston. There's no need to keep the thirty-nine acres useless when Witherston is surrounded by the forested Appalachian mountains."

"And the second reason?" Tabby asked.

"Witherston's elderly need handicapped-friendly cottages for their declining years."

"Those reasons I've heard before. I ask, why build the cottages on Potter's Woods? Is there a third reason?"

"The third reason is that I'm offering you a stake in the project. I can give you either ten thousand dollars now or a ten-percent share of the profits. You would keep this deal confidential, of course." Sam opened his briefcase.

"I'm not interested."

"There's a fourth reason, then."

"Which is?"

"I can prove you are Robin Hood. I can get you convicted of extortion."

"If you try, I'll get you convicted of attempted blackmail, Mr. Farthy. You don't know whom you're tangling with. I can make you fear for your life." Tabby stood up. "Let me show you the door."

Sam Farthy closed his briefcase, put down his empty glass, grabbed his jacket, and left without speaking another word.

"We're here!"

"We're early! Happy winter solstice, Aunt Lottie!"

"Happy birthday, boys," Lottie called from her bedroom. "I'll be right out."

"I invited Tabby Grammer to join us," Jaime said.

"Terrific!"

Jorge and Jaime walked through Lottie's back door into her kitchen, ready for Lottie's annual winter solstice/birthday party. Jorge carried a six-foot-tall purple perch into the living room and set it up by the Christmas tree.

"Here's a hostess gift for you, Aunt Lottie. Actually, for Doolittle. It's your favorite color."

Doolittle noticed and flew onto the platform.

Lottie's living room walls, painted a soft mauve, were covered floor to ceiling with local art. She supported the artists of the north Georgia mountains by buying something from each one she met. And she supported the craftsmen too. On the dining room wall she had hung a purple and yellow quilt, and in the dining room corner she had placed a four-foot high chainsaw-carved black bear.

Jorge and Jaime had dressed up. They wore black slacks, black leather shoes, and white turtlenecks. They'd cut their curly brown hair short. Jorge had shaved his beard, and Jaime had shaved his mustache. They were indistinguishable.

Lottie came out of her bedroom in a lavender sweater and gray slacks.

"Good lord," Lottie exclaimed when she saw them. "You all look grown up."

"We're turning nineteen years old, Aunt Lottie."

"We're men now, Aunt Lottie."

Lottie's guests included only Jorge, Jaime, Mev, and Paco. Tabby Grammer had not come after all. They dined on spinach salad, saffron rice with peas, Paco's garlic shrimp, crusty French baguettes, and Priorat, Lottie's favorite Catalonian red wine. For dessert, dark chocolate truffles.

After dinner, Jaime and Jorge opened their presents. Jaime got a fancy harmonica from Lottie and a microscope from his parents. Jorge got a set of oil paints from Lottie and an easel and canvases from his parents.

The doorbell rang. Tabby Grammer stood on the front porch carrying three baskets overflowing with red and green tissue paper.

"I'm so sorry I'm late, Lottie. I had an unexpected visitor this afternoon."

"Come in, Tabby. Come in. We are happy you're joining us."

"These baskets are for you, Jorge, and Jaime. They contain books I've written. And this basket is for you, Lottie. It holds a Pecorino Italian cheese wheel."

"Thank you, Tabby! We are all fond of Pecorino cheese," Lottie said.

"Wow," Jaime said. "Thanks so much for *Paving Gaia*! I'll share it with Jorge."

"And I'll share *OnlineCrime* with Jaime."

"And with your parents too, I hope," Paco said.

Lottie prepared a plate of food for Tabby and poured her a glass of wine.

Jaime clicked his glass with his spoon. "Hey, everybody," he said. "Jorge and I have something really important to report, really, really, really important. We found a skeleton in the basement of the Gertrude Withers School."

"Actually, it was a heap of bones in the ground. The basement had no floor," Jorge said. "Just dirt."

"Hamlet dug up the bones," Jaime said. "The bones had been buried. I mean, the body had been buried. Behind the stairs."

"Neel took a piece of bone to a lab in Atlanta for a DNA test. He thinks the skeleton is human."

"The body was buried in the basement to hide it," Jaime said. "Or else it would have been buried in a graveyard. So, folks, easy question. Why wasn't the body buried in a graveyard?"

"Because the person who buried the body didn't want it found," Jorge said.

"You got it! The person who buried the body was a murderer."

"Jaime and Jorge, what are you imagining?" Mev exclaimed.

"When do you think the body was buried?" Lottie asked.

"We don't know," Jaime said. "The DNA will tell."

"The body could not have belonged to Harry Withers," Lottie said, "because Harry Withers was buried in the graveyard behind Witherston Methodist Church. I visited that graveyard. That's how I got the birth and death dates of all the Withers."

"Maybe it's Patrick Potter's body," Jaime said. "Patrick Potter just disappeared, Aunt Lottie."

"Right. He was never found. That is, his body was never found. By the way, in my column I explained a possible source for the bad blood between the Potters and the Withers. Did you all read it?"

"Sure."

"Of course."

"Let's see it."

Lottie opened her lap-top and turned it around so everybody could read her column.

"That's important, Aunt Lottie," Jorge said.

"When Patrick Potter learned that he had gotten only thirty-nine acres in the 1832 Land Lottery and his neighbor Hearty Withers had gotten forty-one acres, Patrick Potter must have been livid," Tabby said.

"And Harry Withers was building his wife's school on the very land that Patrick Potter thought was his," Lottie said.

"Here's my theory," Jorge said. "Patrick threatened to kill Harry over the judge's decision. But Harry killed Patrick first. Then Harry buried Patrick's body in the school basement."

"You're speculating, son."

"He has to speculate. We don't have a video of the murder," Jaime said.

"Go on, Jorge," Lottie said.

"Then Patrick's son Mark found out that Harry had murdered his father. So Mark killed Harry."

"The wounded warrior murdered the draft dodger."

"Mark must have despised Harry," Lottie said.

"Could we prove that the bones belonged to Patrick Potter if we got DNA from Timothy Potter?"

"Possibly, Mev," Lottie said. "How do you propose to get Timothy Potter to give a sample?"

"We could ask him."

"Where is Timothy Potter, anyway?" Paco asked. "What do we know about him?"

"Not much," Lottie said. "I googled Timothy Potter and found that he earned a PhD in Indigenous Studies from the University of Alaska in 1977, that he taught Alaskan history and art at Kuput High School in Fairbanks from 1977 until 1986, and that he was arrested numerous times for demonstrating on behalf of Alaska Natives. I found a

1982 high school newspaper interview with him in which he identified himself as Inuit and said that he was fluent in Inuktitut, his Inuit mother's language. And I found a record of his father's will, probated in 1986, bequeathing him Potter's Woods."

"Anything after 1986?" Mev asked.

"Nothing. Nothing at all. After 1986 Timothy Potter disappeared. I wondered where he'd gone."

"That's bizarre," Jorge said.

"Let's have another glass of wine," Paco said. He poured a round.

"Did you find anything else interesting?" Tabby asked.

"A locked treasure chest," Jorge said. "It could contain gold."

"Jorge! The Withers wouldn't have kept their gold in a chest in a schoolhouse," Mev said.

"You don't know that, Mom."

"Any pots, quilts, clothing, tools, guns?" Tabby asked. "Objects of everyday life? For our future museum? That's what I'd like to see."

"There could be all of that," Jaime said. "The basement was pretty dark. There was a lot of stuff on the shelves."

"There were some paintings in a cabinet. I took pictures," Jorge said. He pulled out his phone. Here's one of a Carolina parakeet, which is a real parrot that has gone extinct."

"Magnificent," Lottie said.

"And here are ones of a Red-tailed hawk, a Barred owl, and a Mallard duck."

"I'd like to see those paintings," Tabby said.

"We couldn't stay down there long," Jaime said. "The building reeked of kerosene and paint."

Jorge got a text message.

"Hey, folks, It's Neel. Neel just talked with Amadahy about our work at the schoolhouse."

"We'll get a story in OnlineWitherston tomorrow," Jaime said.

"I hope the story doesn't draw a crowd to the schoolhouse," Mev said.

"Neel sent pictures to her," Jorge said. "Who are you calling, Jaime?"

"Whom," Mev said.

"Okay. Whom are you calling, Jaime?"

"Annie." Jaime was FaceTiming his former girlfriend.

"Hey Annie, you okay?"

"I'm fine, Jaime. Happy birthday! You want to come up some time?"

"Is Seq gone?"

"Yes, Jaime. He just came for a little while. How about coming over tomorrow night?"

"Sure. What time? I'll show you my new harmonica."

"Come at seven."

"I'll bring dinner."

———— ◆ ————

DING. MEV CHECKED HER EMAIL.

RE: REQUEST FOR INFORMATION
Dear Chief Arroyo:
   I hope I can answer your questions satisfactorily.
   I do not know Robin Hood. I do not know who wrote the letter.
   The Indigenous Peoples Reparations Initiative was endowed in 1987 by Pilip Pitka to reimburse America's indigenous peoples for the appropriation of their land.

The IPRI office address, which is my home address, is 200 Gastineau Channel Road, Juneau AL 99801. The telephone number is 907-811-3665.

Although I disapprove of extortion—and this letter constitutes extortion—I hope that IPRI may keep the $15 million. IPRI can put that money to good use.

Yours truly,
Kallik Kootoo
Director of IPRI

Mev forwarded the email to Detective Hicks with the message, "Find out who Pilip Pitka is."

———•·———

ANNIE TURNED OFF HER LANTERN AND PULLED THE blanket over her body. But she could not sleep. It was the first Christmas holiday she'd spent alone. She was not unhappy, but she had much on her mind. She knew that the decisions she made now at the age of nineteen would determine where she'd be at the age of twenty-nine, thirty-nine, forty-nine, fifty-nine. There would be no turning back, no redoing the past.

In the past four months handsome, gentle Seq had entered her life. Eleven years older than she and eleven years wiser, he had become her north star, her guiding light, her spiritual leader. Seq was schooling her in the ways of his Cherokee forefathers, and day by day he was bringing her into his Cherokee world. She was almost there. If she married him she would join Tayanita Village. He wanted marriage. Did she? She wanted a simple existence. So did he. She wanted children.

But now Jaime had become part of her life, again. Why was this choice so difficult?

Jaime was not her guiding light. He was six months younger than she. But he was her spiritual twin. When he smiled at her she knew his smile was coming from deep within. When he laughed she laughed. When he held her hand she wanted to kiss him, to sleep with him, to wake up with him. If she returned to him, she would be embracing his academic future. He would get a PhD in ecology and become a professor. Could she still sing in a band? She wanted children.

———•———

When she arrived home Tabby went straight to her study, sat down at the computer, and composed a letter to the editor.

She emailed it to OnlineWitherston.

"This will annoy Sam Farthy," she said to herself.

———•———

Doug Hanley knew his father was on the line, but he answered his cell phone anyway.

"Yes, Father."

"I don't appreciate your embarrassing me last night, Douglas. You knew I was in the audience."

"Father, I am twenty-two years old. I speak for myself. And before I say something I for sure don't think, 'What would my distinguished lawyer parent want me to say?' I know what you'd want me to say. You've told me all my life."

"And your letter to the editor this morning. You think you comprehend what Tabby Grammer was talking about? You don't. You can't. You have no education. And no bank account. You have a lousy job and an arrest record."

"You got it, Father."

"If you and your buddy Trey had spent your Withers money on tuition instead of fancy cars, you'd have good jobs by now."

"Thanks for reminding me, Father."

"Why can't you be like your brother? All you do is embarrass me—with your tattooed neck and your black clothes, which stink of cigarette smoke by the way."

"It's not about you, Father."

"It is."

"Okay, it is. I'll be happy if you interpret everything I do or say as being about you."

Doug ended the call and punched in Trey Bennington's number.

"Do you want to go for a drink, Trey?"

———•·•———

ONCE DOUG AND TREY HAD SEATED THEMSELVES IN their usual booth at Teke's Tavern, Doug opened his tablet.

"I googled Tabby Grammer and found an interview she did with *Awohali Monthly*," Doug said. "*Awohali Monthly* is a Cherokee magazine. Look at what she said."

> **Editor**: *Thank you for visiting with me, Mrs. Grammer. I liked "Paving Gaia" very much, especially your declaration: "We owe reparations to Gaia." What do you mean by that?*
>
> **Tabby Grammer**: *If we can identify with Gaia—Earth— for a fleeting moment, we can feel the wounds that industrialized civilization has inflicted on her. Think of automobiles, asphalt, coal mines, oil drilling, fracking, bombs, and all the toxic waste, including nuclear waste. How do we heal Gaia? We make reparations.*

Editor: Reparations? Like reparations white people owe Native Americans for genocide?

Tabby Grammer: Comparable. What Gaia and Native Americans have in common is the damage industrialized people have done to them.

Editor: What form would reparations to Gaia take?

Tabby Grammer: Money. Money contributed by countries around the world to clean up pollution, to restore Gaia's forests, marshes, oceans, and other vital natural areas, and to develop non-toxic sources of energy.

Editor: Where would the money come from?

Tabby Grammer: Taxes, of course. Taxes on the richest among us, and on the biggest polluters.

Editor: Do you favor reparations to Native Americans?

Tabby Grammer: Yes. And to other groups that have been wronged.

Editor: Where would the money come from?

Tabby Grammer: Taxes.

Editor: How did you arrive at this notion of reparations for Gaia?

Tabby Grammer: Once I thought of Gaia as a "whole," I understood that if all parts of the whole are not healthy the whole is not healthy. Right now, Gaia is unhealthy. So is the human species, of which some members are wealthy, well fed, well clothed, and well educated, and others are poor, ill fed, ill clothed, and uneducated. Justice will require reparations for humanity as well as Gaia.

Editor: Thank you, Tabby Grammer.

"Christ, Doug. This woman wants to take our money and give it to Indians. She's like Robin Hood."

"She is Robin Hood. Can't you see, Trey?"

"I guess you're right. She calls for 'reparations,' just like Robin Hood did."

"I'm going to expose her."

CHAPTER SEVEN

Sunday, December 22, 2019

OnlineWitherston.com

NEWS

BONES FOUND IN GERTRUDE WITHERS SCHOOL BASEMENT

Yesterday Dr. Neel Kingfisher, Jorge Arroyo, and Jaime Arroyo discovered bones in the unfinished basement of the Gertrude Withers School for Children. The basement had been boarded up for at least eighty years.

Dr. Kingfisher has sent a bone sample to a lab in Atlanta to determine the skeleton's age and gender. He judges the skeleton to be human.

Dr. Kingfisher's team also found farm tools, a rifle, household items, art supplies, a locked wooden chest, and four amateur paintings of birds, including one of a Carolina parakeet, now extinct.

—AMADAHY HENDERSON, EDITOR

NORTH GEORGIA IN HISTORY
By Charlotte Byrd

I will interrupt my columns on Potter's Woods to reminisce about Robin Hood, not our extortionist who calls himself "Robin Hood," but the fabled thirteenth-century outlaw of Nottinghamshire, England.

According to stories told in the late Middle Ages and thereafter, Robin Hood was a skilled archer of noble birth who robbed the rich to give to the poor. He and his band of "merry men" hid out in Sherwood Forest near the Major Oak, an enormous English oak tree which is still standing after a thousand years. Robin Hood is a folk hero.

Some of you may remember this ballad from the British 1950s television show "The Adventures of Robin Hood."

> *Robin Hood, Robin Hood,*
> *Riding through the glen,*
> *Robin Hood, Robin Hood,*
> *With his band of men,*
> *Feared by the bad, loved by the good,*
> *Robin Hood! Robin Hood! Robin Hood!*

The countless songs, books, and films that tell of Robin Hood's deeds carry one message: Robin Hood was a good-hearted bandit who brought about social justice.

Although our local extortionist may be an arrow short of good-hearted, he or she may consider himself or herself a modern-day Robin Hood transferring wealth from the rich to the poor.

LETTERS TO THE EDITOR

To the Editor:

Mr. Tankard thinks I would be happy if he saved Big Yellow alone. I would not.

Mr. Tankard does not know that no living organism thrives alone.

A forest is an interconnected family of trees and shrubs and fungi and organic debris, as well as birds, mammals, insects, worms, and bacteria, all dependent upon each other. Mother Trees help the family survive by facilitating their exchange of nutrients. In turn, the family helps its Mother Trees survive.

Big Yellow is a Mother Tree. Big Yellow will not live long without her family.

—Annie Jerden

To the Editor:

As a televangelist, I denounce Ms. Tabby Grammer's interpretation of Genesis. Mrs. Grammer ignores the Biblical truth that mankind was divinely created to be distinct from the beasts of the field. Mrs. Grammer sees humans as simply one species among many, not any more important than fish.

Let it be known to all: Mrs. Grammer is a heretic.

And she is an unapologetic heretic. She keeps a goat named Allie Baba for a pet.

I demand that her book "Paving Gaia" be banned from Witherston's public library and from Witherston's public schools.

—The Reverend Conrad Carmike

To the Editor:
I have evidence that Tabby Grammer is Robin Hood. Her house is full of Native American relics.

The FBI should interrogate Tabby Grammer, search her house, and impound her phone and her computer for evidence of her connection with the Indigenous Peoples Reparations Initiative.

As we know, "Robin" is often a woman's name.

—*Sam Farthy*

To the Editor:
I suspect that "Robin Hood" is a resident of Tayanita Village. Tayanita Village would benefit from Cherokee reparations.

I request that the FBI investigate Tayanita Village, particularly this newcomer named Sequoyah.

—*Ruth Griggs*

To the Editor:
I object to two actions taken by Witherston: the sale of Potter's Woods to Thomas Tankard, a developer; and the awarding to Mr. Tankard of a building permit.

I object on the grounds that Potter's Woods belongs to the Cherokees who lived in these mountains for a thousand years. The 39-acre piece of land (I will not call it a "property") should not have been given to Patrick Potter in the first place, because it was not the Georgia governor's to give. The governor and his white predecessors stole it from the Cherokees.

Therefore, Potter's Woods should be returned to the Cherokees.

I suggest that Potter's Woods be transferred to Tayanita Village to maintain as an old-growth forest.
—Sequoyah Waters

To the Editor:

Chief Arroyo of the Witherston Police has called my attention to a letter, signed by Robin Hood, extorting citizens of Witherston to support the Indigenous Peoples Reparations Initiative.

I have no idea who Robin Hood is, or why he named the IPRI as the recipient of the $15 million he is trying to raise.

However, I can tell you what IPRI would do with $15 million if we had it. IPRI would endow an Indigenous Peoples College in the the greater Seattle area to provide free four-year education to anybody in the North America who identified himself or herself as Native American.

IPRI is grateful for whatever financial contributions are made to this cause.

Thank you.

—Kallik Kootoo
Director of the Indigenous
Peoples Reparations Initiative
Juneau, Alaska

To the Editor:

To save Earth's residents we must challenge the assumption that ownership of a piece of land entitles the owner to do what he wants with it.

We would not allow an individual to own a river. The river belongs to all of us. So does the air. So do the birds who disperse seeds, the bees who pollinate flowers, and the worms who aerate soil.

And I say, so do the old-growth forests, which regulate green-house gases, preserve biodiversity, and slow climate change.

Air, rivers, birds, worms, bees, and 300-year-old trees are all part of Earth. Earth should not be for sale—at least not the way Earth's surface is for sale.

We humans live on Earth's surface. We should not be permitted to damage Earth.

And that's what Thomas Tankard would be doing if he leveled Potter's Woods to satisfy his desire for money. Thomas Tankard may have bought the 39-acre plot, but he should not think he owns the old-growth forest. The forest belongs to Earth.

—Tabby Grammer

To the Editor:

Mr. Tankard can't see the forest for the trees.

Forests provide a home for rabbits, deer, raccoons, bears, coyotes, foxes, possums, skunks, moles, voles, squirrels, chipmunks, and many, many, many species of birds, including hawks, owls, vultures, cardinals, jays, and robins, as well as snakes, snails, turtles, salamanders, frogs, toads, insects and worms.

Where do the animals go when the chainsaw comes?

Save Potter's Woods from Mr. Tankard's chainsaw—for all of us.

—Jorge Arroyo

CHAPTER EIGHT

Sunday, December 22, 2019

Mev put the cheese omelette, biscuits, sausage, and orange juice on the table. Paco poured the coffee. Jaime was feeding Hamlet. Jorge was looking at his tablet.

"Holy moly!"

"It's breakfast time, Jorge," Paco said. "Put your tablet away and join us."

"Golly jeez!"

"What are you reading?" Jaime asked Jorge.

"Tabby Grammer has written a column for the *National Post-Herald*. And she quotes Robin Hood's extortion letter in full."

"In full?"

"Yes, Mom. In full. Fully, totally, completely, entirely."

"Witherston, Georgia, is making national news," Jaime said. "First time that's happened."

"After quoting the letter, Mrs. Grammer gives an argument for reparations to both Native Americans and African Americans. But she doesn't favor financial reparations." Jorge showed them the article. "Read this, starting here."

Robin Hood has illegitimately raised a legitimate issue worthy of discussion. Robin Hood proposes financial reparations for indigenous peoples—that is, Native Americans.

The long-term value of financial reparations is questionable.

Financial reparations cannot adequately reimburse a group for centuries of discrimination, poverty, insufficient education, and lost economic opportunities. The government cannot redistribute the nation's wealth to compensate sufficiently all those whose families have suffered the consequences of enslavement, genocide, and theft of land and gold.

Reparations in the form of education, however, can compensate the disadvantaged for generations to come. I propose that free higher education, for four years in public institutions, be made available to all Americans under the banner of 'reparations.'

Why everybody? Primarily because we see no reason to continue the unequal opportunity for education that has kept discrimination and poverty in place. The provision of universal free education will not discriminate between those who can trace their ancestry back to group discrimination and those who cannot. And finally, a better educated populace will be a wiser one.

[Tabby Grammer is the author of Paving Gaia and a series of murder mysteries. She makes her home in Witherston, Georgia.]

"It's a good essay," Jaime said. "I agree with her."

"I do too! I'm just surprised that she gave Robin Hood national attention," Jorge said.

"Maybe she thought Robin Hood's extortion letter could be used to promote reparations, reparations in the form of free education."

"I wish I had written it," Jorge said. "I would have said. 'A better educated populace will vote more intelligently.'"

"I wonder why she didn't tell us she was writing the piece," Mev said.

"She writes so much she can't recall all she's written," Jaime said.

"I wanna be like her," Jorge said.

While they ate, Jorge looked again at his tablet.

"Here's a letter from Kallik Kootoo. Remember who he is? Robin Hood made him the recipient of our contributions."

"Of the extorted money," Mev corrected Jorge.

"Okay." Jorge read aloud Kallik Kootoo's letter. "Kallik Kootoo and Tabby Grammer ought to get together. They both want free college for anybody who wants it."

"Aha," Jorge said. "I found something fun. It's ten o'clock. Let's listen to the Reverend Conrad Carmike's Sunday morning service." Jorge turned up the volume on his tablet. First they heard music, an orchestral version of "You Raise Me Up." Then Conrad Carmike's thunderous voice.

"Must be the voice of God," Jorge said. "Let's hear what he says."

It's ten o'clock on Sunday morning, the Reverend Conrad Carmike Hour. Hello, all you God-loving congregants. Time for listening to the Lord and me, the very Reverend Conrad Carmike, who will change your life. We've got four thousand souls in Union County, all sitting by their television sets waiting for today's message. And the message is: Remember Adam, who was created by God. Forget Eve.

Now let me tell you why you must remember Adam.

Many of you attended an event in Pinetops Hall Friday night where our godless woman mayor bestowed the Key to the City on an even more godless woman writer. Who is this godless woman writer? She is Tabby Grammer, who worships not God but Gaia, a pagan goddess of the earth. Tabby Grammer is a heretic.

Tabby Grammer says, "Gaia first." Not God first, not Jesus first, not even man first, but the earth. Tabby Grammer is a heretic.

Tabby Grammer claims to see creation from the viewpoint of the earth, from the viewpoint of dirt and water and worms and grass and trees and beasts. To Tabby Grammer, dirt and water and worms and grass and trees and beasts are being hurt by man. To her, therefore, dirt and water and worms and grass and trees and beasts are more important than man.

Let me tell you: In creation's hierarchy, God is on top, then the angels, then man, then woman, then beasts, and then trees and grass and worms and water and dirt.

Tabby Grammer may as well say, "Dirt first!"

Tabby Grammer denies the truth of the Bible, that God made man to rule over beasts.

Hear me! Tabby Grammer is a heretic.

Tabby Grammer calls for war against mankind.

Hear me! Tabby Grammer is a heretic!

And pay particular attention to this. Tabby Grammer is an egalitarian. If she had her way she would take your hard-earned money and give it to people less worthy than yourselves.

Hear me! Tabby Grammer is a heretic!

Let me ask you: Is her attitude compatible with the teachings of the Bible? I say No! It is not. It is heresy.

I ask you not to buy Tabby Grammer's book, not to attend any of her book-signings, not to read anything she writes, and not to listen to any of her interviews, such as the radio interview she has scheduled with Jorge Arroyo this noon.

And finally, stop Tabby Grammer. Tabby Grammer is a heretic. Tabby Grammer is your enemy.

"Well I'll be fiddled!" Jorge shouted. "Reverend Carmike plugged my show! I just got a thousand new listeners. And Tabby Grammer just got a thousand new readers."

"Whoa, son. Not so fast. Lots of Conrad Carmike's listeners will do anything he tells them to do. He just told them to stop Tabby Grammer."

"Whatever he meant, it will not be good for Tabby," Mev said.

———•———

"And . . . it's twelve o'clock noon! This is Jorge Arroyo, at WRVL-AM 570 on your dial, welcoming mountain listeners to my Sunday program 'Interview with Jorge Arroyo.' Today I have the honor of speaking with Tabby Grammer, author of the Appalachian Murder Mystery series, the children's book *Gaya Says,* and the non-fiction book, just out, titled *Paving Gaia.*

"Thank you for coming on my show, Mrs. Grammer."

"Call me Tabby, Jorge. And the honor is mine."

"Let me first ask you why you turned from writing mysteries to writing non-fiction."

"I really enjoyed writing mysteries, Jorge. I liked developing characters as human beings with recognizable and, for the most part, endearing personalities. I liked making funny dialog. I liked creating a puzzle and figuring out how my characters could solve the puzzle. But I became dissatisfied with entertainment."

"You call novels entertainment?"

"Not novels. Mysteries. Mysteries are mostly entertainment. I was a mystery writer, not a novelist. Novelists probe more deeply into the nature of things."

"So why didn't you write a novel?"

"Well, I'm probably incapable of being a serious novelist. I don't have the talent Barbara Kingsolver has. But may I tell you about an event that changed my life?"

"Go ahead."

"One night I dreamt that Earth was convulsing, as if it were in the throes of death. Trillions of ant-like creatures covered every square inch of the sphere's surface. They were turning the surface black. Earth shuddered—and I shuddered—and then Earth exploded. The ants all disappeared."

"What happened then?"

"I awoke, but not completely. I envisioned Earth at rest. Its surface was green and blue. I felt calm. Suddenly I realized that I had dreamt the catastrophe from the viewpoint of Earth, not from the viewpoint of the creatures on its surface."

"So from your perspective, from Earth's perspective, the ants on Earth's surface were Earth's enemy."

"Right, Jorge. They caused Earth to convulse and explode. And then they disappeared."

"I get it, Mrs. Grammer. The ants represented us, us humans. In your dream we are Earth's enemy, and we are killing Earth."

"Yes, Jorge. We are killing our home, since Earth is where we live. I thought of Gaia."

"Tell us who Gaia is."

"In Greek mythology Gaia is Earth, the mother of all life and the ruler of nature. In the secular twenty-first century, some of us speak of Earth as Gaia when we consider Earth as a single planetary ecosystem."

"So Gaia is a metaphor."

"Yes, Jorge. A useful metaphor. If we view Earth as Gaia we can see that if we harm Gaia, we harm ourselves. I've written a letter to the editor for OnlineWitherston to publish tomorrow explaining Gaia as a metaphor."

"In your imagination, will Gaia convulse again?"

"Yes. Climate change is a convulsion. Climate change will affect everyone on Earth."

"You've said you view life from Gaia's perspective. Does that mean you value Gaia more than any individual human?"

"I guess it does, Jorge."

"Our time is almost up, Mrs. Grammer. So I'll ask you one final question, a big one."

"Go ahead."

"If you were Gaia, and could talk, what would you say is the second biggest problem humans have, after climate change?"

"The unequal distribution of wealth. It's the greatest cause of unhappiness on Earth."

"I guess I agree, Mrs. Grammer. Thanks for talking with me."

"I appreciate your having me on the show, Jorge."

"Well, mountain listeners, our time is up. I thank Tabby Grammer, author of *Paving Gaia*, for joining us today. This is Jorge Arroyo saying 'Good-bye for now but not for long.'"

CHAPTER NINE

Sunday, December 22, 2019

Pil Pitka looked at the thermometer. Three degrees Fahrenheit. Too cold for a sixty-nine-year-old man to take a walk. He fixed his breakfast of oatmeal and coffee, put a log on the fire, and opened his tablet.

Pil—that is, Oki Yukon—had no friends in Nome. He couldn't take a chance. When in need, he relied on blood relatives, such as Toklo. Recently widowed, and lonely, Toklo had suggested that Pil live with him in Utqiagvik. Pil might sometime take him up on the invitation.

Pil found companionship online, in Witherston. Witherston was the site of a crime he knew well, a crime that Robin Hood would rectify.

He was curious about the body in the basement of the Gertrude Withers School. Had a Withers been killed there? Or had a Withers killed somebody there? There must have been a misdeed of some sort.

He thought about Tabby Grammer, who according to Sam Farthy collected Native American "relics." What did Sam Farthy mean by "relics"? Sam Farthy wouldn't call the Mona Lisa a "relic." He googled Sam Farthy and hit Farthy Construction Company. Yes, Farthy was an enemy. Was he a Withers's beneficiary? Yes. He had lived in Witherston since 1990.

Pil read Tabby Grammer's letter to the editor.

That's it. She's on my side. She thinks like me.

Pil googled Tabby Grammer and found her resumé, in addition to many images of her.

She was attractive.

Through the website YourIndigenousKin.com, Pil had discovered Sequoyah Waters, who was a fairly recent arrival at Tayanita Village. Sequoyah Waters would be a good surrogate for Robin Hood. He might be susceptible to suggestion. He had written an excellent letter.

He saw Kallik Kootoo's letter. "Well done, Cousin."

Pil googled Annie Jerden and found her picture. "Very pretty. She's on my side too."

He googled Rhonda Rather. How was she reacting to the letter from Robin Hood? How would Witherston react if she died?

He googled Thomas Tankard and landed on the Tankard Developers website, which said, "Specializing in home construction and remodeling for handicapped accessibility." No surprise there.

Pil closed his tablet and picked up a piece of soapstone. Today he would sculpt an otter. Tonight he would watch *The Deer Hunter.*

———— • • ————

"Hello, Lydia. I'm so glad you came over. Would you like a glass of wine?"

"I would. Thank you, Tabby."

As they sat by the fireplace, Lydia spoke tearfully of her departed spouse.

"Since my husband died last summer, I've been lonely on the farm. I've never lived by myself before. I'm seventy years old, I've got arthritis, I use a cane, I occasionally fall, and I can't take care of the animals anymore. I have to sell the farm."

"Oh, Lydia. I'm so sorry you've been lonely. I should have gone out to see you. How thoughtless I've been."

"Three weeks ago I sent Arthur Hanley a down payment for a cottage in Potter's Woods Retirement Community. I came to see you because we will find ourselves on opposite sides of your proposal at Wednesday's Board meeting."

"Oh, no."

"I respect your position on saving the forest, but I must tell you mine. I want to live in a community where I can socialize, play bridge, join book clubs, and have meals served to me in a dining room. I want to live in a hand-icapped-accessible cottage. I want to have access to an assisted living facility if I need it. Potter's Woods Retirement Community will provide all that on its campus."

"Campus?"

"Yes, it will be called a campus. Potter's Woods Campus. I can show you an architect's drawing."

On the coffee table Lydia unrolled a large architect's pen-and-ink rendition of the future Potter's Woods Retirement Community. It was labeled "Potter's Woods Campus." Tabby counted some ninety cottages and an assortment of larger buildings all situated on straight streets that intersected at right angles. She saw tennis courts and a golf course. And sidewalks, lawns, bushes, fountains, and perhaps a dozen trees.

"The architect saved Big Yellow," Lydia said, pointing to one of the trees depicted in the drawing.

"But a dozen trees don't make a woods," Tabby said. "I'm sorry that I must oppose this development, Lydia. I can't countenance the exchange of an old-growth forest for a subdivision."

"You're thinking abstractly, Tabby. You're steeped in knowledge about ecosystems and climate change and the function of old-growth forests. You're capable of seeing the planet as Gaia. I will read *Paving Gaia*, and I'll probably like it. But while you're identifying with Gaia, I'm identifying with me, one human who needs a retirement home, a retirement home in Witherston, not one in Atlanta or Gainesville."

"Oh, Lydia. You are right. I didn't think of the retirement community from a prospective resident's viewpoint."

"I am not alone, Tabby. Lots of people of my generation are realizing that we may not have many years ahead of us, and what years we have may not be good years. We must move while we can still pack up our things and sign our checks. You are in your thirties. You don't have such worries."

"I know, Lydia. I know. But I can't let go of my conviction that we humans have to protect our natural environment from ourselves."

"It's a matter of viewpoint, isn't it?"

"Maybe it is."

"It's time for me to go, my friend. Thank you for the wine. I will see you on Wednesday."

"I will try to think of a good alternative for the retirement community, Lydia. Maybe it doesn't have to be in Potter's Woods."

Tabby shut the front door and through the window watched her friend make her way to her car, slowly and carefully, leaning on her cane.

"Will the meeting of Tayanita Village please come to order. Thank you."

Village Chief John Hicks stood in the middle of the large circular yurt that served as the Village Council House. Above his head, at the top of the pitched canvas ceiling, was the seal of the Cherokee Nation.

John Hicks was admired by the Villagers for his knowledge of the Cherokee civilization and by the Witherston Police for his investigative skills. He had been elected Village Chief a month after being promoted to Detective.

On wooden benches facing John sat the fifteen other Villagers who had traced their heritage to the Cherokees of north Georgia and western North Carolina. Their experiment of living communally, growing their own vegetables, keeping chickens and goats, and taking turns cooking had been a success.

"Tonight we must discuss an impending FBI investigation. Mrs. Ruth Griggs has accused us of writing the Robin Hood extortion letter, saying that our Cherokee community would benefit from reparations. Special Agent Debra Danzer informed me today that she may talk with a few of us."

"We are Francis Hearty Withers's beneficiaries and therefore targets of Robin Hood's letter. We'll each have to pony up five thousand dollars," one Villager said. "Nobody should be suspicious of us."

"I'm not a beneficiary," Seq said. "I didn't join Tayanita Village till last spring. And I'm not rich."

"Agent Danzer knows that, Seq," John said. "She asked about you specifically. She wanted to know your original name, the name you had before Sequoyah Waters. I knew your first name was Andrew, but I didn't know Waters was not your last name. Anyway, Ms. Danzer will contact you."

"We should defend ourselves against Mrs. Reynold's accusation," Seq said. "Witherston needs to know we're good and honest citizens of this community."

"I propose that we do two things," said Amadahy. "First, we each pay our five thousand dollars immediately. Then in a letter to OnlineWitherston we reject in advance any reparations that might be offered us."

"Good idea. We're already affluent, by most standards. We don't need reparations."

"I'll write the letter as Village Chief," John said.

"I want to know if we're going to do anything to protect Potter's Woods," Seq said. "It belonged to our Cherokee ancestors before the Georgia legislature gave it to Patrick Potter. Our Cherokee ancestors would expect us to save this vestige of their homeland."

"What do you propose, Seq?" John said.

"Give Annie more publicity, for one thing. And show up at the Town Council meeting."

"All of us?"

"Yes, all of us. Wearing our green Deer Clan sweatshirts."

"Great idea!"

"I'm up for that!"

"I have another suggestion," Amadahy said. "Let's approve a resolution that I can report as news in OnlineWitherston."

"Do you have one ready?"

"Yes." Amadahy read from her tablet. "Because we know that a frog does not drink up the pond where he lives, we Cherokees of Tayanita Village oppose any effort to consume the planet that supports life."

The Villagers clapped.

"Any discussion?" John waited a moment. "Then all in favor please raise your right hand."

BETTY JEAN CRAIGE

All did.

"It's unanimous. Amadahy, you may report our action in OnlineWitherston."

"Will do."

"Now our historian will give us our topic for meditation. Let us stand and bow our heads."

The Villagers stood.

Seq spoke. "Tonight we'll listen to Chief Seattle, leader of the Suquamish people."

We know the sap that courses through the trees as we know the blood that courses through our veins. We are part of the earth and it is part of us. The perfumed flowers are our sisters. The bear, the deer, the great eagle, these are our brothers.

"Thank you, Seq," John said. "The meeting is adjourned."

"I'm worried about Annie," Amadahy said to Seq. "Will you stay with her tonight?"

"No. Annie has a date with someone else."

———•—

JAIME FOLLOWED A DEER TRAIL TO BIG YELLOW. THE SUN had set, and a full moon was rising. He reached the top of the rope ladder, climbed onto the platform that Seq and Annie had assembled in Big Yellow's branches, and entered the tent.

"Nice," Jaime said. "It's warm. I could live here." He greeted Annie with kisses on both cheeks.

"I do live here," Annie said.

"I've missed you."

"I've missed you too."

"I brought you a book, Tabby Grammer's *Paving Gaia*. It's really profound. I read it in bed last night. And I brought both of us dinner," Jaime said, taking a bottle of Penedés, a bottle opener, and a warm vegetarian pizza out of his backpack. "The wine is from Aunt Lottie. The pizza is from me."

Sitting cross-legged they ate their meal around the lantern and the heater as if around a campfire.

"Tell me about Seq," Jaime said. "Is he important to you?"

"Yes, Seq is important to me. He is teaching me Cherokee ways of thinking. Yesterday we talked about health. Seq said that when we treat our bodies as separate from everything else we can't be healthy. He said that a life spirit flows between our bodies and our natural environment. We can be healthy only when that flow is uninterrupted, only when we are in a harmonious relationship with our environment. Seq says that white people brought bad health to this continent by interrupting the flow of the life spirit. They thought they could separate themselves from their natural environment."

"That makes sense."

"I understand what Seq is saying, Jaime. That's why I'm trying to save Potter's Woods."

"So Seq is a teacher to you?"

"Yes. Seq says that when we allow ourselves to float down the river of time, enjoying what we encounter, not looking behind at what has gone, not trying to grab overhanging branches, not trying to swim upstream, we find health."

"That makes sense."

"I tell him that health is like music. We feel good when we are carried away by a melody."

"Like we do when you sing and I play the guitar."

"Right."

"Is Seq just a teacher to you, Annie?"

"What are you getting at, Jaime?" Annie touched his cheek.

"Are you in love with him?"

"Seq is my teacher. And he's eleven years older than I am. I look up to him."

"Do you look up to me?"

"Jaime! Where are we going with this conversation? I don't look up to you, and I don't look down on you. I look straight at you, into your beautiful blue eyes, into your mind, into your heart. And you look straight at me, into my eyes, into my mind, into my heart. You and I are equals. We are on the same wave length. We've been friends since our first year in high school."

"Yes, Annie. But just friends?"

"Okay. You and I are birds of a feather."

"Can we nest together?"

Annie laughed.

"Seq says he loves me. That's why he built me this platform. He put it together in Tayanita Village and brought it over in his pickup with the rope ladder. And he gave me this painting." Annie showed Jaime a very detailed watercolor of Big Yellow.

"Very impressive. Seq is good."

"He did this painting last fall, when Big Yellow was big and yellow."

Jaime changed the subject. They talked about their studies. About the satisfaction Jaime got from ecology. About the satisfaction Annie got from music. And finally about why they'd broken up.

"You need to date people at the University of Georgia," Annie said.

"No, I don't," Jaime said. "I see all these women at UGA and the woman I think of is you. Let's go back to the way we were. Let's be together again."

They listened to the sounds of the forest at night: the hoot of an owl, the high-pitched bark of a fox, the whine of a coyote.

About nine o'clock, Jorge pulled aside the tent flap.

"Look, Annie! The moon is so bright you can see the whole forest. And the old Gertrude Withers School building. And Bear Lodge. What a great look-out you have here! The wind's picking up. It's really cold. May I stay a little longer?"

"Sure. Come inside. Let's hear your new harmonica."

Jaime played the blues. They shared a joint.

Annie rested her head on Jaime's chest.

"Can you come back tomorrow night?"

"Sure, Annie."

— · —

Jorge was drawing a cartoon for OnlineWitherston when Jaime got home.

"You seem happy, Jaime."

"I am happy. I think Annie is coming back to me."

"What about Seq?"

"She likes him and looks up to him, but she doesn't love him. At least that's what I guess."

"Here's my picture of Annie in Big Yellow. Like it?"

"How about putting me in there, Jorge? Then I'd really like it."

"Will do, bro."

Jaime picked up his guitar and strummed it softly. Soon he was singing John Denver's "Annie's Song," softly.

You fill up my senses, like a night in a forest
Like the mountains in springtime,
  like a walk in the rain
Like a storm in the desert, like a sleepy blue ocean
You fill up my senses, come fill me again

———•———

TABBY GRAMMER SENT AN EMAIL TO KALLIK KOOTOO.

REPARATIONS
Dear Kallik Kootoo:
  I appreciated your letter in OnlineWitherston.
Let's talk.
  Call me at 1-706-883-4838.
  I attach a column I wrote for the National Post-Herald.
  Sincerely,
  Tabby Grammer, Witherston, Georgia

———•———

MEV AWOKE TO THE DING OF AN EMAIL. IT WAS ONE twenty in the morning.

ARRIVAL IN FAIRBANKS
Hello, Chief.
  Patty and I caught a flight out of Atlanta at 2:15 pm today and, with a stop in Seattle, arrived in Fairbanks at 8:35 pm their time (4 hours difference between Witherston's time and Fairbanks's time).
  We're staying at the Fairbanks Airport Hotel.

It's minus 10 degrees here now. But tomorrow the weather will warm up to 5 degrees. Lots of snow on the ground.

Tomorrow (Monday) we'll go to the courthouse, to the newspaper archives, and to Timothy Philip Potter's last known address.

On Tuesday morning early, we'll fly to Juneau to visit Kallik Kootoo. I got your message about Pilip Pitka. I'll see what I can ascertain.

On Christmas Day we may take a helicopter ride over Juneau and the islands.

And on Thursday, we'll catch a 9:00 am flight out of Juneau to Seattle and on to Atlanta.

We'll send you information as we get it.

Merry Christmas to you and Paco and Jaime and Jorge.

I'll see you Friday morning.

John

Mev went back to sleep.

CHAPTER TEN

Monday, December 23, 2019

OnlineWitherston.com

NEWS

Tabby Grammer Takes "Robin Hood" National

Author Tabby Grammer has brought national attention to Robin Hood's extortion demand.

In a column titled "Reparations Through Education," published yesterday in the National Post-Herald, Mrs. Grammer quoted in its entirety the letter sent to Online-Witherston last Friday that was signed by Robin Hood.

Then, in apparent approval of Robin Hood's call for reparations to indigenous peoples, Mrs. Grammer proposed that "free higher education, for four years in public institutions, be made available to all Americans under the banner of 'reparations.'"

This morning her column reappeared in the New York Times, the Atlanta Journal-Constitution, the Honolulu Star-Advertiser, the Fairbanks Daily News-Miner, the Juneau Empire, the Nome Nugget, and the Bismarck Tribune.

—Amadahy Henderson, Editor

Investigation into Extortion Case Continues

Chief Mev Arroyo has communicated with Kallik Kootoo, director of the Indigenous Peoples Reparations Initiative in Juneau, Alaska. In response to Chief Arroyo's questions, Mr. Kootoo said that he was unaware of the Robin Hood letter.

Chief Arroyo has dispatched Detective John Hicks to Alaska to make further inquiries regarding the use of IPRI funds. IPRI has a current endowment of $105,000, from which it makes small grants annually.

FBI Special Agent Debra Danzer is conducting an investigation into the identity of Robin Hood.

—Amadahy Henderson, Editor

Tayanita Village Supports Annie Jerden

At its regular Sunday meeting, Tayanita Villagers approved unanimously the following resolution:

RESOLVED: Because we know that a frog does not drink up the pond where he lives, we Cherokees of Tayanita Village oppose all efforts to consume the planet that supports life. Therefore, Tayanita Village endorses Annie Jerden's efforts to preserve Potter's Woods.

—Amadahy Henderson, Editor

NORTH GEORGIA IN HISTORY
By Charlotte Byrd

Back to the Potters and the Withers!

On August 10, 1869, Mark Potter, still suffering the effects of his amputated leg, married Mary Alice McCoy in Dahlonega. They moved to Savannah, where Mark became a surveyor. Mark never returned to Potter's Woods.

According to Savannah courthouse records, Mary Alice gave birth in 1870 to their son Nathaniel Gray Potter. Nathaniel, who struggled economically during Reconstruction, inherited Potter's Woods when Mark died but never visited the plot.

In 1902, getting news of the Alaska gold rush, Nathaniel moved to Fairbanks, Alaska, to a place called Barnette's Trading Post, in search of riches. Failing to make his fortune in the gold mines, Nathaniel went to work on the Alaska Railroad, married an Alaska Native named Muuka, and produced four daughters and a son, Chauncey Philip Potter, who eventually inherited Potter's Woods.

Chauncey and his Inuit wife Akna Pitka produced one son, Timothy Philip Potter, who inherited Potter's Woods in 1986.

— ◆ —

"Annie Jerden Saving Big Yellow," by Jorge Arroyo

LETTERS TO THE EDITOR

To the Editor:

I wish to report that fifteen Tayanita Villagers have each transferred $5,000 to the bank account of

Online Witherston for the Indigenous Peoples Reparations Initiative. That adds up to $75,000.

Furthermore, Tayanita Village rejects in advance any funds collected by IPRI for Native American reparations.

—*Village Chief John Hicks*

To the Editor:

I have given Mr. Arthur Hanley a down payment of $20,000 for a cottage in the Potter's Woods Retirement Community. So have eighteen other people.

I find Tabby Grammer to be insensitive to the needs of elderly Witherston citizens.

I urge the Council to reject her proposal to buy back Potter's Woods from Thomas Tankard.

—*Ruth Griggs*

To the Editor:

I am compelled to respond to Tabby Grammer's letter of yesterday.

First, removing 39 acres of woods from the million wooded acres of the surrounding mountains will not cause any harm to "Earth." (Why does Mrs. Grammer have to capitalize "earth," anyway?)

Second, Mrs. Grammer wants government to regulate individuals' use of their own property. I see government control of our property as an infringement on our freedom. It leads to communism.

Third and most important, in building the Potter's Woods Retirement Community, I am serving an urgent need, the need for humane treatment of our oldest citizens. Many of these Witherston residents, ranging in age from 70 to 100, have nowhere else to go. Some of them have no children to care for them when they can no longer drive, cook, bank, walk, hear, or see. Others do not want to move in with their children when they cannot take care of themselves. Still others suffer from dementia and need full-time nursing.

Mrs. Grammer obviously does not understand.

—Tom Tankard

To the Editor:

Sequoyah Waters is not who he says he is. If Sequoyah Waters does not publicly disclose his past, I will.

—Sam Farthy

To the Editor:

If you wonder who Robin Hood is, read Revenge of the Brave.

—Trey Hamilton

CHAPTER ELEVEN

Monday, December 23, 2019

A t ten o'clock Jaime and Jorge met Neel Kingfisher at the old Gertrude Withers schoolhouse. Neel passed out shovels.

"Let's start in the basement, boys," Neel said. "I mean men. Sorry. I have thought of the three of you as boys since you were fourteen."

"We're men now," Jorge said. He carried an LED lantern down the decaying steps and set it in the middle of the room.

"This place was used to store farm equipment," Jaime said, pointing to a wagon wheel, a plow, and a saddle.

"Whoa," Jorge said. "Where's the chest? Someone stole the chest."

"Oh, no!"

"Here's the chest," Neel said, pointing his LED flashlight under the stairs. "Someone opened it and dragged it over here."

"He dragged it over the bones!" Jorge said.

"He or she," Neel said.

"He or she broke the lock," Jaime said. He illuminated the chest's dusty interior with his phone's flashlight. "There's glitter in here!"

Neel approached with his flashlight. "We're looking at gold dust, boys. This chest probably held some nuggets."

"Harry Withers stored his valuables in this basement," Jorge said. "Corpses and gold nuggets."

"Who stole the gold?"

"I suspect Trey and Doug," Jaime said.

"Don't touch the chest," Jorge said. "The police will try to get some fingerprints off it."

"Let's solve that mystery after we level the floor," Neel said. "Who knows? We may find more bones."

"Or gold," Jorge added.

The group worked until noon without finding either bones or gold. They did find a pale blue velvet purse in the dirt. It contained a white handkerchief and a gold cross on a gold chain.

"Gertrude Withers was religious," Jaime said."

"Poor Gertrude. She must have known about the corpse," Jorge said, putting the purse on a shelf with other household items.

"Let's finish up here," Neel said. "Time for lunch."

They stacked the farm equipment against a wall and moved the chest under the stairs.

"I'll ask Tabby to inventory the contents of the schoolhouse," Neel said.

———•◦•———

"I appreciate your coming in this morning, Mr. Farthy. Have a seat."

Sam Farthy dusted the snow off his heavy leather coat, sat down across from Special Agent Debra Danzer, and lit a cigarette. He looked at his watch. It was nine o'clock.

"Will this take long?" Sam Farthy asked her.

"No, Mr. Farthy. I want to interview you regarding your knowledge of Tabby Grammer. You wrote a letter to the editor suggesting Tabby Grammer was Robin Hood. I'm trying to determine whether that is the case. What evidence do you have?"

"Besides her public advocacy for reparations to Native Americans? Let me tell you. I visited her in her home. I took pictures, including this one of a document in her desk drawer.

Sam showed it to Agent Danzer. It was a list of organizations.

DONATIONS FOR 2019

ACLU

Food Bank of Northeast Georgia

Stone Clean Streams in Atlanta

Greenpeace

American Indian College Fund

Native American Rights Fund

IPRI

Sierra Club

Ocean Conservancy

World Wildlife Fund

"Do you notice that IPRI is on the list?" Sam asked.

"Yes. Can you forward your photo to me?"

"Sure, Agent Danzer. Do you want to see my other pictures?"

"Yes, thank you. Was Mrs. Grammer aware that you took these pictures?"

"She was not."

As the FBI agent looked through the photos on his camera, Sam talked.

"Tabby Grammer has a museum's worth of Native American paraphernalia on display. In cases, in curio cabinets, on the wall. You know, she considers herself part Cherokee."

"Is there any reason I should not suspect you of false accusation, Mr. Farthy?"

"Me? Why?"

"Is it to your advantage to have Tabby Grammer arrested? Aren't you a partner in Thomas Tankard's Retirement Community project?"

"I am. But . . ."

"One last question. Why did you accuse Sequoyah Waters of hiding his past?"

"Because he is hiding his past. He should not be considered a credible witness against Tom Tankard."

"What is he hiding?"

"He's hiding the fact that his father is in prison. That's why he changed his name."

"Thank you for speaking with me today, Mr. Farthy. Have a good afternoon."

⸺ ◆ ⸺

Kallik Kootoo read with excitement Tabby Grammer's "Reparations" piece. He showed it to his wife.

"We ought to work with Tabby Grammer," Kallik said to Kirima. "We'll have fifteen million dollars from Robin Hood. With matches from Wallace Scout and Everett Sail we'll have a total of forty-five million. We'll be able to establish the college."

Kallik had met Kirima Pitka when they were graduate students at the University of Washington in Seattle. He was finishing an MBA, and she was finishing a certificate in Indigenous Studies. They married in 1980, moved to Juneau the following year to be closer to their Alaska relatives, got good jobs, and raised their daughter Ahnah, who now taught women's studies at a small college in Idaho. They lived with a huskie named Yuka in an A-frame log home facing the Gastineau Channel. The interior walls were lined with bookshelves.

With the hundred-thousand-dollar endowment gift from Kirima's older cousin Pilip Pitka in 1987, Kallik had set up the Indigenous Peoples Reparations Initiative. Over the years he had increased the endowment by five thousand dollars from small donations.

The dream of establishing an Indigenous Peoples College with IPRI funds was hers. The responsibility for raising funds for it was his. Kallik had been courting two Native-friendly billionaires from Seattle, Wallace Scout and Everett Sail, who had each promised to match whatever donations he could bring in.

"Are you thinking of Tabby Grammer for our Board of Directors?" Kirima asked.

"Yes. She has made small gifts to IPRI from time to time."

"What if the police don't allow us to keep the fifteen million?"

"The police won't halt the payments till they catch Robin Hood."

"I think they will catch him."

"I think they will not. Anyway, I'll call Tabby Grammer."

"Be careful what you say, Kallik."

"Of course."

Kallik called 1-706-883-4838. Tabby Grammer didn't answer, so he left a message with his cell phone number for her to return his call.

———•———

"It's an honor to meet you, Mrs. Grammer. I read your mystery *OnlineCrime*. As an FBI agent I found your knowledge of illegal internet activities very impressive."

"Thank you, Agent Danzer. I wasn't expecting your call. I was on my way to the Gertrude Withers School."

"Why would you be going over there?"

"I need to inventory the items in the basement. I'll be curator of the museum."

"This won't take long, Mrs. Grammer. If you don't mind, I will record our conversation."

"I don't mind."

"I heard that you stirred up a hornet's nest Friday night, both before and after the audience learned of Robin Hood."

"I did."

"What made your audience—at least some of your audience—angry at you?"

"I threatened their investments."

Agent Danzer raised her eyebrows. "Financial investments?"

"Yes. And social investments, religious investments, investments in what they held to be true. I challenged their deeply held, long-standing opinions."

"Go on."

"I told them that Earth wasn't created for us humans. Shocker. Let's say I gently tugged at the string that held their hierarchical world together. And they feared I'd pull it harder and unravel everything they believed in. Such as God, their superiority over others, their money, their righteousness."

"Their relationship with Native Americans?"

"Yes. Lots of people with inherited wealth believe they deserve their good fortune, even if their ancestors acquired their wealth by theft from Native Americans."

"What did you say to your audience Friday night? As I was told, you were there to accept the Key to the City."

"Yes, and I was also asked to talk about *Paving Gaia*. So I did. I explained what the world looked like from Gaia's viewpoint. And what humans looked like from Gaia's viewpoint."

"Did you say you favored reparations to Native Americans?

"I did. And I do."

"Do you believe that your fellow citizens of Witherston owe their wealth to Native Americans?"

"I do."

"Mrs. Grammer, are you Robin Hood?"

"Why would you think that?"

"You and Robin Hood both assert that Native Americans deserve reparations."

"True."

"Why do some accuse you of being Robin Hood?"

"They think I want to take away what they have, like Robin Hood aims to do."

"Do you?"

"Not all of what they have, but a portion of it. I'd do it through taxes."

"If you were arrested, Mrs. Grammer, how would you prove you are not Robin Hood?"

"That would be hard to do. It's difficult to prove a negative, you know."

"Can you explain this preface to *OnlineCrime*?" Agent Danzer showed Tabby a highlighted paragraph.

Robin Hill, defender of the down and out, computer hacker, and extortionist par excellence, transferred funds electronically from wealthy individuals engaged in illegal activities to a non-profit organization established to feed the hungry. Was Robin Hill engaged in crime? Or was Robin Hill pursuing social justice? Was Robin Hill a twenty-first-century Robin Hood?

"*OnlineCrime* is fiction, Agent Danzer. Do you believe that every mystery is based on true events? I don't base the mysteries I write on true events."

"How did you get the idea for *OnlineCrime*?"

"From my imagination, of course. I asked myself, What crime would serve justice? What crime would make a better world? And I thought of transferring lawbreakers' ill-gotten gains to the needy. Robin Hill became a character worthy of admiration."

"Do you consider the extortionist Robin Hood worthy of admiration?"

"I won't stoop to answer that question, Agent Danzer."

"Have you ever communicated with Kallik Kootoo?"

"Yes, I emailed him yesterday after I read his letter to the editor."

"What did you say?"

Tabby looked at her phone and read the message aloud.

"Can you forward your email to me?"

"Of course." Tabby forwarded the email.

"Has Kallik Kootoo spoken with you since then?"

"No, he hasn't."

"Did he email you back?"

"No."

"Had you ever been in contact with him before now?"

Tabby hesitated. "Yes."

"On what occasion?"

"I have made hundred-dollar donations to IPRI five or six times." Then she added, "Every November I contribute a hundred dollars each to ten organizations. IPRI is only one of them. Kallik Kootoo sends me a thank-you note."

"Which are the others?"

"I'll email you the list for 2019. But off the top on my head I remember Stone Clean Streams in Savannah, the ACLU, Greenpeace, the American Indian College Fund, and the Native American Rights Fund. There are a couple of others I've forgotten."

"So you and Kallik Kootoo are friends."

"Acquaintances. Not friends."

"Thank you, Mrs. Grammer." Agent Danzer turned the recorder off. "You may leave now."

Tabby went home. Before she changed clothes she emailed Mev.

FBI INTERVIEW
Dear Chief Arroyo:
>*I think I'm being framed. Can we talk tomorrow?*
>*Thanks.*
>*Tabby*

She got an immediate reply.

Re: FBI INTERVIEW
Hello, Tabby.
>*Come see me in my office tomorrow morning at 10:00.*
>*Mev*

"Tell me about yourself, Seq." Tabby Grammer said after the waiter had poured their glasses of Cabernet.

Tabby had dressed up. She wore knee-high black boots, tight black jeans, a mauve sweater, and a pale pink lambskin leather jacket, plus dangling turquoise and silver earrings. She took off the jacket. She had looked forward to the evening, but now she had other things on her mind.

They were seated in front of the great hearth in the crowded dining room of Bear Lodge. The fire crackled.

Tabby raised her glass in a toast. "Here's to Gaia and to those who love her."

"To those who love her," Seq repeated.

They clicked glasses.

"And thank you, Tayanita Village," Tabby said, "for treating Gaia gently."

"And thank you, Tabby Grammer, for accepting honorary membership in the Village."

They both looked around at the mounted heads of wild animals adorning the wood paneled walls: two bucks, a bear, and a bobcat.

"I've seen all these animals in the mountains near here, in the flesh," Seq said. "I'm not a hunter though. I'm a birder and a painter. I paint feathers and trees. I'll give you one of my water colors."

"Thank you. I'd love one."

"I'll give you a painting I just finished of a Screech owl feather."

"Tell me how you came to Witherston."

"I was born on April twenty-second, thirty years ago, in Dahlonega, where I grew up and learned carpentry from my father. After high school I enrolled at the University of North Georgia but dropped out because I ran out of money. Actually, I had a family—a wife and a daughter—whom I needed to support. I got a job with the U.S. Forest Service and worked in Dahlonega for eight years until I was laid off."

"What happened to your family?"

"My daughter, Celeste, died of a brain tumor at the age of two. My wife became depressed, and she left me. We're divorced."

"Oh! I am so sorry!"

"I try not to think about her. My daughter, I mean."

"Why did you come to Witherston?"

"I discovered a website called YourIndigenousKin. I joined the group and made some friends. One of them was John Hicks of Tayanita Village. I'd heard of Tayanita Village. I didn't want to live alone. So I talked with John Hicks, who was impressed with my carpentry skills, and he invited me to live there. I told him that I had traced my mother's Cherokee ancestry to Chief Sequoyah and that I was taking the name Sequoyah. Seq for short."

"Was that true?"

"Somewhat," Seq paused and smiled.

Tabby was startled to find herself attracted to Seq. He was tall, handsome, and clean-shaven, with short black hair and hazel eyes. He'd worn a royal blue wool sweater. He looked older than thirty. She hoped she looked younger than thirty-six.

"How did you get interested in birds?"

"The first week I was here I rescued a baby Barred owl. I cared for him until he was three months old and he flew away. He left behind some beautiful feathers. I got hold of some watercolors and did a painting of one. Then I did a painting of an eagle feather. I'd always liked to paint. And I've always been fascinated by birds. Now I had an obsession."

"A great obsession. With a great obsession you're always on the hunt."

"Do you have an obsession, Tabby?"

"I do. But I'm a collector, Seq. I collect Native American art. I want you to come over and see my collection. Maybe tomorrow. It will include the feather painting you bring me."

"You're also a writer. Writing is a great obsession. You and I both make gifts for others."

Their dinner arrived. Roasted vegetables, kale, and mushrooms for Tabby. Shrimp, wild rice, and spinach for Seq. And freshly baked multi-grain rolls.

Seq poured them each a second glass of wine.

"Let's speak softly, so we won't be overheard. Since you're famous, lots of people might be trying to hear what you're saying."

Tabby looked around. "Good idea. I see a few people I know who may not be friendly."

"Anyway, I started studying the Cherokee civilization and really liked their way of living, I mean their way of living before the white settlers came. Until the nineteenth century the Cherokees belonged to the land. They belonged to each other. They belonged to their past. They did not consider themselves separate from the mountains, the forests, the waters, and the animals around them."

"Nature was not separate from them."

"Right. As far as I can find out, the Cherokee had no sense of nature as a 'thing' outside themselves. In fact, I couldn't find a Cherokee word for 'nature' that corresponded to our word for 'nature.' The traditional Cherokee people—I mean the Cherokee people who lived here for a thousand years—seemed to consider themselves part of what we'd call nature. Nature was everything. Nature was the world. Europeans didn't think like that."

"For the Cherokees, nature was Earth."

"Yes. And they were part of Earth. I was taken with the Cherokees' sense of belonging. I wanted to belong somewhere. I wanted to escape the loneliness I'd felt since I was a boy and was told to be independent and to take responsibility for myself."

"It seems that you find belonging and independence to be opposites."

"Actually, I find belonging and separation to be opposites, Mrs. Grammer."

"Seq, please call me Tabby. I don't call you Mr. Waters. By the way, is 'Waters' your original surname?"

"No. I took the name Waters when I took the name Sequoyah. I won't tell you my original surname now. I'll tell you sometime. But tonight let's talk about belonging and separation."

"Okay. Let's see. In your view of Cherokee culture you see as 'belonging' what I see as 'interconnected.' Belongingness equals interconnectedness, right?"

"Belongingness. That's nice. That's what I'm looking for."

"What would give you belongingness personally?" Tabby asked.

"A family. Tayanita Village suits me temporarily, but I want a family of my own. A wife and children."

"Do you have anyone in mind?"

"It's not much of a secret, I guess. I would like to marry Annie Jerden. But I'm not sure she would like to marry me."

"Not yet."

"Not yet."

"Go after what you want, Seq. Go see her tonight."

A moment of silence passed.

"Now it's time for you to tell me about yourself, Tabby. I listened to your interview with Jorge Arroyo today, which was very interesting. And I've read all your books. Now I want to know more about you."

"That's only fair, I guess. I was born in Savannah, grew up there, went to law school, practiced law in Savannah for five years, wrote a murder mystery called *Interred in the Low Country*, led a movement to save a state park, led a movement to clean up a stream, and wrote a couple more mysteries. Then I lost interest in writing fiction and moved here. The beauty of these mountains inspired me to write *Paving Gaia*. In doing the research for the book, I evolved from an ordinary environmental activist to a Gaia-centrist."

"That's an impressive resumé, Tabby, but it's just a resumé. What happened to your soul when you evolved into a Gaia-centrist?"

"You want me to dig deeply, Seq?"

"Yes, Tabby, dig deeply."

Tabby looked into the flames of the fireplace.

"I'm asking you what made you what you are, Tabby."

"What made me? Okay. First, my mother, whose maiden name was Wolf, instilled Native American values in me. So going from her teachings to Gaia-centrism was not a leap."

"Your mother was Native American?"

"Yes, half Cherokee. So I'm a fourth Cherokee. Anyway, I told Jorge about a dream in which I saw the world from the hypothetical viewpoint of Earth, and not from the viewpoint of a human. That dream was my turning point. But even before then I was gradually realizing that my environmentalism was human-centric, that I wanted to keep Earth healthy for us humans to enjoy. We humans were trying to manage Earth for our benefit. After the dream, trying to manage Earth seemed not only wrong but ludicrous."

"I agree."

"Being truly Gaia-centric, which would be to abandon the human viewpoint, is not easy. I accomplish it only momentarily from time to time, and, if I were totally honest, only theoretically. Gaia-centrism is an ideal, not a way of life. But it is an ideal that can serve Earth well."

"So what happened to your soul, Tabby?"

"Okay. I've never dug this deep before, Seq. Give me a minute."

Tabby took a sip of wine.

"When I let go of my ambitions—to be a lawyer, to write a best-seller, to lead environmental causes, to find another husband—I relaxed, maybe for the first time in my life. But I did more than relax. I shed the lifelong conviction that I needed something beyond what I had and that I needed to compete with others for that something. I shed the belief that I was autonomous, independent, self-sufficient."

"I'm with you, Tabby."

"Shedding those convictions was huge, let me tell you. It allowed me to see Earth as my home in which I was connected to others, in which all Earth's inhabitants were connected to one another and dependent on one another, in which we helped each other. Anyway, now I feel whole. Not independent or autonomous, but whole in myself and part of a larger whole. As you would say, I belong to Earth."

"For you, autonomy and interconnectedness are opposites. For me, separation and belongingness are opposites. Same thing, right?"

"Yes, Seq, yes. Now let me tell you about something that happened to me when I had just moved to Witherston. I was driving up Hope Avenue not far from here, and I saw the car ahead of me hit a squirrel running across the road. The car drove on, but I braked. The squirrel twitched and died before my eyes. Suddenly I felt kinship with the squirrel, and I said to myself, 'My life is no more, and no less, important than this squirrel's life. This squirrel and I and all the other trillion animals on Earth, live, love, twitch, and die. And after we're gone and our molecules enter the soil other squirrels and humans take our place. We all belong to Earth. And nobody is in charge.'"

"Nobody is in charge. Good thing."

"Humans are trying to take charge, Seq. That's not serving Earth well."

"How did your intellectual conversion affect your personal life? Are you still looking for a husband?"

"I am not," Tabby said. "For the first time in my life I feel happy. I did get a goat, however. I named her Allie Baba. And a month ago I got a kitten. Smoky."

"You don't have children?"

"I don't. For years I looked back in my life to revisit decisions I'd made, thinking that if I'd gone in a different direction I'd have children and I'd be happier. After my 'conversion,' as you call it, I realized that I can't change the past. So I ride the winds of the present."

"Are you open to new relationships?"

"Yes. But I no longer view relationships only in terms of mates. Relationships can take many forms. I am open to new relationships now, to friendships."

"I'm still in the seeking mode."

"You are, because you're young. You want a wife and children."

"Are you writing another book, Tabby?"

"I am. My next book will be called 'Gaia's Revenge.'"

"Gaia's Revenge on us humans, I bet."

Tabby raised her wine glass and took the last swallow. "Here's to Gaia."

Seq raised his. "And to those who love her."

"I have to tell you something, Seq. I am worried that I might be arrested for extortion. Agent Danzer thinks I'm Robin Hood."

Tabby told Seq about her interview with the FBI officer.

"That's absurd. How could she think you're Robin Hood?"

"I didn't distinguish myself ideologically from Robin Hood. I was honest."

"She won't arrest you, Tabby. She's interviewing lots of folks, including me, tomorrow."

"The end of the interview was particularly disturbing. She seemed to know about my contact with Kallik Kootoo—as if she'd been in my computer, or my desk."

"You're in contact with Kallik Kootoo?"

"Yes, but not about Robin Hood. I have contributed to the Indigenous Peoples Reparations Initiative."

"There's nothing illegal about that. The FBI can't arrest you for donating to an organization."

"I hope you're right. I could not bear being tried for extortion. I would not go through it."

"Don't worry, Tabby. I have your back. I know you're not Robin Hood, not Robin Hood the extortionist. Besides, you don't have the temperament of Robin Hood the extortionist. You're more like Robin Hood of Sherwood Forest."

"And why am I like Robin Hood of Sherwood Forest?"

"Robin Hood of Sherwood Forest was a spirited leader of a band of merry men. He wasn't lonely. Like you, he was connected with others. I'd guess that the extortionist Robin Hood is not connected with anybody. I'd guess he's a loner. He's like a solitary cat who enjoys watching the mice scramble."

A young man dressed in a tux sat down at the piano by their table and began playing Scott Joplin's "Maple Leaf Rag."

Over the music, Tabby spoke more loudly.

"Something just occurred to me. Sam Farthy paid me a visit on Saturday. He wanted me to withdraw my proposal to the Town Council. I wonder whether he got into my desk when I was in the kitchen fixing his scotch."

"What did he say?"

"He offered me shares in the Potter's Woods Retirement Community, and when that didn't work he threatened to expose me as Robin Hood. I threatened to get him convicted for attempted blackmail. I ended the visit."

"He drank your scotch and then tried to blackmail you?"

"Yes."

"You should tell Chief Arroyo."

"I intend to tell her. Tomorrow."

"You have found serenity, Tabby. Don't let go of it."

The waiter returned Tabby's credit card.

"Thank you so much for inviting me to dinner, Tabby. Our next dinner is on me."

"I hope that will be soon."

Seq kissed Tabby on her forehead, got into his truck, and departed.

Tabby zipped up her jacket, retrieved an LED camping lantern out of her car, and walked across the highway to the Gertrude Withers School.

CHAPTER TWELVE
Monday, December 23, 2019

With her lantern lighting the way Tabby descended the rickety stairs into the schoolhouse basement. She looked around the cavernous space.

Against the north wall she saw farm tools, horse tack, a wagon wheel, a shovel, a rifle, and an easel. On a ledge she saw pliers, a saw, a hammer, a hatchet, and a handgun.

The east wall was covered floor to ceiling with shelves. She spotted an iron, pots and pans, a set of blue pottery dishes and bowls, drinking glasses, a pitcher, water color paints, and brushes. In the drawers of a dresser she found a quilt, dresses, shoes, bonnets, ribbons, and a hairbrush. What a trove. She opened a built-in cabinet and found the paintings. She imagined them hanging on the museum walls.

Tabby set her lantern on the ground, took her cellphone from her purse, and documented her findings with a video.

"Where is the chest?" she asked herself. She panned the room and found the disturbed grave. She videoed the bones. She saw the chest, lid open, under the stairs.

Then she heard footsteps. The wood floor creaked above her. Somebody was walking around the schoolroom.

"Hello," she called out. "Who's there? I'm Tabby Grammer. I'm in the basement."

She headed toward the stairs. She smelled kerosene, then smoke. "Oh, no! Fire!"

The explosion knocked her to the ground. Flames blocked her exit. The smoke intensified. She couldn't breathe. She dropped the phone.

———•———

Seq returned to his yurt in Tayanita Village.

He had inherited the dark green canvas yurt from John Hicks when John and Patty got married. It was twelve feet in diameter, eight feet high, with a skylight, solar panels, two screened windows and a wooden door facing Tayanita Creek. Inside, six of his feather paintings hung on the walls. A heater-lamp kept the space warm even on the coldest nights. A small refrigerator cooled his beer, and a hot plate heated his soup. A small bathroom with a shower was attached. With electricity and running water he was comfortable.

Seq charged his phone, put Cherokee flute music into his CD player, opened a beer, and composed an email to Tabby Grammer.

THANK YOU
Hi, Tabby.
Thank you very much for the special evening.
Our souls touched tonight.
We are related in spirit.
Would you like to join YourIndigenousKin?
Your devoted friend,
Seq

Seq lay back on his pillows and fell asleep.

After a dinner of venison, cabbage, and potatoes, Pilip Pitka sat down by the fire with his beer and his tablet.

Pil noted that Detective John Hicks was in Alaska snooping around. What would Hicks find? Not any clue to Oki Yukon of Nome, for sure. But no doubt he would find the official documents of Timothy Philip Potter of Fairbanks: birth, military service, marriage, divorce, inheritance, taxes.

Would Hicks get access to his record in Vietnam? His medical records?

Would Hicks discover that Timothy Philip Potter had become Pilip Pitka?

Pil recalled the theme of Tabby Grammer's *Revenge of the Brave*. "Every contact leaves a trace." He pulled *Revenge of the Brave* off his bookshelf and found the reference in the preface. It was "Locard's Principle," named for a French detective named Edmond Locard.

"Traces." Every crime, every action, every decision made in the past leaves traces in the present. What traces did thefts in the past leave on the present? The distribution of wealth, obviously. What traces did rape leave? The distribution of DNA. He himself had been born of more than one crime.

In Vietnam he had committed more than one crime.

Could the crimes of the past ever be undone? No. Could reparations ever compensate the victims of those crimes? No. Not the original victims, but maybe their descendants. Could a crime in the present rectify a crime in the past? Not fully. But worth the effort, Robin Hood would say. Would such a crime really be a crime? Or would it be an adjustment?

Pil opened another beer and read "Reparations Through Education" in the *Nome Nugget*. Excellent. Should he contact Tabby Grammer, anonymously of course? No. That would be leaving a trace.

Next Pil visited OnlineWitherston.com/contributors. Two thousand nine hundred fifty-five. Impressive show rate.

Robin Hood was serving the cause of justice, and he merited admiration for his self-sacrifice, if it came to self-sacrifice. Because of Robin Hood's crime of extortion in the twenty-first century almost three thousand individuals who owed their wealth to a crime of theft in the nineteenth century were giving a small part of it to the victims' descendants.

Would Robin Hood be captured? What traces had Robin Hood left?

Pil read Sam Farthy's letter to the editor. Interesting.

He ordered *Into the Wild* from Amazon Prime, stoked the fire, and watched the movie.

———•◦•———

Jaime brought a bottle of Cabernet and four pieces of Kentucky fried chicken. He climbed the rope ladder carefully.

"Hello, Annie. I brought your Christmas present early." Jaime unzipped his backpack and handed her a box wrapped in red foil.

Annie kissed Jaime on both cheeks and opened the box. She removed a pair of night-vision binoculars.

"Oh, Jaime! Thank you! We are going to have fun tonight! The moon is still full. We'll be able to see the nocturnal animals."

"Foxes, skunks, raccoons, owls. I'll have to spend the night up here, don't you think?"

"I think," Annie said.

Using the binoculars they spotted a fox, two owls, and a coyote before they got hungry and went inside the tent to eat.

"Do you know why owls turn their heads two hundred and seventy degrees, Jaime? Because they have fixed eye sockets."

"Cool." Jaime raised his glass of wine. "Here's to you, Annie."

"Here's to us, Jaime."

"Annie, I've been thinking. If you transferred to the University of Georgia you could major in music and study voice. You could even study opera, if you like. You know, you can really sing."

"I don't want to study opera, Jaime. I just want to sing, like last year when you played the guitar and I sang in Tony Lima' Band."

"Do you want to sing all your life?"

"Yes, all my life."

"Then come back with me to Athens, Annie. I'm in a band called Folk. You can sing with us."

"What about Seq?"

Jaime fell silent.

"I mean, how do I let Seq down easy, and not hurt him terribly?"

"Did you see Sam Farthy's letter this morning? He's trying to blackmail Seq."

"Sam Farthy is a creep," Annie said.

"Do you know what Seq is hiding?"

"I do, but I promised to keep his secret."

"Seq must hate Farthy."

"I'm sure he does now."

"Annie, will you come back to Athens with me?"

"I'll think about it."

"Would you live with me?'

"I'll think about it."

Jaime took her into his arms.

After an hour or so, Annie said, "I smell smoke. I mean, smoke from burning wood." She pulled aside the tent flap. "Oh, my God! The forest is on fire!"

The fire surrounded Big Yellow. Flames were ascending the rope ladder.

"I'm calling nine-one-one!"

"Do you have a knife? We've got to cut down the ladder."

"Here!"

Jaime leaned over the edge of the platform and severed the rope.

The fire was spreading through the trees, consuming the underbrush. It had already obliterated the trail to the Witherston Highway. It was destroying the Gertrude Withers School building.

Jaime saw no way for them to get down from the tree. He called Jorge.

Soon they heard sirens.

"The Fire Department volunteers can't put out this conflagration, Jaime," Annie said. "The forest debris is too dry. It has to burn from time to time. Naturally. That's how a forest stays healthy. Seq explained it to me."

"Does Big Yellow have to burn? Do we have to burn?"

"Big Yellow will be okay. We will too. But we won't be able to go down till the all dead leaves, fallen branches, rotten logs, and brush have completely burned. Or till it rains or snows."

"How will we go down without a ladder?"

"Good point. You'll have to live here with me until Seq makes another ladder."

"Look, the fire engine has stopped near Bear Lodge."

"So has the patrol car. Your mother is getting out."

"Amadahy Henderson just pulled up in her van. She must have heard about the fire on the police scanner."

Jaime answered his cell phone. "Hi, Mom. We're up in Big Yellow. Stuck."

"You all are safe up there. Jorge and your father are on their way."

The fire got hotter and brighter. Jaime and Annie watched it spread through Potter's Woods, taking down the shorter pines and the undergrowth. They saw a buck and two does dash out of the woods and cross the Witherston Highway.

Soon Jorge's red Corolla pulled into the Bear Lodge parking lot. Jorge and Paco got out.

"Hi, Jorge. We're fine." Jaime said on his cell phone. "We're just watching the forest debris burn. A forest fire is a natural occurrence."

"Someone set it," Jorge said. "I know that someone set it. Someone who is trying to scare Annie out of Big Yellow."

"Who would that be?"

"Someone who wants the development to go through."

"Would Thomas Tankard do it?"

"I don't think he'd risk his reputation by setting the woods on fire. Besides, he's old. I think he's in his fifties," Jorge said.

"It's snowing, Jaime!" Annie had stuck her head through the tent flap. Big wet snowflakes adhered to her down jacket.

"It's snowing!" Jaime said to Jorge on the phone. "It's snowing!"

Jaime and Annie huddled together on the edge of the platform where they could watch the fire. Jorge pulled the blanket over them, and they passed the bottle of wine back and forth till they'd finished it. By midnight the forest fire was out.

"Do you hear something, Jaime?"

"It's a helicopter."

Jaime answered his phone. "Hi, Mom."

"Hello, Jaime. The Georgia State Patrol has sent a helicopter to get you and Annie out of the tree. Help her into the harness, so she can be hoisted up first. The harness will descend again for you. The State Patrol will bring you all to Bear Lodge."

The helicopter landed in the parking lot.

The snow kept falling.

"You all come in for some cider," Billy Gardner said.

"I've got to put a story online," Amadahy said. "And get home to my family."

"Time for us to go home too," Mev said. "You boys stay if you wish."

"We wish."

Billy Gardner, age fifty-nine, was the loquacious and amiable proprietor, innkeeper, bartender, and executive chef of Bear Lodge. He was also a locally prominent chainsaw artist. Bear Lodge attracted the same guests year after year, not just for its beautiful setting and gourmet meals but also for the life-size bears Billy carved out of fallen logs. Bears sat on benches in the entranceway. Bears climbed the exterior log walls to peek in the bedroom windows. A bear occupied a chair in the dining room. A bear stood at the front desk. A bear sat on a barstool at the end of the bar.

Jaime, Jorge, and Annie walked into a wood paneled great room.

"Wowzer," Jorge said. "I want to have a place like this some day."

"Move, Bud. Move, Busch. Move." Billy ordered his German Shepherds off of a leather sofa in front of the hearth. The dogs jumped onto another leather sofa farther away.

"Now you all can sit close to the hearth. Or wherever you wish."

Warming themselves by the fire, Jorge, Jaime, and Annie drank hot apple cider and listened to Billy.

"I just knew something was up tonight," Billy said. "I could feel it in my bones. The change of weather, you know, but also the folks in my restaurant. Monday night always draws a crowd. It's the half-priced wine and the piano man. Anyway, there were lots of town folks here. The usual guests. The Benningtons with their son Trey, and Sam Farthy. Also the Meltons. And others. But what made this Monday night different was the famous author. What's her name?"

"Tabby Grammer?"

"Yes, that's her. Everyone was watching her. She was with a younger guy from Tayanita Village, Sequoyah something or other. Know him? Handsome fellow. They acted like a couple, whispering and all. And they were both dressed up. She was wearing these pretty turquoise earrings. Looked like they were on a date."

"That's nice," Jaime said. "Did they seem to be having a good time?"

Annie laughed at Jaime.

"Yeah. They were having a good time. For sure. They came at seven and didn't leave till nine or so. It looked to me like a really good first date, though she looked a bit old for him. Not old, I mean, just older. She was eye-catching. I could tell he liked her. And she was totally taken with him. When they left they hugged. And he kissed her."

"On the lips?" Jaime asked.

"On the forehead, as I recall," Billy answered. "Anyway, I listened to the piano man play ragtime for a while, till the dining room and bar were empty. Then a little before ten I turned out the lights and headed toward my cabin. It's behind the lodge, in sight of the old schoolhouse. There's a path to it. That's when I spotted the fire. It was just a little fire, at first. I called nine-one-one."

"Where did you see the fire, Billy?" Jorge asked. "Would you be able to show us tomorrow exactly where you first saw it?"

"Where I was standing? I was on the path to my cabin."

"No, Billy. Where did you see the fire start?"

"Sure. I can tell you now. I saw it inside the schoolhouse. And in front of it. The wind was blowing, so the fire was spreading fast. Instantly, I'm telling you. I watched it. So did my son Will. By the time the firefighters got here the whole damn forest was blazing. I worried about you, Annie. And I would have worried about you too, Jaime, but I didn't know you were with Annie in Big Yellow."

"Thanks, Billy."

"I care for you kids. I've watched you grow. You know Will was a year behind you all in school."

"Where's Will now?"

"He's gone back to his own cabin on the other side of the Lodge."

"Time for us to go home too, Billy. And my brother needs a shower. He smells like smoke."

"Me, too," Annie said.

"You all come visit me again, you hear?"

"We will, Billy," Jaime said.

MEV READ THE EMAIL FROM DETECTIVE HICKS.

NEWS FROM FAIRBANKS

Hey, Chief.

You asked me to find out who Pilip Pitka was. Well, I did. Pilip Pitka is Timothy Philip Potter!

Patty and I went to the Fairbanks courthouse this morning. Here's what we learned:

1) Timothy Philip Potter spent one year in Vietnam, 1968-1969. He won a Purple Heart for being wounded. We couldn't ascertain the nature of the injury.

2) Timothy Potter got BA, MA, and PhD from the University of Alaska.

3) Timothy Potter taught history at Kuput High School in Fairbanks from 1977 through 1986.

4) Upon his father's death on January 8, 1986, Timothy Potter inherited Potter's Woods, a house, and the remainder of his estate, worth approximately $100,000.

5) Timothy Potter sold the house in May of 1986 for $84,000.

6) In December of 1986 Timothy Potter divorced Mary Lou Potter and legally changed his name to Pilip Pitka. Pilip is the Inuit form of Philip. Pitka was his mother's maiden name.

7) Pilip Pitka taught history at Chena High School in Fairbanks from 1987 to 2016. He retired in 2016, at the age of 66.

8) Pilip Pitka seems to have left Fairbanks. Fairbanks has no tax records for Pilip Pitka after 2016.

After lunch we went to the archives of the Fairbanks Daily News-Miner. We found numerous references to Pilip Pitka as a leader of a group of Alaska Natives called IPRI. You guessed it. Indigenous Peoples Reparations Initiative. Pilip Pitka was arrested on at least four occasions for disrupting the peace: 1999, 2001, 2011, and 2015.

We also went shopping.

By the way, we've been using Arctic Taxi to get from one place to another. Arctic Taxi has big all-wheel-drive black trucks that are really nice.

Tomorrow we'll take a 10:00 am Alaska Airlines flight to Juneau. We're expecting a snowy Christmas day.

Merry Christmas!

John Hicks

So Pilip Pitka is, or was, Timothy Potter, Mev thought. Why had he disappeared?

CHAPTER THIRTEEN

Tuesday, December 24, 2019

OnlineWitherston.com

NEWS

POTTER'S WOODS CATCHES FIRE

At 9:46 last night Bear Lodge innkeeper Billy Gardner reported a small fire across the Witherston Highway in the Gertrude Withers School. By the time the Witherston Fire Department got there, the Gertrude Withers School was burning and the forest was ablaze.

"The firefighters couldn't control the fire," Gardner said. "The heat was too intense. All they could do was protect Bear Lodge and wait for precipitation."

Fortunately precipitation came. About 11:00 pm snow started falling heavily, and within an hour the fire had gone out.

Gardner expressed concern for Annie Jerden.

"She was up in that tree saving Potter's Woods," he said. "Good thing she was high off the ground."

Annie Jerden said that the fire would not stop her campaign to save Potter's Woods. "Fire is a natural and necessary occurrence in old-growth forests," she said. "Fire does not disrupt the underground exchange of nutrients among the trees and bushes. It does not destroy the arboreal family the way logging does."

Annie Jerden said that she would continue her campaign to save Potter's Woods and that she would return to the branches of Big Yellow right away.

"The fire does not change Potters Woods's status as a valuable old-growth forest," she said.

Chief Mev Arroyo will investigate the cause of the fire.

—Amadahy Henderson, Editor

———•———

Bones at Gertrude Withers School Are Human

Late yesterday Neel Kingfisher received the results of DNA analysis on the bones discovered in the basement of the Gertrude Withers schoolhouse. They belong to a male 50-60 years of age who died approximately 150 years ago.

Dr. Kingfisher is investigating historical records of the period in an effort to determine the man's identity.

The mystery is: Why was the corpse not buried in a graveyard?

The Witherston Methodist Church graveyard is the resting place of five generations of Withers, including Harry Withers, who was killed in 1866.

—Amadahy Henderson, Editor

———•———

NORTH GEORGIA IN HISTORY
By Charlotte Byrd

Today is Christmas Eve. It is time to be aware of our blessings and to remember where they came from.

"Robin Hood," whoever he may be, reminds us beneficiaries of Francis Hearty Withers that our financial blessings have come from gold and land stolen from the Cherokees.

We may not want to believe that the source of our wealth was a crime. Even if we do acknowledge that crime, we can't unravel the past and reweave the course of events. And if we want to rectify injustices how far back in time do we go? We may discover that civilization was built on thefts and conquests.

Hearty Withers's wealth was passed down from generation to generation, growing greater and greater through lucrative investments, until it amounted to more than a billion dollars when his great-great-great grandson Francis Hearty Withers died and passed his wealth onto the residents of Witherston.

That's where our financial blessings came from: Cherokee gold and land.

By the way, midnight tomorrow is the deadline Robin Hood gave Witherston's residents for contributing $5,000 to the Indigenous Peoples Reparations Initiative.

———•·•———

LETTERS TO THE EDITOR

To the Editor:

I've been doing some research. I find three individuals who could be Robin Hood: Tabby Grammer, Sequoyah Waters, and Timothy Potter. Here's why I consider them all suspects.

1. Tabby Grammer wants reparations for Indians and knows about "OnlineCrime."

2. Sequoyah Waters seems to resent us for receiving Francis Hearty Withers's money. And he identifies with Indians.

3. (Long shot) Timothy Potter, who may hate Witherston for foreclosing on Potter's Woods and then selling "his" property to Thomas Tankard.

Of the three, I think Tabby Grammer is the most likely Robin Hood. I wonder if she would really kill Mayor Rather.

By the way, I see Mayor Rather drive past my house on Azalea Avenue every morning at 9:50. Why can't she get to her office before 10:00?

—Ruth Griggs

CHAPTER FOURTEEN
Tuesday, December 24, 2019

"Oh no, oh no, oh no, oh no!"

From the kitchen Paco, Jaime, and Jorge could hear only Mev's side of the phone conversation. Mev had taken the call as she was preparing to leave the house. They could see she was distraught.

"I'll meet you there at eight thirty," she said. "First, I want to tell my family."

Mev sat down at the breakfast table.

"What happened, Mom?"

"That was Officer Pete. Tabby Grammer is dead. A few minutes ago Billy Gardner's dogs found her body in the basement of the schoolhouse. The building burned to the ground. What could she have been doing there?"

"Neel asked her to inventory the contents of the basement," Jaime said.

"I can't believe she's gone," Mev said.

"She was only thirty-six years old," Paco said.

"And she'd just published *Paving Gaia*," Jaime said.

"I wish I'd read it and talked about it with her," Jorge said.

"I did read it. I wish I'd told her how much I liked it," Jaime said.

"She was an original thinker," Jorge said. "She was not

afraid to be outlandish."

"Outlandish. Good word, brother."

"I've got to go now," Mev said. "See you all later." Mev left.

"I wonder if Tabby Grammer was Robin Hood," Jorge said. "Jaime, have you looked at OnlineWitherston today?"

"Yes. I'm reading Lottie's column."

"I'm referring to Ruth Griggs's letter to the editor. She says Tabby is Robin Hood."

"Well, she's wrong," Jaime said.

"So now everyone will relax, thinking that Robin Hood is dead," Jorge said. "And some folks will save five thousand dollars."

"I'm betting that Robin Hood is Cherokee," Jaime said.

"Or at least Native American."

"I just thought of Mrs. Grammer's goat," Jaime said. "Who will take care of Allie Baba?"

"Tayanita Village could give her a home," Jorge said. "Maybe Seq would take her."

"I'll ask Seq," Jaime said. "How about Smoky?"

"We can give Smoky a home," Paco said.

"We'll surprise Mom."

"I want to write Mrs. Grammer's obituary," Jorge said. "I'll call Amadahy."

"What do you know about Mrs. Grammer, Jorge?"

"Not much, so I'll google her. Then, *voilà*, I'll have what I need."

"I'll go over to Tabby's house to get Smoky," Jaime said. "Tabby doesn't lock her door."

"Tabby didn't lock her door," Jorge said.

— ◆ —

Chief Mev Arroyo left her Forester by Tabby's Prius in the Bear Lodge parking lot and walked through the snow to the ruins of the Gertrude Withers School. When she entered the yard Officer Pete was taking pictures. Billy Gardner was poking at the few remaining embers with his walking stick.

"Hey, Pete. What do you find here?"

"Hello, Chief. The smell of gasoline. Somebody set the fire with Tabby trapped in the basement."

"Could the smell be of kerosene? That's what I smell."

"Could be."

"Where was her body?"

"At the foot of the stairs. She probably died of the intense heat. The medical examiner is on his way."

"She should have taken Sequoyah with her," Billy said. "But she must have wanted to go there alone. I noticed her car in my parking lot this morning, but not his pickup."

"Did they come in separate vehicles, Billy?"

"Yes, Chief Arroyo."

"Here comes Amadahy," Pete said.

Amadahy Henderson got out of her van with notebook in hand.

"What happened?" Amadahy asked.

Mev told her what she knew.

"So the case is homicide."

"Don't put that into your article," Mev said. "We have no idea that anyone intended to kill Tabby."

"I've got to put something in OnlineWitherston."

"Just say that a fire trapped Tabby inside the log cabin, and the building went up in flames very quickly."

"Billy, can we talk?" Amadahy said, turning to Billy.

"Sure."

"I'll call Mayor Rather," Mev said.

"Aha," Officer Pete said. "Here comes the medical examiner."

———•———

AT NINE THIRTY DOUGLAS HANLEY AND HIS FATHER, attorney Arthur Hanley, arrived for the interview with Agent Danzer.

Arthur Hanley spoke first.

"Agent Danzer? I am Arthur Hanley, my son's attorney. I will accompany him today."

"Pleased to meet you, Mr. Hanley. Sit down. I will be recording this interview."

"I would like to know the reason you are interrogating my son."

"I am talking to individuals who have accused Tabby Grammer of extortion," Agent Danzer said. "May I ask your son some questions?"

"Go ahead."

"Thank you for coming in, Mr. Hanley," Agent Danzer said, addressing Doug. "First, do you have any animosity toward Tabby Grammer?"

"I have a philosophical disagreement with her."

"Please explain."

"I view her Gaia-centrism as dangerous to our way of life. She is anti-capitalist, the sort of person Robin Hood is. And I found proof that she favors reparations."

Doug removed from his backpack a copy of Tabby's interview with the *Awohali Monthly* and laid it on the table. He had highlighted in yellow the word "reparations" wherever it appeared.

"Is this all the proof you have, Mr. Hanley."

"I guess so."

"Do you have any other reason for suggesting that Tabby Grammer is Robin Hood? That is a significant accusation, I'm sure you realize. You are accusing her of extortion, a crime meriting imprisonment."

"No, ma'am."

Agent Danzer's phone *dinged*. She looked down. Without changing her expression she read the online news bulletin.

"Mr. Hanley, are you aware that Tabby Grammer died in the fire last night?"

"What? No!"

"Did you have anything to do with the fire?"

"No! Why would you suspect me?"

"Have you ever been convicted of a crime?"

Doug looked at his father.

"Tell her, Douglas. Your record is public knowledge."

"I spent six months in jail for a prank."

"What was that prank?"

"A friend and I set fire to Witherston High School's football field."

"Why did you all do that?"

"For fun, I guess. And to stick it to the jocks and the cheerleaders."

"Who was your friend?"

"Trey Bennington."

"Thank you, Douglas Hanley. Thank you, Attorney Hanley."

NEWS BULLETIN

Author Tabby Grammer Is Dead

9:30 am. Author Tabby Grammer died in the fire last night.

At 7:45 am today, Billy Gardner, proprietor of Bear Lodge, reported that his dogs had found the body of Mrs. Grammer in the basement of the old Gertrude Withers School for Children.

According to Chief Mev Arroyo of the Witherston Police, Mrs. Grammer had been trapped inside last night when the schoolhouse caught fire a little before 9:46 pm.

The fire burned the building to the ground and scorched some 12 acres of Potter's Woods until it was extinguished by snowfall about 11:00 pm.

This morning Chief Arroyo said he smelled kerosene on the site.

Billy Gardner opined that Ms. Gardner had gone to the schoolhouse about 9:00.

"Mrs. Grammer ate here at the Lodge last night with that young fellow Sequoyah Waters," Mr. Gardner said. "Mr. Waters must have left after dinner, because his pickup was gone when I saw the flames. I found Mrs. Grammer's white Prius in the parking lot this morning."

Mrs. Grammer was 36. She left behind no immediate family.

—Amadahy Henderson, Editor.

Mayor Rhonda Rather read the news bulletin and composed a letter to the editor.

"Mr. Trevor Bennington, the third, I presume?"
"Yes, but you can call me Trey."

"Have a seat, Mr. Bennington," Special Agent Debra Danzer said. "And please put out your cigarette." She slid an ashtray across the conference table.

"Yes, ma'am."

"Thank you for coming in today. I am interviewing a few individuals who offered an opinion on the identity of Robin Hood."

"Yes, ma'am."

"Did you read all of Tabby Grammer's novel *Revenge of the Brave*?"

"No, ma'am. My father showed me a few pages. He read the whole book."

"Do you really think Tabby Grammer is Robin Hood?"

"Yes."

"Why?"

"Robin Hood has got to be one of us. I mean, someone from Witherston. Witherston is divided between supporters of my father who like our country the way it is and supporters of Mayor Rather who criticize everything our country stands for. Robin Hood could be Tabby Grammer or Sequoyah Waters or Annie Jerden or some other left-wing Indian lover. I put my money on Tabby Grammer. But you ought to interview Sequoyah Waters and Annie Jerden too. They could have cooked up the extortion scheme together."

"Why do you think Robin Hood is from Witherston?"

"Who else would know about the so-called crime? It was two-hundred years ago. As I see it, the statute of limitations has run out. Who else would know about Francis Hearty Withers's bequest? And who else would read OnlineWitherston and know our population?"

"Do you know that Tabby Grammer died last night?"

"No. Really? She died?"

"Yes. She died in the Potter's Woods fire."

"Oh. I didn't know. I'm sorry."

"Were you in Potter's Woods yesterday?"

"No."

"Were you in the Gertrude Withers School yesterday?"

"No. Are you suggesting that I burned the school down?"

"No."

"Do I need a lawyer?"

"Not now. I am finished with our interview. You may go. Merry Christmas."

———◆———

At eleven o'clock Seq sat down across the table from FBI Special Agent Debra Danzer in the Witherston Police Department's conference room.

"Thank you for coming, Mr. Waters," Agent Danzer said. "This conversation with you is not the only one I'm having today, and it's a friendly conversation. I hope to eliminate you as a person of interest in the Robin Hood extortion case."

She put a small recorder on the table. "Do you mind if I record our talk?"

"No, ma'am."

Seq had worn his only suit and tie to the interrogation. He was nervous.

"First, let me ask you your name and address."

"Sequoyah Waters, Tayanita Village, Witherston, Georgia."

"Is Sequoyah Waters your original name?"

"No, ma'am. I took the name Sequoyah in honor of Chief Sequoyah, inventor of the Cherokee syllabary. I like to think that I am descended from him."

"What was your original name?"

"Andrew."

"Was Waters your original surname?"

"Am I required to answer that question?"

"Let me say that you don't want to lie to the Federal Bureau of Investigation."

Seq looked down.

"My original surname was Jackson. I was Andrew Jackson, Jr., until I came here and legally changed my name to Sequoyah Waters."

"Why did you change your name, Mr. Waters?"

"For two reasons. First, I read books about Georgia history when I worked for the Forest Service and learned that President Andrew Jackson issued the order to evict the Cherokees from their homeland. I didn't want to be associated with him. That's when I started thinking about changing my name. And I was also getting interested in the Cherokees."

"And your second reason?"

"I'll tell you. Folks in Dahlonega know what happened. And if Sam Farthy has his way, everyone in Witherston will know too. My father, Andrew Jackson, Sr., went to prison. I didn't want to be associated with him."

"I'm so sorry, Mr. Waters. That must have been hard on you. And I know this conversation with me is difficult. Still I must ask you, why was your father sentenced to prison?"

Seq was beginning to like Agent Danzer. She was pretty, with wavy brown hair and blue eyes, and she was gentle. She seemed kind. Not what he had expected in a FBI officer.

"My father was a construction worker, a good one when he was sober. He carried a gun. He should not have had a gun, but he somehow got a license. One night about four years ago, when he'd had too much to drink, he shot and killed his boss."

"That must have been awful for your mother."

"She died when I was fifteen. She was a good mother, very warm, very caring. She said she was Cherokee. She looked Cherokee. I resemble her."

"Is she why you came to Tayanita Village to live?"

"Partly. Mainly, I wanted to start over with a new name and a new identity. I wanted to belong somewhere, where people would know me for the man I am now."

"Who are you now, Mr. Waters?" Agent Danzer asked softly.

"I am a good man. An honest man. A Cherokee. At least I have a Cherokee spirit."

"Are you Robin Hood, Mr. Waters?"

"No, no! Of course not! Why would you ask me that question?"

"I had to ask you that question, Mr. Waters. I am trying to find Robin Hood before he or she kills somebody."

"I could never kill anybody, not ever."

"Where were you last night?"

"I was having dinner with the writer Tabby Grammer at Bear Lodge."

"Could Tabby Grammer be Robin Hood?"

"No! She could not."

"Why not?"

"Extortion is what a man does. Tabby Grammer is a woman."

"Did you talk about Robin Hood?"

"No. No, we didn't."

"What time did you all finish eating?"

"Let me think. We had a long dinner, so we might have finished as late as nine o'clock."

"Then did you go home?"

"Yes. I went directly back to Tayanita Village.

"Did Tabby Grammer leave at nine o'clock with you?"

"She had her own car. I think she left at the same time, but I can't be sure. Why are you asking me about her? We had a wonderful time at dinner, a really personal conversation, and we are now close friends. We're going to have dinner together again."

"I regret to give you terrible news. Tabby Grammer died last night in the fire. She was found in the basement of the Withers School. I don't have further details."

"Oh no, no, no!" Seq started shedding tears.

"Do you know why she would have gone there?"

"No."

"I'm so sorry, Seq. How did the two of you happen to have dinner together? She was a bit older than you."

"We wanted to talk about Cherokees. She invited me."

"And you all parted amicably?"

"Oh, more than amicably." Seq was audibly crying now.

"We've talked enough for today," she said softly. "I'm sorry your friend died."

"Thank you, Agent Danzer."

— • —

MEV WAS IN HER OFFICE WHEN OFFICER PETE CALLED to say he had found Tabby Grammer's phone.

"It's locked, Chief, but you can probably unlock it. Many folks, especially women, use their birthdate for their password. Find out her birthdate. I'll be there in twenty minutes."

While waiting for Pete to deliver Tabby's phone, Mev sent Rhonda an official email. She copied Detective Hicks.

INVESTIGATION UPDATE
Dear Mayor Rather:
    I would like to update you on Tabby Grammer's death and the police investigation of the Potter's

Woods fire.

The medical examiner determined that Tabby Grammer died of smoke inhalation before her body burned. He estimated the time of death to be between 9:30 and 10:00 pm, taking into consideration Billy Gardner's statement that the schoolhouse was on fire by 9:46. The medical examiner found no evidence that Tabby Grammer was murdered before the fire.

Officer Pete Koslowsky recovered Tabby Grammer's phone.

We are seeking proof of arson. Detective Hicks and I both smelled kerosene around the schoolhouse. We have not yet ascertained whether the kerosene was poured on the schoolhouse or on the path into Potter's Woods. And we do not know who had the motive and the opportunity to set the woods on fire.

We also do not know Tabby Grammer's reason for going to the schoolhouse. Her body was found at the foot of the stairs. Had she gone into the basement looking for something when the fire trapped her there? Or had she gone into the basement to escape the fire when the fire blocked her exit? The fire did not consume the basement.

On an unrelated matter, Agent Danzer has concluded her interviews related to Robin Hood's identity, and she will release her report tomorrow.

I will keep you informed.

Sincerely,

Mev Arroyo, Chief of Police

Witherston

Then Mev called Rhonda and invited her to Christmas Eve dinner.

Ten minutes later Officer Pete brought in Tabby's phone. "It's all yours," he said. "I'll be in my office."

After getting Tabby's birthdate from Jorge—October tenth, 1983—Mev tried a few numbers. 1983? That didn't work. 10101983? That didn't work either. How about 19831010? Yes! That was Tabby's password!

Mev entered Tabby Grammer's private life.

Mev went to the camera app. She clicked on the video. She saw photos of farm tools, a rifle, an easel, pots and pans and dishes, water color paints, and the contents of a drawer, followed by a swift panorama shot of the whole room with Tabby murmuring, "Where is the chest?"

On the video she heard loud footsteps. And Tabby's voice. "Hello! Who's there? I'm Tabby Grammer. I'm in the basement." A pause. "Oh, no! Fire!" The video ended with Tabby's screams and a view up the stairs where smoke filled the doorway.

"Oh my god!"

Officer Pete Koslowsky walked into the chief's office.

"You called me?" Pete smiled.

"I think I've witnessed Tabby's murder, Pete. Watch this video." Mev replayed it.

"Now we've just got to identify the footsteps," Pete said. "You know, everybody's walk is unique."

"So all we have to do is to record the footsteps of every adult in Witherston and compare the recordings to this video. Good idea," Mev said.

"Not everybody's footsteps," Pete said. "Just the suspects' footsteps."

"And who might the suspects be?"

"I'll put my mind to it," Pete said. "Do you need me this afternoon? I'm thinking of going home soon for Christmas Eve. I need to pick up one of Billy's bears as a present for my wife. You can text me if you need me."

"Go on home, Pete. And give your wife my Christmas greetings."

Alone again in her office, Mev went through Tabby's sent emails. The first email that caught her eye was one to Kallik Kootoo:

REPARATIONS
Dear Kallik Kootoo:
    I appreciated your letter in OnlineWitherston.
    Let's talk. Call me at 1-706-883-4838.
    I attach a column I wrote for the National Post-Herald.
    Sincerely,
    Tabby Grammer

Were they acquainted? What was her relationship with Kallik Kootoo? Why had she put "Reparations" in the subject line? Mev needed to ask Kallik Kootoo about his acquaintance with Tabby.

Mev found correspondence with Sequoyah Waters regarding their dinner date, with Neel Kingfisher regarding the key to the city, and with Annie Jerden regarding Potter's Woods, as well as correspondence with her publisher and with a contact at the *National Post-Herald*. She found a dozen letters to the editor, most of them sent to Online-Witherston but several to the *Atlanta Journal-Constitution*. She found none that would give her a clue to Tabby's murder.

No texts.

What about recent phone calls? A missed phone call from Kallik Kootoo on Monday, December twenty-third, at seven thirty in the evening. She must have been dining with Sequoyah Waters when the call came through. Either she didn't hear it or she ignored it. Kallik Kootoo must have been responding to Tabby's email. Could Tabby Grammer have been Robin Hood after all? Mev couldn't bring herself to believe that.

She noticed that Tabby had taken a two-minute call at twelve fifteen on Sunday afternoon, December twenty-second, from Lydia Gray.

Going further back she saw that at three seventeen on Saturday, December twenty-first, Tabby had taken a one-minute call from Sam Farthy. How odd. Sam Farthy and Tabby Grammer had little in common. Maybe she should talk to Sam Farthy.

Before going home Mev send Kallik Kootoo an email.

TABBY GRAMMER
Dear Mr. Kootoo:

With much regret I inform you that Tabby Grammer died in a fire last night.

I have learned that she was in communication with you.

Could you please tell me how you knew her?
Thank you.
Sincerely,
Chief Mev Arroyo, Witherston Police Department

Within ten minutes Kallik Kootoo wrote back.

RE: TABBY GRAMMER

Dear Chief Arroyo.

I am shocked and saddened to hear of Tabby Grammer's death.

I tried to call Mrs. Grammer yesterday to invite her to join the board of our projected Indigenous Peoples College. She has been a donor to the Indigenous Peoples Reparations Initiative at the $100 level for six years.

I have just finished reading "Paving Gaia." Mrs. Grammer was an iconoclastic thinker.

My wife and I have great respect for Mrs. Grammer as a writer and as an advocate for Native American causes.

Yours truly,

Kallik Kootoo

Director of IPRI

CHAPTER FIFTEEN

Tuesday, December 24, 2019

B y the time Jaime reached Big Yellow the snow had stopped falling and the sun had come out.

Chief Bobby Bracker of the Witherston Fire Department had brought a sixty-foot aluminum ladder from the fire station that he was securing to Big Yellow's trunk. Seq was helping him. Annie was attaching to the base of the tree a white bedsheet on which she'd painted Save Potter's Woods.

"What can I do to help?" Jaime asked.

"Do you have any contacts in the national media? Like the *New York Times* or CNN? We need publicity."

"I don't have contacts, but Amadahy might," Jaime said. "I'll call her."

Jaime called Amadahy.

"Amadahy is sending Mrs. Grammer's obituary to the Associated Press. Jorge wrote it."

"Four cheers for Jorge," Annie said.

"Hey, Seq. Would you like to give Tabby Grammer's goat a home? Allie Baba needs a home."

"Sure, Jaime. I like goats. Tayanita Village already has a couple. Thanks. I'll take special care of Allie Baba. I'll go get her."

"Would you like me to stay with you tonight, Annie?" Jaime asked.

"Would you like us both to stay with you?" Seq asked. "You decide."

"It's Christmas Eve," Annie said. "Jaime, I want you to be with your family. And Seq, I want you to be with your fellow Villagers. I want to be alone under the stars with my mandolin and my night vision binoculars. You all can FaceTime me whenever you like."

⁘

It was an Arroyo tradition for Christmas Eve dinner: a seafood stew, for which Paco was executive chef, sous chef, and server.

The large blue terra cotta bowl, which Paco had placed in the center of the dining room table, was filled with shrimp, crab, clams, scallops, mussels, and lobsters cooked with garlic, saffron, and dry sherry. It was accompanied by Mev's cold beet salad and hot crusted bread.

Lottie contributed cava and a red blend from California.

Rhonda brought a rum cake. She also brought Coco Chanel, to Hamlet's delight.

"Let us raise a glass to Tabby," Rhonda said. "A star has gone out of the firmament."

After the toast, Mev said, "Tabby may have been murdered. As I told Rhonda I smelled kerosene at the site. That would suggest arson."

"Arson! So someone set the fire!"

"Yes, Paco."

"Was the kerosene in the schoolhouse or on the path into Potter's Woods?" Jaime asked.

"We don't know."

"I can't see why anyone would burn the schoolhouse, but I can see why someone would burn the woods. To end its status as an old-growth forest," Jorge said, "to ensure that the development would go through without a problem."

"But Potter's Woods is still an old-growth forest," Jaime said. "I think someone wanted to scare Annie out of Big Yellow."

"It didn't scare her?"

"No, it didn't."

"I read OnlineWitherston's list of contributors, which now includes almost three thousand names, but not quite," Jorge said. "You want to know who's not on it?"

"First tell us who is on it," Paco said.

"All of our friends are on it, including our beloved mayor," Jorge said. "Since Saturday, Annie and Teresa and Patty have contributed. So have John Hicks and the Tayanita Villagers, and other folks we like."

"Now tell us who is not on the list," Mev said.

"You could probably guess who's missing," Jorge said. "The Benningtons, Arthur Hanley, Doug Hanley, Thomas Tankard."

"And probably Ruth Griggs, Mitch and Becky Melton, and of course Sam Farthy," Jaime said. "Right?"

"You got it on the first bounce."

"They must be waiting till tomorrow morning to see if enough other folks contribute that they don't have to," Rhonda said.

"Or to see if Robin Hood is caught or killed," Jorge said.

"Killed?"

"If Robin Hood is dead, then he can't threaten Mayor Rather and another beneficiary with death."

"Crikes! I just had a terrible thought."

"I think I had the same thought, Jaime. What if the arsonist intended to murder Tabby Grammer? What if he knew she was in the schoolhouse and set it on fire to kill her?"

"Because he thought she was Robin Hood?"

"Could she have been Robin Hood?"

"I don't think so. I see her as totally non-violent," Jaime said.

"The killer might have killed her for any number of reasons," Mev said. "Number one. The killer might have thought she was Robin Hood, as you say."

"The suspects with that motive would include a few people at the key-to-the city- ceremony Friday night," Jaime said.

"Correction, Jaime. The suspects would include everybody in Witherston who didn't want to pay five thousand dollars," Jorge said.

"Number two. The killer might have wanted to stop her campaign to save Potter's Woods," Mev said.

"The suspects would include Thomas Tankard and a number of local businessmen. Such as Trevor Bennington," Jaime said.

"But I can't picture those stuffed shirts going into the woods after dark to start a fire," Rhonda said.

"Trey could."

"Number three. The killer might have considered her a heretic," Mev said. "If that's the case, then any devotee of Reverend Conrad Carmike could have killed her."

"If we could figure out the killer's motive, we could figure out the killer," Jorge said.

"Or if we could figure out the killer, we could figure out the killer's motive," Mev said. "Actually, we can't prove that the arsonist knew that Tabby was inside the building."

"What do you all think of Seq Waters?" Jaime asked. "Annie and I are meeting up with him at Big Yellow at three o'clock."

"We hardly know Seq," Jorge said, "but he seems like an okay cat to me."

After dinner, Jaime played Christmas music on his guitar and Rhonda sang. They concluded their duet with "Children, Go Where I Send Thee."

Rhonda produced from her red handbag a copy of *OnlineCrime*.

"I started reading Tabby's last mystery at noon today, feeling bad that I hadn't opened it before she died. But I couldn't get past this sentence in her preface," she said, opening up the book.

> *Robin Hill, defender of the down and out, computer hacker, and extortionist par excellence, transferred funds electronically from wealthy individuals engaged in illegal activities to a non-profit established to feed the hungry.*

"Don't jump to conclusions, Rhonda," Mev said. "Perhaps the person who calls himself "Robin Hood had read Tabby's book."

"Yes, and had gotten the idea from the book to transfer Withers's fortune to the Native Americans who needed it," Jaime said. "I don't think Mrs. Grammer was Robin Hood."

"I don't think so either, Jaime, but we don't have another suspect," Jorge said.

"It would be convenient if Tabby Grammer were the extortionist, Rhonda," Paco said, "because then you wouldn't have to worry about losing your life."

"And neither would any other Withers's beneficiary who preferred not to hand over five thousand dollars," Jaime said.

"But my feelings would be hurt—to think that she would have sacrificed me for the good of Native Americans. She knows I give to all sorts of liberal causes, including the American Indian College Fund."

"Tabby wouldn't sacrifice you, Rhonda," Jorge said. "She was not capable of murder, I'm convinced."

"And according to her article in the *National Post-Herald* Mrs. Grammer favored reparations in the form of education, not money," Jaime said.

"I should tell you that Agent Danzer planned to submit her report to the FBI this afternoon," Mev said. "She's supposed to give me a heads-up before she makes it public tomorrow."

"What if Agent Danzer announces that Tabby Grammer was Robin Hood?" Jorge mused. "Would that provoke the real Robin Hood, or whoever is the real Robin Hood, to send another letter?"

"It might provoke the real Robin Hood to kill me!" Rhonda exclaimed.

"Oh, yeah, you're right," Jorge said. "Sorry."

"Oh, Rhonda! I should have asked how you're doing. You must be so worried."

"Not really, Mev. I just don't want the extortionist to be Tabby."

"Maybe by tomorrow night three thousand Witherston citizens will have contributed five thousand dollars each to satisfy Robin Hood."

"I wish," Rhonda said.

Jorge opened his tablet. "The list of contributors numbers only two thousand nine hundred and sixty nine."

"Close," Jaime said.

"Not close enough," Rhonda said. "Some hold-outs, whom we probably know, are waiting to see if thirty-one others contribute so they won't have to."

Mev got a *ding* on her phone, indicating the arrival of an email.

"Hey, folks," she said. "I have a message from Agent Danzer."

ROBIN HOOD CASE CLOSED

To Chief Mev Arroyo, Witherston Police Department:

I am terribly sorry that Tabby Grammer lost her life last night in the fire.

And I am further saddened to report to you the results of my investigation of Robin Hood.

I submitted my report to the FBI at 7:00 this evening. I want to give you a heads-up, as the report will be made public tomorrow.

After seeing evidence that Tabby Grammer was in contact with Kallik Kootoo, and after conducting numerous interviews, including one with Tabby Grammer herself, I determined that Tabby Grammer was "Robin Hood."

When asked, Tabby Grammer did not deny being "Robin Hood."

Although I regret very much Tabby Grammer's untimely death, I am glad that Mayor Rather and the community of Witherston need no longer fear for their lives.

I have recordings and transcripts of the interviews, which I will send you. The interviewees included Trey Bennington, Sam Farthy, Douglas Hanley, Tabby Grammer, and Sequoyah Waters.

The FBI considers the case closed.
Sincerely yours,
Debra Danzer, Special Agent
Federal Bureau of Investigation

"Great God!" Mev exclaimed. "How can she have come to this conclusion? I don't consider the case closed."

"What conclusion?"

Mev read them Debra Danzer's report. "I will forward this to Detective Hicks."

"I wonder how much evidence she has."

"Mrs. Grammer left a paper trail of her thoughts, like any writer," Jorge said, "Her paper trail led Agent Danzer to think she was the perp."

"There's got to be a connection between Tabby's death and her support for Potter's Woods," Mev said.

"And Robin Hood?" Jorge said.

"Tabby emailed me yesterday that she was being framed," Mev said.

"By whom?" Rhonda asked.

"She didn't say. She asked to see me this morning. We made an appointment for ten o'clock in my office. I'll request the transcripts of the interviews," Mev said. She replied to Agent Danzer's email.

"Time for me to go home," Rhonda said, putting her empty glass on the table. "I've got to read more of *OnlineCrime*. Good-bye everybody. Merry Christmas! Thank you all so much! I had a wonderful evening!"

Rhonda and Coco Chanel departed.

The time was eleven o'clock. Jaime FaceTimed Annie.

"All's well, Annie?"

"All's well, Jaime."

Betty Jean Craige

Annie Jerden sat inside her tree tent listening to the sounds of the woods on a winter night.

She glanced at her watch and continued writing in her journal. Eleven forty-five, on Christmas Eve. She thought of the pagan roots of the Christian holiday, the celebration of the winter solstice, the longest night of the year. The nights thereafter would get shorter and shorter, and the crocus would bloom, and then the daffodils, and then the forsythia. And the redbuds, dogwoods, azaleas, rhododendron, magnolias, and poplar trees. Big Yellow would blossom in June, and so would all the other poplars in Potter's Woods, converting the sun's energy into golden glory. Humans could burn the forests, pollute the air, and poison the land with nuclear and toxic waste, but humans could not slow the earth's turning. Humans could not slow the arrival of spring, although humans would eventually not be here to witness it.

Annie stopped writing and closed her eyes.

An hour later she woke up suddenly to the screech of an owl. She heard other forest noises. Did she hear footsteps? She grabbed her night-vision goggles and pulled aside the tent flap to look. Oh, no! She saw somebody silently approaching Big Yellow. He was wearing dark clothes. He was not using a flashlight. Why would he not turn on a flashlight? He had almost reached the base of the tree when she found the police siren app on her cell phone. She turned the siren on.

She heard a rock hit Big Yellow. She saw a man run away.

Pil Pitka disliked Christmas. Even though many modern Inuits observed the holiday, he did not. He couldn't fathom why Inuits would celebrate a boy's birth two thousand years ago in the Middle East unless they needed to worship someone or to subordinate themselves to authority. Christianity certainly provided authority, as well as a hierarchy in which a father-god was above earth.

The belief in an unearthly, supernatural, omnipotent, omniscient, ever-lasting father-god was totally foreign to traditional Inuit values. Traditional Inuits believed in no supreme ruler, no heaven, no hell, no divine father or mother, no final authority. Traditional Inuits were not worshippers. His mother had taught him that spirit inhabited everything on earth—animals, plants, forests, streams—here and now. So how could traditional Inuits adopt a religion that required adulation? Because the whites had replaced the Inuits' traditional egalitarian values with their own hierarchical values. That was an aspect of the conquest.

Pil grabbed a beer, sat down in his recliner, and opened his tablet. He went to Amazon.com and ordered *Paving Gaia*. The Kindle version arrived in thirty seconds. He read the preface.

> *In Genesis 1:28, God ordered humans to "Be fruitful, and multiply, and replenish the earth, and subdue it: and have dominion over the fish of the sea, and over the fowl of the air, and over every living thing that moveth upon the earth."*
>
> *And that's what we did. We multiplied so well that we now number eight billion people. We subdued the earth by replacing wilderness with cities, displacing the animals and plants that once lived there. We*

took control of the land, the sea, and the air. We took
dominion over every living thing on Earth.
  We turned the living stuff of Earth into commodi-
ties for us humans.

Yes, yes, yes. He would like *Paving Gaia.*
  Wait. He reread God's words. The indigenous peoples did not subdue the earth. The indigenous peoples
did not take dominion over every living thing. The
indigenous peoples must not have heard God's order.
Whom was God addressing? Not the indigenous peoples
of North America.
  Why would Inuits, or Cherokees, or any other Native
people, take the Bible as their holy book? Why would Inuits
become Christians? Pil was becoming angry. He downed
his beer and got another.
  Then he went to OnlineWitherston.com. What did
those wealthy retirees do on Christmas? Give each other
expensive presents. They could do that because they had
inherited money from Francis Hearty Withers.
  "Oh, no!" Tabby Grammer was dead! She died in a fire
set by an arsonist! In the Gertrude Withers School, of all
places. How symbolic was that? Was she murdered? Was
she murdered for deriding the Bible? Was she murdered
for defending Potter's Woods against development? Or
was she murdered by someone who thought she was Robin
Hood? Several people considered her a suspect. She had had
dinner with Sequoyah Waters. What did they talk about?
Did Sequoyah Waters find her attractive?
  The fire could have killed Annie Jerden too. Who would
want to kill both Tabby Grammer and Annie Jerden? Pil
couldn't think of anyone.

Maybe the arsonist just wanted to torch the woods. That was a real possibility. But why would an arsonist set Potter's Woods on fire? Because he liked fire? Or because he wanted to destroy the old-growth forest to help Thomas Tankard?

From what he knew about ecology, Potter's Woods would still be considered an old-growth forest, fire or not. Forests benefitted from periodic fires.

Pil read Amadahy Henderson's story about the bones. Very interesting, he thought. Those bones must have belonged to a victim of murder. And who else but Harry Withers would have had access to the school's basement to hide a crime? And whom did Harry Withers hate? Patrick Potter. Harry Withers murdered Pil's ancestor. That made sense. That was why Patrick's son Mark, who had lost his leg in the war, moved to Savannah. He wanted to get away from the Withers. And that was why Patrick's grandson Nathaniel went to Alaska, to find gold and also to get away from the Withers.

Pil read Charlotte Byrd's column. Charlotte Byrd grasped that the Witherston citizens' financial blessings came from a crime, from gold and land stolen from the Cherokees.

Pil viewed the contributors. Interesting. Robin Hood had scared quite a few of Francis Hearty's beneficiaries into forking over five thousand dollars but not three fourths of them. And not the investors in the Potter's Woods Retirement Community.

According to Annie Jerden, the investors were Thomas Tankard, Sam Farthy, Arthur Hanley, Trevor Bennington, and Mitch Melton.

———◦———

LATE THAT NIGHT, MEV RECEIVED TWO EMAILS. THE first came from John Hicks:

NEWS FROM JUNEAU

Hey, Chief.

Patty and I are very distressed about Tabby Grammer's death. Tabby was an honorary member of Tayanita Village. Patty read "Paving Gaia" on the plane and says it will be as important as Rachel Carson's "Silent Spring."

No way could Tabby Grammer have been Robin Hood. Tabby Grammer is a philosopher. Robin Hood is not. Tabby Grammer explains. Robin Hood extorts. Tabby Grammer thinks like a woman. Robin Hood thinks like a man.

Thanks for keeping me informed.

We had a cold day in Juneau. Lots of snow. High 30, low 26. And the sun barely rose above the horizon.

In courthouse tax records we learned that IPRI was endowed in 1987 with a $100,000 gift from Pilip Pitka (formerly Timothy Potter).

We found Kallik Kootoo, owner of P.O. Box 76992 and director of IPRI, and interviewed him at his home on the Gastineau Channel. Kallik is an Alaska Native about 60 years old, genial but probably not forthright. He claimed that he did not know the whereabouts of Pilip Pitka, whom he called Pil. When we questioned him, he said that Pil Pitka was an "Alaska Native activist" who had founded the Indigenous Peoples Reparations Initiative "to reimburse the Natives for the whites' theft of their land."

We went back to the courthouse and discovered Kallik's wife's maiden name: Kirima Pitka. So Kallik Kootoo and Pil Pitka are probably related by marriage.

Patty and I will spend Christmas day here and will fly home on Thursday.
I'll be in the office on Friday.
Merry Christmas!
John Hicks

The second came from Special Agent Debra Danzer.

Dear Chief Arroyo:
I attach the transcripts of my interviews with Trey Bennington, Sam Farthy, Douglas Hanley, Tabby Grammer, and Sequoyah Waters.
I also left hard copies for you at the Police Station.
Sincerely yours,
Debra Danzer, Special Agent
Federal Bureau of Investigation

Before turning the light off, Mev skimmed the transcripts.

BETTY JEAN CRAIGE

CHAPTER SIXTEEN

Wednesday, December 25, 2019

OnlineWitherston.com

NEWS

Tabby Grammer Was Robin Hood, FBI Says

In a report to the Federal Bureau of Investigation, Special Agent Debra Danzer concluded that author Tabby Grammer wrote the letter to the editor signed "Robin Hood."

If Agent Danzer is correct, Mayor Rather is safe and so are the beneficiaries who did not contribute to the Indigenous Peoples Reparations Initiative. As of 7:00 am today, the contributors number only 2,970.

—Amadahy Henderson, Editor

Police Chief Arroyo Opens Arson Investigation

Chief Mev Arroyo has officially opened an investigation of arson and possible homicide in the Potter's Woods fire.

Chief Arroyo found evidence of kerosene where the fire started, presumably inside the old Gertrude Withers School or very nearby.

As previously reported, Tabby Grammer died in the fire, in the basement of the abandoned building.

Apparently, Tabby Grammer went to the schoolhouse at approximately 9:00 pm, after dining with Sequoyah Waters at Bear Lodge.

Questions have arisen:

Why did Mrs. Grammer visit the Withers School Monday night?

Why did she go down to the basement, where her body was found?

Did she go down there to photograph artifacts because she had been appointed curator of the future museum?

Or did she go down there to escape the fire, which may have blocked the door?

Was Mrs. Grammer an intended victim of the arson?

Chief Arroyo asks that anybody with pertinent information contact the Police Department.

—Amadahy Henderson, Editor

TIMOTHY POTTER MAY BE ALIVE

Timothy Philip Potter, aka Pilip Pitka, is presumed to be alive, although he has not been located.

Detective John Hicks reports that in 1986, upon the death of his father Chauncey Potter, Timothy Potter changed his name to Pilip Pitka and in 1987 gave $100,000 of his inheritance to the Indigenous Peoples

Reparations Initiative.

Timothy Potter/Pilip Pitka never replied to the Witherston Tax Assessor's foreclosure letter of 2017, which informed him that $1.2 million were owed in back taxes for Potter's Woods.

Potter/Pitka apparently left Fairbanks in 2016, after retiring from high school teaching.

—*Amadahy Henderson, Editor*

ANNOUNCEMENTS

Town Council Meeting is Postponed

In honor of the late Tabby Grammer, the Witherston Town Council will postpone its December meeting until 6:00 pm on Friday, December 27.

The sole agenda item is the following proposal, which will be presented by Charlotte Byrd:

PROPOSED (by Tabby Grammer): That the Witherston Town Council allocate $1 million to buy back Potter's Woods from Thomas Tankard because of its value to the community as an old-growth forest.

Ruth Griggs has withdrawn her proposal to allocate $15 million to meet the demand of Robin Hood.

—*Neel Kingfisher*
Chair of Town Council

Robin Hood Fails to Reap $15 Million

After Tabby Grammer's tragic death the number of contributors to the Indigenous Peoples Reparations Initiative has remained at 2,970. That makes the

*total $14,850,000, which is $150,000 short of the
$15 million the extortionist intended to collect from
Withers's beneficiaries.*

—Amadahy Henderson, Editor

———◦———

NORTH GEORGIA IN HISTORY
By Charlotte Byrd

*In 2019, thanks to the transformation of newspapers and
courthouse documents into digital form, marriages, births,
divorces, and deaths do not fade into oblivion. Everybody
has a record now, a permanent record that proves we existed.
Courthouse records and old newspapers no longer disappear.*

*The first chart tracks the ownership of Potter's Woods.
The second chart tracks Timothy Philip Potter's life. I thank
Detective John Hicks for his research.*

POTTER'S WOODS

*1832—Hearty Withers won 40 acres in Georgia Land
Lottery.*

1832—Patrick Potter won 40 acres in Georgia Land Lottery.

*1862—Mark Potter, drafted by the Confederacy, lost his
leg in battle.*

*1862—John Sando, hired by Harry Withers to fight in his
place, lost his life in battle.*

1866—Patrick Potter disappeared.

1866—Harry Withers was murdered.

1873—Patrick Potter was declared dead.

1873—Mark Potter inherited Potter's Woods.

1881—Mark Potter bequeathed Potter's Woods to

Nathaniel Potter.

1902—Nathaniel Potter moved to Alaska.

1940—Nathaniel Potter bequeathed Potter's Woods to Chauncey Potter.

1986—Chauncey Potter bequeathed Potter's Woods to Timothy Philip Potter.

2017—Timothy Philip Potter lost Potter's Woods, through foreclosure, to Witherston.

TIMOTHY POTTER/PILIP PITKA

1910—Nathaniel Gray Potter married Muuka.

1911—Chauncey Potter was born to Nathaniel and Muuka Potter.

1948—Chauncey Potter married Akna Pitka.

1950—Timothy Philip Potter was born to Chauncey and Akna Potter.

1960—Chauncey and Akna Potter divorced, in Fairbanks.

1968—Timothy Potter was drafted into the Army for service in Vietnam.

1969—Timothy Potter was wounded and honorably discharged with a Purple Heart.

1972—Timothy Potter married Mary Lou Ellison.

1977—Timothy Potter got a PhD from the University of Alaska.

1986—Chauncey Potter died.

1986—Timothy Philip Potter inherited Potter's Woods.

1986—Timothy Philip Potter and Mary Lou Potter divorced, without progeny.

1986—Timothy Philip Potter changed his name to Pilip Pitka.

2016—Pilip Pitka retired from Chena High School in Fairbanks.

Pilip Pitka has no public record in Fairbanks after 2016. He seems to have disappeared.

— • —

OBITUARY
By Jorge Arroyo

Tabby Grammer, nationally renowned author and environmental activist, died in a deliberately set fire on December 23, 2019, in an old-growth forest outside of Witherston, Georgia. She was 42 years old.

Born in Atlanta on October 10, 1977, Tabitha ("Tabby") Grammer was the daughter and only child of Martin and Sara Grammer. Tabby Grammer got a BA from the University of Georgia, where she graduated Summa Cum Laude, and a JD from the UGA School of Law, where she graduated second in her class. As a defense attorney in Savannah, she represented the serial murderer George Mash, known as the "Savannah River Strangler." In 2004, as president of Stone Clean Streams, she led Savannah's effort to clean-up its waterways. In 2010, she left her law practice to write fiction. In 2016, having achieved commercial success with her mysteries, Mrs. Grammer moved to Witherston and wrote the children's book "Gaia Says" and the non-fiction book "Paving Gaia," which came out in early December, 2019.

Mrs. Grammer became a subject of controversy in recent weeks for espousing an earth-centered vision of nature that was incompatible with Christian dogma. In "Paving Gaia," Mrs. Grammer evaluated human actions according to their impact on the earth, which she called "Gaia." She ridiculed the belief that God had ordered humans to be fruitful and multiply and have dominion over every living thing.

That was not the only thing Mrs. Grammer did that aroused the ire of Witherston. She also campaigned to save Potter's Woods, an old-growth forest, from a developer. And she supported reparations to Native Americans. She was even suspected of being Robin Hood, the extortionist who demanded $5,000 from the beneficiaries of Francis Hearty Withers for the Indigenous Peoples Reparations Initiative.

Thus when the brilliant Tabby Grammer died in an arson fire, those of us who knew and liked her wondered whether her death was a homicide.

Tabby Grammer had no living relatives.

In her will Tabby Grammer specified that her body be cremated.

A memorial service organized by Ms. Lottie Byrd will be held at 8:00 pm on Thursday, December 26, in the Witherston Inn's Pinetops Hall.

LETTERS TO THE EDITOR

To the Editor:

I ask Robin Hood: Are you still alive?

If so, please reply to this email.

—Rhonda Rather, Mayor

To the Editor:
Could Tabby Grammer and Sequoyah Waters have concocted the extortion scheme together?

Also, could Tabby Grammer have committed suicide? She probably knew that she would be identified as Robin Hood. She was facing jailtime.
—Trey Bennington

To the Editor:
Notice that Tabby Grammer, a heretic, died in a fire.
—The Reverend Conrad Carmike

To the Editor:
Could that Indian Sequoyah Waters have killed Tabby Grammer after they had dinner together at Bear Lodge?

If Tabby Grammer had discovered that Sequoyah Waters was Robin Hood, he would have had motive to kill her.

The FBI should reopen the case.
—Ruth Griggs

CHAPTER SEVENTEEN

Wednesday, December 25, 2019

"For me?" Mev exclaimed, when Jorge put the cat on her lap. Smoky wore a green ribbon on his collar.

"Yes, for you, Mom! Merry Christmas!"

"Merry Christmas, Smoky! You have a new home." Mev kissed the purring cat.

Jorge and Jaime had kept Smoky in their bedroom all night, giving Smoky and Hamlet the opportunity to become acquainted.

"He comes with provisions," Jaime said. Jaime had wrapped Smoky's gourmet cat food, a litter box, and a cat bed in brown paper and put them behind the tree.

After the Christmas presents had been opened—a ceramic cookware set for Paco and Mev, cameras for Jaime and Jorge, a DVD of Ken Burns's *Country Music* for Lottie, and Nylabones for Hamlet—Paco poured everybody a cup of non-alcoholic eggnog.

"Here's to Tabby Grammer, who used her gift of words to do good for the world," he said, raising her cup. "Let's remember her."

Jaime spoke first. "Mrs. Grammer was a leader. She was an independent thinker. She wrote *Paving Gaia* to explain how our civilization is damaging Gaia, which is our home."

Jorge said, "She showed us that Gaia is not ours, even though it's our home. And that Gaia will destroy us before we destroy Gaia."

Lottie said, "She was an egalitarian."

Mev said, "She was a writer whose convictions cost her her life."

"Mom, you're saying she was murdered?"

"I am. The burning of Potter's Woods was the accident, not the burning of the schoolhouse. The inflammatory agent was kerosene, and kerosene was already in the schoolhouse. Tabby's death could have been a crime of opportunity, not premeditated murder. Anyway, if the schoolhouse fire was deliberately set, then Tabby's death was at least manslaughter, if not second-degree murder."

"So why was she murdered?"

"If we knew that, we'd know who murdered her," Mev said.

"I'll bet she was murdered because she wanted to save Potter's Woods. And she had a vote on the Town Council," Lottie said. "If that's the reason, then the suspects are Thomas Tankard and his associates."

"Who are Trevor Bennington, Arthur Hanley, Sam Farthy, and Mitch Melton," Jorge said.

"And Trey Bennington," Jaime added. "Trey works for his father now."

"So Trey has an actual job," Paco said. "Must be the first time."

"We were talking about murder," Jorge said.

"A murder of opportunity usually has a very immediate cause," Mev said. "Nobody brought the cans of kerosene to the schoolhouse. They were already there."

"And the arsonist must have been a smoker. Non-smokers don't have matches in their pockets," Lottie said. "So who smokes?"

"Trey Bennington and Doug Hanley," Paco said. "They've been smoking since tenth grade."

"And Sam Farthy," Lottie added.

"Only Seq could have known that Tabby was going to the schoolhouse," Jaime said.

"Maybe somebody followed her there from Bear Lodge," Mev said. "I'll get a list of the diners there on Monday night."

"Why was Agent Danzer so sure that Tabby Grammer was Robin Hood?"

"I don't know. I'll ask her for her evidence."

"It's nine o'clock," Jaime said. "I'm FaceTiming Annie."

"Go ahead."

"Hi, Annie. Merry Christmas!"

"Merry Christmas to you, Jaime."

"How was last night?"

"Weird. Scary. I woke up a little before two because an owl hooted real loud, like in my ear. So I got out the night-vision binoculars you gave me and opened the tent flap to look. I didn't see the owl, but I did see someone walking very surreptitiously toward Big Yellow. He was dressed in black, with a ski mask. I turned on my phone's police siren app, and he threw a rock at Big Yellow. Then he ran. Oh my god did that man run! He ran to the Witherston Highway and sped away."

"Could he have been Trey Bennington?" Jaime asked.

"I couldn't tell."

"Jiminy Christmas! What did you do then?"

"Billy Gardner must have called the police, because Officer Pete showed up in a half hour."

"Annie, you're not safe up there all by yourself. I'm coming over now. Could you identify the guy? Or his vehicle?"

"Officer Pete asked me that question, of course. I told him that I couldn't identify the man. But I could see he drove a pickup."

"Everybody drives a pickup. Seq does."

"It wasn't Seq. It might have been Trey or Doug. They both drive pickups."

"Annie! That is scary! Talk to Mom."

Annie talked to Mev.

"Are you determined to stay in the tree, Annie?"

"I'm not coming down till the Council saves Potter's Woods, Chief Arroyo. I hope that will be on Friday. If not, I'm not."

"I'll send Officer Pete to stand guard."

"I'm coming too," Jaime said. "I'll be there in thirty."

———•———

BY THE TIME JAIME REACHED BIG YELLOW OFFICER PETE was already there. He was taking pictures of boot tracks in the snow.

"These boot tracks were left by somebody wearing hiking boots, size nine or nine and a half," Pete said. "A man, weighing a hundred and fifty pounds more or less, who is not very tall. If he were tall he'd have bigger feet."

"That could be Trey," Jaime said. "He wears hiking boots, and he's about five feet seven. He's skinny."

"It could be Trey, or it could be Trey's buddy Doug Hanley, who's about the same size."

"I think the man was Trey," Annie said. "Trey hates me."

"How could anybody hate you, Annie?"

"He hates me because I don't love him. Actually, I find him repugnant, and I've let him know."

"And because you threatened to expose his misdeeds," Jaime said, "whatever they were."

"Jaime, are you going to stay with Annie today? If so, I'll go back to the station," Pete said.

"I'll stay as long as Annie lets me stay."

"Here comes Seq," Annie said.

"Then you'll be in good hands, Annie," Pete said. "I'll head out."

Seq shook Jaime's hand. "Merry Christmas. I brought you all gifts." He unzipped his backpack and took out two small tubes, one wrapped in red tissue paper, the other in green. He handed the red one to Annie and the green one to Jaime.

Annie received a watercolor of a peacock tail feather.

"It's exquisite, Seq. Thank you, thank you. I love it. I will frame it."

"Neel gave me the feather, Annie, so I painted it."

Jaime received a watercolor of a wild turkey tail feather.

"This is incredible, Seq. So much detail. You must have spent hours and hours on it."

"Hours and hours and more hours. But that's what I like about painting. When I paint I forget about time. I forget about the world. I think only about trying to represent something beautiful, to make it mine. To me, feathers epitomize nature's splendor. They are little miracles. I have a collection of feathers."

"You are the John James Audubon of feathers, Seq," Jaime said.

"Thanks. I wish I were as good as Audubon. Audubon lives in my head. I am trying to paint feathers of all the birds that inhabit the Smoky Mountains. I've painted thirty so far, not including the small ones like these that I give to my friends."

Seq turned to Jaime. "I want us to be friends, Jaime, and friends need to know each other's soul. I paint with my soul. These paintings tell people who I am."

"I sing with my soul," Annie said. "And Jaime plays the guitar with his soul. Our songs tell people who we are."

"Seq, you had dinner with Tabby Grammer. Do you think she could possibly have been Robin Hood?" Jaime asked.

"No! No, no, no. Tabby Grammer was too gentle. She probably wouldn't kill a roach if she found it on her kitchen floor. Robin Hood would kill the roach and more. He would kill a human being."

"How do you know?" Annie asked.

"He likes to scare people. That's more a man thing than a woman thing."

———•———

PILIP PITKA HAD NOT LEFT HIS CABIN FOR A WEEK. THE temperature remained below zero, and the wind off the Bering Sea would freeze his face if he ventured outside without a mask. In November he had stocked enough cereal, rice, beans, canned fruit and vegetables, canned milk, bourbon, brandy, and beer in his pantry to last him till March, but he was restless. He needed a break. Should he go visit his cousin in Juneau for a few days?

Pil put another log on the fire, finished his breakfast, and opened his tablet to his favorite website. He scanned the news of Witherston.

"So the deceased Tabby Grammer gets to be Robin Hood," Pil said aloud. "And nobody doubts the FBI."

How convenient for the Withers beneficiaries. The FBI agent's verdict, on top of Tabby Grammer's death, relieved them of their debt to the Indigenous Peoples Reparations Initiative. And it would bring the hunt for Robin Hood to a halt. That would be convenient for Robin Hood.

Pil read Amadahy Henderson's report of Chief Arroyo's investigation. "Oh, no! Damn! Damn, damn, damn." How did Detective Hicks discover his name change? What should he do now?

Pil had ignored the tax assessor's letter because he was trying to disappear. And because he didn't have a million dollars. That official missive had been forwarded to him from the Fairbanks post office in June of 2017, right after he had relocated to his deceased mother's home in Nome. When he sold her house and moved into the cabin, he had revoked the forwarding address. He'd intended to disappear. He still wanted to disappear. He still had to disappear.

He read Charlotte Byrd's column. "She got it right," he muttered.

Now what should he do?

Pil didn't think that authorities would track him to Nome. But he didn't want them to try.

Would the Witherston police suspect him of being Robin Hood?

Wait. Maybe he should take the lead. Maybe he should go to Witherston, spend a day or two there, deflect attention from Nome. Using his anonymity app he emailed Mayor Rather an invitation.

THE PLEASURE OF YOUR COMPANY
Dear Mayor Rather:

As a descendant of Patrick Potter, the original owner of Potter's Woods, I would like to visit Witherston and to meet you.

I would be honored if you would join me for coffee at 10:30 this Friday at the Witherston Inn.

Most sincerely,
Pilip Pitka (formerly Timothy Philip Potter)

Pil pressed SEND.
He emailed Charlotte Byrd.

THE POTTERS AND THE WITHERS
Dear Ms. Byrd:

I greatly appreciated your genealogy chart showing the relationship of the Withers and the Potters over the past two hundred years. I congratulate you on your outstanding research.

Let me introduce myself. I am Pilip Pitka of Alaska, formerly Timothy Philip Potter.

I changed my name in 1986 when my father died because I felt greater kinship with my Inuit mother, Akna Pitka, than with my father, Chauncey Potter. I taught Alaska Native history and art in high school and became an activist in the Alaska Native Movement.

You must wonder why I read OnlineWitherston. I read it because I want to know the fate of Potter's Woods. I support the campaign to save it from Tankard Developers in the hope that Potter's Woods may be returned to the Cherokee people to whom it rightfully belongs.

These days I am a hermit. I want to keep my privacy. However, I have decided to visit Witherston to see Potter's Woods.

May I take you to lunch on Friday at 12:30 pm at the Witherston Inn?

I look forward to meeting you.

Most sincerely,
Pilip Pitka

Pil pressed SEND.
Finally he emailed Sequoyah Waters.

VISIT TO WITHERSTON
To Sequoyah Waters:

I am Pilip Pitka of Alaska, formerly Timothy Philip Potter, a descendant of Patrick Potter. I shall be in Witherston on Friday, December 27. I would like to meet you, and I would like to see Potter's Woods.

Could we visit both Potter's Woods and Tayanita Village on Friday afternoon? If you are available, please come to the Witherston Inn at 2:30.

Most sincerely,
Pilip Pitka

Robin Hood had achieved his goal. With over fourteen million dollars Kallik and Kirima could establish their college for the indigenous populations of North America. Robin Hood had provided education for hundreds—eventually, thousands—of Native Americans.

Mayor Rather asked whether Robin Hood was still alive. Of course Robin Hood was alive. For as long as injustice prevailed Robin Hood would live.

Let the people of Witherston continue to fear Robin Hood. Let everyone everywhere fear Robin Hood, everyone everywhere whose wealth came from injustices committed by their ancestors.

The letter had accomplished its purpose. And if those Withers beneficiaries who hadn't contributed to IPRI learned that Robin Hood was alive, they would be afraid for a long time to come. Robin Hood was clever.

Pil composed a letter to the editor of OnlineWitherston. He called Toklo.

Then he booked a round-trip Juneau-Atlanta flight under the name of Pilip Pitka. He would arrive in Atlanta at midnight that night. And he would leave Atlanta late Friday night to return to Juneau. Toklo would fly him to and from Juneau.

He made reservations at the Witherston Inn. He reserved a rental car under the name of Pilip Pitka. He would have Thursday in Witherston to himself.

In a carry-on suitcase, Pil packed his toiletries and his only remaining dress clothes—a navy wool suit, a blue-striped silk tie, a white dress shirt, and black leather shoes. Also four small soapstone animal carvings, for gifts.

He trimmed his white hair and shaved off his beard, dressed as inconspicuously as possible in jeans, gray sweater, black down jacket, black wool scarf, and black cashmere beanie, and took a taxi to the Nome airport. He found Toklo there waiting.

* * *

As she finished her lunch of a banana-strawberry smoothie, Lottie heard her cell phone *ding*. She opened the email and read the message from Pilip Pitka. Heavens! She forwarded the email to Mev.

BETTY JEAN CRAIGE

"This email was sent through an anonymity app." Mev replied. "You have no way to contact him."

"I will accept his invitation."

"Try to get some DNA from him. His DNA could be compared to the DNA of the bones in the schoolhouse."

"Will do."

Lottie called Amadahy.

———•———

MEV RECEIVED A TEXT FROM THE MAYOR.

> Hey, Mev.
> I have been invited to meet Timothy Philip Potter (aka Pilip Pitka) at 10:30 Friday morning at the Witherston Inn.
> Do you want to send Officer Pete to watch over me? Haha.
> Rhonda

———•———

AT FOUR O'CLOCK, MEV MET OFFICER PETE AT THE Withers School. Because the main floor had been destroyed, the basement was open to the sky. The stairs were coated in ice but still intact.

Wearing latex gloves Mev and Pete descended carefully into the pit and found the wooden chest.

Pete dusted the brass lock for fingerprints but found none. The lock had been wiped clean.

"Not even prints from the nineteenth century," he joked.

As Pete inventoried and photographed the contents of the basement Mev heard somebody approach.

"Hello, down there!"

"Hey, Billy," Pete called up. "What are you doing here?"

"I saw the chief's patrol car and thought I'd come over to talk to you all. But first, may I take the concrete body parts for the Lodge? I thought I'd scatter them around the porch."

"Let me photograph them first, Billy, and then you can take them," Pete said.

While loading the broken statues onto the bed of his pickup, Billy talked about the night before.

"I should've mentioned that about the time I saw the fire I heard someone drive a car out of my parking lot. I didn't pay it any mind until today, when I realized that folks should have all been gone by nine thirty, when Bear Lodge closes."

"That's important, Billy," Mev said. "Could you see what make it was?"

"I didn't see it, but I heard it. Seemed like a big car. Some fancy car with a smooth engine. Maybe a Mercedes or a Cadillac."

"Who was at Bear Lodge on Monday night, Billy?"

"Besides Tabby Grammer and Sequoyah Waters? There were the Benningtons and Sam Farthy at one table. Trey Bennington was with them. Mr. and Mrs. Melton were at another table. Ruth Griggs and her bridge group came at six o'clock for the early bird special, played bridge, and left about eight thirty. Those ladies do love their wine."

"Thanks so much, Billy."

"I hope that helps," Billy said.

As he drove away, Mev asked Pete, "Who drives a Mercedes or a Cadillac or some other fancy vehicle?"

"Among those people dining at Bear Lodge last night? Let me think. Trevor Bennington drives a black Lincoln Continental. Mitch Melton drives a big Benz, a silver one.

Sam Farthy drives a maroon Cadillac. Those folks must make a lot of money."

"What does Trey Bennington drive?"

"He usually drives a pickup. It wouldn't have a smooth engine. But he also owns a Jaguar sports car, which roars."

"Thanks, Pete. I think I'll interview Mr. Farthy, but I'll wait till Detective Hicks returns."

CHAPTER EIGHTEEN

Thursday, December 26, 2019

OnlineWitherston.com

NEWS
TIMOTHY POTTER IS ALIVE

Timothy Philip Potter, who now goes by the name of Pilip Pitka, will visit Witherston tomorrow. Although he no longer owns Potter's Woods, Mr. Pitka says he supports the campaign to preserve it.

—Amadahy Henderson, Editor

—·—

ANNOUNCEMENT

In lieu of a funeral, a memorial service for author Tabby Grammer will be held at 8:00 pm tonight in Pinetops Hall of the Witherston Inn. Charlotte Byrd, organizer of the service, will preside.

—·—

NORTH GEORGIA IN HISTORY
BY CHARLOTTE BYRD

Today I honor Tabby Grammer, author of the profound meditation on life titled "Paving Gaia."

In remembering Tabby Grammer on Christmas Eve Jorge Arroyo said, "Tabby left a paper trail of her thoughts, like any writer." I agree.

When the life of a writer—Tabby Grammer—comes to an end, we can keep her alive by reading the books she leaves behind. Her books form her intellectual autobiography. They let us see into her mind and take what we find there. Tabby Grammer will not die.

Nor will her big idea: "All of us creatures—humans and worms alike—come from Gaia, live on Gaia, and return to Gaia. We belong to Gaia. Gaia's health is our health."

"Paving Gaia" will continue to influence readers' thoughts and actions. And those readers will influence the thoughts and actions of their friends, their families, and their fellow citizens of the world, who will ultimately change the world for the better.

At her memorial service we will celebrate her life.

———— ◆ ————

LETTERS TO THE EDITOR

To the Editor:
Shouldn't the contributors get back the money we were extorted into giving to the Indigenous Peoples Reparations Initiative?
—*Ruth Griggs*

To the Editor:
In her letter of Christmas day Mayor Rather asks whether Robin Hood is still alive. Yes, Mayor Rather. Robin Hood is still alive. And Robin Hood will stay alive.

Robin Hood will stay alive for as long as the rich steal from the poor. Robin Hood will stay alive for as long as developers like Thomas Tankard use more than their fair share of the earth's resources to increase their own wealth.

Do not worry: Robin Hood will stay alive for as long as he is needed. Robin Hood will live in the dreams of those who have nothing, in the dreams of those who have been robbed.

Christmas is a good time to remember Robin Hood.

—*Robin Hood*

CHAPTER NINETEEN

Thursday, December 26, 2019

"Well, what do you know? Robin Hood replied to Rhonda's letter." Jaime read the letter to Online-Witherston aloud to his brother.

"Robin Hood just transformed himself from a local extortionist into a mythical hero," Jorge said, "a savior."

"Whom he asks us to remember at Christmas."

"I like him now," Jorge said, "even though he's an outlaw."

"Robin Hood is an outlaw because the law is protecting an injustice. An outlaw is not necessarily an evil person. An outlaw is just someone who breaks the law. The law could be a bad one."

"Right, like the Indian Removal Act."

"Like the Fugitive Slave Act," Jaime said. "And the Jim Crow laws."

"Are we outlaws if we support an outlaw?" Jorge asked. "Robin Hood is protesting the Georgia Land Lottery, which he views as a bad law."

"So do I," Jaime said. "By the way, did you read Mrs. Griggs's letter to the editor?"

"I did. What a stingy old crone! I'm not taking back my five thousand."

"How about our writing a letter to the editor saying we want our donations to go to the Indigenous Peoples College?"

"How about getting our friends to sign the letter with us? We could raise some real money for the college."

"I'll email folks. You write the letter, Jorge."

Jaime sent out an email blast to twenty of their friends, including John Hicks as chief of Tayanita Village. Jorge composed the letter to the editor of OnlineWitherston.

"Jorge, have you ever tried to see the world from someone else's perspective? I mean, empathize with someone else so completely that you get inside her head? Or his head?"

"I've tried to comprehend another person's way of thinking, but I guess I haven't really succeeded."

"I've been trying to get inside Annie's head to see why she likes Seq. So I close my eyes real tight and imagine being Annie, a person whose parents don't support her, a person who is a passionate environmentalist, who wants to leave her mark on the world, who is brave and idealistic, who thinks about her future children, who admires Seq. I'm almost there, seeing the world through her eyes, and then I fall back into myself, and I think of her as smart and pretty and honest and sweet and soft and sexy with blond pigtails. And principled, too."

"That's because you love her."

"I do. I want to live with her forever. I want her to be my girlfriend again, and then my fiancé, and then my wife."

"Do you think it's possible to imagine being someone else?"

"I can imagine being you, Jorge."

"That's because we grew up together. Can you imagine being Mrs. Griggs?"

"No! I can't identify with someone who is mean."

"Try."

"Okay." Jaime closed his eyes. "I imagine being afraid I'll run out of money. Being suspicious that other people aren't doing the right thing. Being old and hurting from arthritis. And wanting to know what everyone else is doing with their life."

"I think you nailed it, Jaime. I'll think more kindly of her after this."

"Now you try."

"I'd fail. It would be easier to imagine being Smoky."

"Okay, let's close our eyes and imagine being Smoky."

"I imagine being on your lap, warm, happy, purring, full, feeling safe. Now close your eyes and imagine being Trey Bennington."

Jaime closed his eyes again. "I imagine loving Annie but getting rejected because I'm not good-looking. Making poor grades in school because I can't concentrate. Resenting the popular kids, which is why Doug and I set fire to the football field. Thinking nobody likes me. Wanting to prove to my parents that I'm smart, but not feeling smart."

Jorge closed his eyes. "Okay. Now I'll put myself in Trey's moccasins. I imagine doing cocaine with Doug, always needing money, always wanting a girlfriend, hating myself."

Jorge opened his eyes. "How did I do?"

"Spot on."

"Here comes the biggest challenge. Imagine that you are Robin Hood, our Robin Hood, our local extortionist Robin Hood. How do you see the world?"

Jaime closed his eyes. "I imagine being bitter about what's happened to me. I hate people with money. I see the world as unfair. I am angry. I am lonely and alone. I am obsessed with the injustices of the past. I could kill. And I read a lot of history."

"Wow. You've profiled a dangerous loner. Let me try." Jorge closed his eyes. "I imagine being proud of my cleverness, proud of my letter of extortion. I enjoy the game I've created. I enjoy watching Francis Hearty Withers's beneficiaries squirm. I watch those beneficiaries like a cat watches a mouse. I want to rectify the injustices of the past. I identify with the Robin Hood of Sherwood Forest because of his association with justice."

Jorge opened his eyes. "Do we have a suspect?"

"I don't know, but I'm writing this down for Mom." Jaime made a list.

CHARACTERISTICS OF ROBIN HOOD

Is bitter

Hates people with money

Obsesses about the past

Feels anger over injustice

Wants to rectify injustice

Is a loner

Considers himself smarter than others

Is capable of murder

Does not want to be caught

"How's that, Jorge?"

"I'd say Robin Hood's desire to rectify injustice should be at the top of the list."

"I agree."

"Neither of us mentioned Cherokees."

"Then we don't put Cherokees on the list."

"The list is good, Jaime. Now what do you think Robin Hood looks like?"

"Jeez, I don't know. And I don't know whether he's from Witherston or Atlanta or somewhere else in Georgia. I don't know whether he's old or young."

"I think he's old."

"Do you think he knows us?"

"I think he knows about us."

"That's creepy. I'll email the list to Mom."

"Copy me."

⸻ • ⸻

As she walked into his office, Mev got a text from Officer Pete.

> *Hey Chief.*
>
> *Mayor Rather veered off Azalea Avenue into Moss Creek this morning.*
>
> *She wrecked her Lexus.*
>
> *I got to the scene of the accident by 9:00, shortly after a 911 caller reported it.*
>
> *The ambulance took her to St. Mary's Hospital.*
>
> *I have her dog.*
>
> *Pete*

Seq Waters appeared in Mev's doorway.

"Well, good morning, Mr. Waters. So nice to see you. What brings you here?"

"Hello, Chief Arroyo. Did you ask people who had information about Tabby Grammer to contact you?"

"I did, Mr. Waters. What can you tell me?"

"You know I had dinner with Tabby Grammer at Bear Lodge Monday night, before the fire. She told me that Sam Farthy had visited her Saturday afternoon and that he had threatened to expose her as Robin Hood if she didn't support Mr. Tankard's development. She told him she'd get him convicted of attempted blackmail."

"That's certainly pertinent information. Thank you."

"Tabby Grammer was not Robin Hood. I knew she was not. So I didn't see how he could expose her."

"Did she say anything else about Sam Farthy?"

"She said she thought Farthy had gotten into her desk."

"Why did she think that?"

"Agent Danzer said something to her in the interview that got her worried."

"Did you see Mr. Farthy at Bear Lodge Monday night?"

"Yes, Chief Arroyo. He was there with Mr. and Mrs. Bennington and their son Trey."

"Thank you very much, Mr. Waters. You were right to come see me. I find this information valuable."

"Thank you, Chief Arroyo. Tabby Grammer was my friend. Please clear her name."

After Seq had left his office, Mev reread Agent Danzer's interview with Sam Farthy.

Then she looked at Jaime's email.

———•———

THE AUDIENCE FOR TABBY GRAMMER'S MEMORIAL SERVICE was considerably smaller than the audience for her book talk the previous Friday.

From her chair on the stage Lottie Byrd counted some fifty mourners, nearly all of them wearing black like herself.

At eight o'clock, Lottie rose to her feet and walked to the podium.

"Good evening, friends. Let me remind you that this memorial service is being broadcast live on local television. So I welcome both our audience here tonight and all our viewers."

Lottie paused, and then continued. "I am distressed to report that our mayor, Rhonda Rather, had a serious automobile accident this morning. She is in St. Mary's hospital."

"Where?"

"How did it happen?"

"Is she okay?"

"Maybe I can answer your questions," Officer Pete said, standing up. "Shortly before nine o'clock this morning Mayor Rather skidded off Azalea Avenue into the Moss Creek ravine. The pavement was icy. The fog was heavy. There were no witnesses. I don't know her condition."

"Maybe somebody forced her off the road."

"I bet it was Robin Hood."

"We don't have evidence for that," Officer Pete said.

"Robin Hood threatened to kill her if we didn't raise fifteen million dollars."

"And we didn't."

"If Robin Hood is alive nobody is safe," Ruth said.

"You're not safe if you didn't contribute to his fund, Ruth," Blanca said. "I contributed."

"If Robin Hood did it, then Robin Hood is not Tabby Grammer."

"Enough," Neel said. "This is a memorial service. Let's proceed with our tribute to Tabby."

"Thanks, Neel," Lottie said. "Friends, now I ask you on this sad occasion to celebrate Tabby Grammer's life. Tabby Grammer was a writer. She lived by her conviction that we should be gentle with each other and with the earth. She believed in persuasion, not coercion. Words change people's minds, whereas coercion generates resistance. I will miss her. I will never believe that she was the Robin Hood extortionist. I know that some of you would like to honor her with your words, and I will recognize you all. Dr. Neel Kingfisher, Chair of the Town Council, will speak first."

Neel went to the podium. He read from *Paving Gaia*.

When you hear the wind, you are listening to the voice of Earth. When you hear the squirrels and the birds and the frogs and the crickets, you are listening to the voice of Earth. When you hear the crash of waves upon the beach, the thunder in the storm, the roar of a tornado, you are listening to the voice of Earth. Don't forget that Earth's voice is older than yours.

Neel said nothing more. He returned to his seat.

Jaime took the stage with his guitar. Annie joined him.

"I am Jaime Arroyo. Annie Jerden and I would like to sing a funny song Tabby Grammer published in her children's book Gaia Says," Jaime said. "It goes to the tune of 'Dem Bones.'"

> *The trees are connected to the biosphere,*
> *The biosphere is connected to the atmosphere,*
> *The atmosphere is connected to the hydrosphere,*
> *The hydrosphere is connected to the lithosphere,*
> *The lithosphere is connected to the human sphere,*

*The human sphere is connected to the
hydrosphere,
And the biosphere and the atmosphere
And the worms and fish and bees and deer,
And soil and water and trees—oh hear,
Hear the humming of Gaia.*

Jaime and Annie returned to their seats.

Jorge approached the podium.

"I am Jorge Arroyo, and I would like to read a prophecy from the Cree Indians of Canada that Tabby Grammer would have liked."

*When all the trees have been cut down,
when all the animals have been hunted,
when all the waters are polluted,
when all the air is unsafe to breathe,
only then will you discover you cannot eat money.*

"Ouch," Thomas Tankard said.

"Oh, hello, Mr. Tankard. I didn't know you were here." Jorge sat down.

Lottie returned to the podium.

"Would anybody else like to speak?"

Sequoyah Waters raised his hand.

"Come up here, Seq," Lottie said.

"I'd like to quote some words Chief Seattle spoke in 1854. Tabby Grammer would have liked them too," Seq said.

*Humankind has not woven the web of life.
We are but one thread within it.
Whatever we do to the web, we do to ourselves.*

All things are bound together.
All things connect.

Seq returned to his seat.

"Would anybody else like to speak?" Lottie asked.

From the back of the auditorium where he sat alone, a man raised his hand.

"I would," he said.

"Then come to the podium," Lottie said. "And tell us who you are."

"I am Pilip Pitka, from Alaska. Formerly Timothy Potter. I just arrived in Witherston tonight."

Lottie heard a collective gasp. The audience turned to stare at the stranger, broad-faced, white haired, clean-shaven, well-dressed, with black-rimmed glasses. Amadahy Henderson took Pilip Pitka's picture.

"I'll speak from here, if you don't mind," Pil said. "In honor of Tabby Grammer, I propose that Potter's Woods be renamed 'Gaia's Woods' and assigned to Tayanita Village for safekeeping."

Lottie heard another collective gasp.

"Thank you for hearing me," Pil said. He turned and walked out the door into the night.

"May I say something?" Thomas Tankard called out.

"Of course, Tom."

"I presume Mr. Potter's proposal will require the munici-pality of Witherston to buy the property back from me. But even if I should agree, I have partners who may not."

Neel Kingfisher rose.

"This is not the place for such debate, Tom. I will invite you and Mr. Potter and anybody else who has an interest in Potter's Woods to the Town Council meeting tomorrow."

"Thank you, Neel," Lottie said. "Now let us observe a moment of silence to remember Tabby Grammer as a woman who thought like Gaia."

With that Lottie concluded the memorial service. "Thank you all for coming. Drive safely."

Before anybody could leave Jorge stood up. "Aunt Lottie? What did you think of Robin Hood's letter to the editor today?"

"I think that Robin Hood the extortionist was reminding us that Robin Hood the legendary outlaw was a figure of our imagination who restored justice. A figure of our imagination does not die."

"Why did Robin Hood the extortionist say we should remember Robin Hood the legendary outlaw at Christmas?" Jaime asked.

"Probably because Robin Hood the legendary outlaw gave hope to the poor."

"Do you think Robin Hood the extortionist should be arrested?"

"Yes. For extortion."

———•·•———

LOTTIE EMAILED NEEL KINGFISHER A REVISION TO THE proposal on the Board's agenda.

CHAPTER TWENTY

Friday, December 27, 2019

OnlineWitherston.com

NEWS

Timothy Potter Visits Witherston

Dr. Timothy Philip Potter, now known as Pilip Pitka, has traveled to Witherston, where his great-great-grandfather won Potter's Woods in a Georgia Land Lottery.

At last night's memorial service for Tabby Grammer, Dr. Potter proposed that Potter's Woods be renamed "Gaia's Woods" in honor of Mrs. Grammer, author of "Paving Gaia."

Dr. Neel Kingfisher invites Mr. Potter to tonight's Town Council meeting.

—Amadahy Henderson, Editor

Mayor Rather Wrecks Her Lexus

Mayor Rhonda Rather was involved in a one-car accident yesterday morning on Azalea Avenue. Her Lexus went over a steep embankment into Moss Creek within two blocks of her home.

In the dense fog nobody witnessed the accident. An early-morning runner noticed the red Lexus upside down in the creek at 9:46 am and called 911.

The mayor was rushed by ambulance to St. Mary's hospital where she underwent emergency surgery.

—Amadahy Henderson, Editor

NORTH GEORGIA IN HISTORY
By Charlotte Byrd

Pilip Pitka, who was born Timothy Philip Potter, can help solve a 153-year-old mystery during his visit to Witherston today by providing a sample of his DNA.

We have reason to believe that on December 18, 1866, Harry Withers murdered Pilip Pitka's ancestor Patrick Potter and that Withers hid the body in the basement of the Gertrude Withers School.

We have a DNA sample from the bones found under the basement stairs. If we had a DNA sample from Mr. Pitka we could determine whether he might be a descendant of the deceased.

I imagine that Dr. Pitka, an historian, will be eager to learn who was buried in the Withers schoolhouse so many years ago.

ANNOUNCEMENT

Updated Agenda for Town Council Meeting

The Town Council will meet in the Mayor's Conference Room at 6:00 pm today to consider two proposals.

The proposal to buy back Potter's Woods, which will be presented by Annie Jerden and Lottie Byrd, was revised late last night as follows:

PROPOSED (by Tabby Grammer and Lottie Byrd): That the Witherston Town Council allocate $1 million to buy back Potter's Woods from Thomas Tankard because of its value to the community as an old-growth forest; that the Witherston Town Council assign it to Tayanita Village for safekeeping; and that the old-growth forest be renamed "Gaia's Woods."

PROPOSED (by Mayor Rhonda Rather): That the Witherston Town Council allocate $10 million to rebuild the Gertrude Withers School for use as the Witherston Museum of Material Culture.

—Neel Kingfisher
Chair of Town Council

LETTERS TO THE EDITOR

To the Editor:

In response to Mr. Finley's letter requesting a refund for his contribution to the Indigenous Peoples Reparations Initiative, we say let him have his. We the undersigned are happy to contribute our share of $5,000 each to the Indigenous Peoples College. We invite others to join us.

Jorge Arroyo
Jaime Arroyo
Annie Jerden
Lottie Byrd
Paco Arroyo
Mev Arroyo
Neel Kingfisher
Amadahy Henderson
Patty Hicks

Teresa Fuentes
John Hicks
Tayanita Villagers

—*Jorge Arroyo*

To the Editor:
Is it too late to contribute my $5,000 to the Indigenous Peoples Reparations Initiative? I wish to save Mayor Rather from any more attempts on her life.

—*Ruth Griggs*

From the Editor:
No, it is not too late. In fact, between Tabby Grammer's memorial service and 11:30 last night, twenty additional Withers beneficiaries contributed $5,000 each, making the total collected $14,900,000.

That is still short of the $15,000,000 Robin Hood demanded.

—*Amadahy Henderson, Editor*

CHAPTER TWENTY-ONE

Friday, December 27, 2019

D*ing*. Mev awakened to an email sent at 6:46 am.

SEND CHOCOLATES
Hey there, Chief Arroyo.
Spread the word: I survived the surgery.
Robin Hood will be disappointed.
My arm is now in a splint.
No flowers, please. Flowers make me sneeze.
Chocolates would be nice. Bourbon even nicer.
Rhonda

By eight o'clock Mev was interviewing the mayor in her hospital room. He learned that a black vehicle had followed Rhonda out of Azalea Circle onto Azalea Avenue when she left her house for work at nine forty, that the driver wore a black beanie, and that he had forced her off the icy road at the top of the hill where the road curved.

"What make of vehicle, Rhonda?"

"I don't know, Mev. Maybe an SUV, maybe a small truck. I couldn't tell in the fog. Anyway, I don't think he intended to kill me. He just wanted to scare me, but I don't scare easily."

"He could easily have killed you," Mev said. "The driver could have been Robin Hood."

"If he was, then Tabby Grammer wasn't Robin Hood," Rhonda said. "Anyway, please tell Lottie I regret missing Tabby's memorial service."

"I will, Rhonda," Mev said as she put a chocolate bourbon ball on her tray. "Call me when the hospital releases you, and I'll take you home."

⸱•⸱

"Thank you, John!"

Detective John Hicks had deposited on Mev's desk a box marked Alaska Native Arts and Crafts.

"Open it, Chief," John said. "It's from Patty and me for you and your family. Merry Christmas!"

Mev unwrapped a soapstone dancing bear.

"Wow, John. Nice present!"

"The piece was carved by an Inuit from Nome."

"Thank you." Mev turned it over and saw a signature. "It's signed Oki Yukon."

"Whoever Oki Yukon may be," John said. "Now let's solve our two mysteries: Who set the fire that killed our writer and who sent the letter that threatened our citizens."

"And who ran the mayor off the road." Mev told John of Rhonda's mishap.

"The events must be connected."

"We have a clue to the arsonist who burned the Gertrude Withers School."

Mev showed John the video on Tabby Grammer's phone. "Listen to the footsteps," she said. She replayed the video several times.

"Well, it's not anyone from Tayanita Village," John said.

"We Cherokees tread lightly."

"So we're not hearing the footsteps of Sequoyah Waters?"

"No way," John said. "These are the steps of someone who feels important, someone who struts when he walks, someone who doesn't care what he disturbs, someone who is heavy."

"Agent Danzer interviewed five people: Seq, Tabby, Trey Bennington, Doug Hanley, and Sam Farthy. Farthy gave Agent Danzer the list of Tabby Grammer's charitable contributions that included IPRI. That's why Agent Danzer named Tabby as Robin Hood."

"Farthy may have framed her."

"Right. She feared she was being framed."

"How about setting up a walking test? Right on this hardwood hallway? To start, we can bring in Seq, Trey, Doug, and Farthy. I'll record their footsteps, and we can compare them digitally with the footsteps Tabby recorded in the schoolhouse."

"I'll send out invitations for tomorrow morning," she said. "I'd like to invite Trevor Bennington and Mitch Melton too."

Mev told John what he'd learned from Billy Gardner.

"Don't tell them we want to hear them walk, Chief. Just invite them to your office to talk. And give me the schedule. I'll be underneath on the first floor with my recording equipment. From the first floor I can always hear folks coming down your hall."

PILIP PITKA AWOKE IN HIS HOTEL ROOM AT NINE O'CLOCK. It was just five o'clock in Alaska. Not enough time to eat breakfast. But enough time to read OnlineWitherston.

Lottie entered the Withers Inn Dining room a minute early. Pilip Pitka sat at a table by the window. He was impeccably dressed in a navy suit, white shirt, and blue silk tie. He stood when she approached and helped her take off her coat.

Lottie found the man attractive and his manners faultless. She sat down.

"Good day, Ms. Byrd. I've ordered us a bottle of Cava."

"How lovely! And please call me Lottie."

"And you may call me Pilip. I am honored to meet you, Lottie. First, I must say that I regret not meeting Mayor Rather. I read about her accident in Online Witherston. We were to have coffee this morning. How is she?"

"She will be okay. She is recovering from surgery to set a broken arm."

"I am relieved." Pil put a small package on the table. "I admire your historical research, Lottie. I have a gift for you."

Lottie unwrapped a soapstone carving of a dancing bear. "How delightful! Did you carve it, Pilip?"

"I did. That's what I do during the long Alaskan winter nights."

"You are talented! Do you sell your art?"

"I do, through a gallery in Fairbanks."

The waiter brought the Cava and poured them each a glass.

"I am so happy to get to know you, Pilip. I like your suggestion that we rename Potter's Woods 'Gaia's Woods.' In fact, I am presenting your proposal at the Board meeting this evening."

"Thank you, Lottie. The name change is appropriate. Potter's Woods no longer belongs to a Potter. It should never have belonged to a Potter. It should belong to the Cherokees from whom it was stolen two centuries ago. Or it should belong to the earth."

Over shrimp and grits, Pil told Lottie his story.

"We are both historians," he said. "I believe that historians are the mainstays of social change."

"How is that?"

"Historians find evidence in the present of events in the past. Or as I prefer to say, historians find the causes of present social injustice in the crimes of the past."

"Is that why you studied history, Pilip?"

"In retrospect, yes. I study the crimes of the past to explain the present."

"So for you, Pilip, teaching history is a form of activism."

"Yes. I taught my students to connect our heritage with human rights, environmental preservation, and climate. Warming temperatures are wiping out Alaska Natives' traditional ways of life, particularly those of the Inuit. I taught my students that violence against the earth is linked with violence against our people and violence against women. I taught them to resist the incursion of industry on our land and on our culture."

"Go on," Lottie said.

Pil poured them each a second glass.

"We Alaska Natives are committed to protecting our land and our wildlife, because for a thousand years our land and our wildlife protected us. This commitment makes conflict with the whites, as we Natives call them, inevitable."

"I'm on your side," Lottie said.

"I know. Anyway, I entered the struggle in Fairbanks for Native civil rights, and I got arrested a few times in demonstrations. Nothing major. Disturbing the peace, mostly. At any rate, I had no family and wanted no family, so when I retired I left Fairbanks."

"Where did you go?"

"I moved to one of the Aleutian Islands, where I live as a hermit. Alone. Far away from civilization. I like it there. I have privacy. I enjoy listening to the sea and sculpting figures of otters, bears, and walruses out of soapstone. I have a television, a smart phone, and a tablet, and I can download books, music, and movies. I don't need much else."

"You are an interesting man, Dr. Pilip Pitka."

"Enough about me. What about you, Lottie?"

"I retired from the *Atlanta Constitution* and came to Witherston where I spent my childhood. My writing gives me purpose."

"I read *Moccasins in the Mountains*. You are a good writer. Why do you write?"

"To lose myself in another world, a world of individuals far away whose passions for living and loving, suffering and celebrating, and sometimes killing and dying, are as powerful as the passions I've known. Speaking of killing, I have a request to make of you."

"You would like a DNA sample from me?"

"Yes, Pilip. Would you mind?"

Pil Pitka paused. He poured himself a third glass of Cava and called for the check. "Would you like to finish off the bottle?" he asked Lottie.

"No, thanks. I've had a gracious sufficiency, Pilip."

Pilip poured the rest of the bottle into his glass. "As an Alaska Native activist I've seen the government misuse DNA samples. I want to preserve my privacy. I like my hermit status. However, if you want to use it to identify the remains, that is of interest to me too."

"Thanks, Pilip." Lottie brought out a small vial from her purse. "Please give me a sample of your saliva in this vial."

Philip did.

"You promise you'll use it only for this purpose?"

"I promise."

"I have enjoyed getting to know you, Lottie," Pil said, rising to his feet. "If I lived here I'd want us to get together again."

"And I you, Pilip. I hope to see you at the Board meeting."

———•———

LOTTIE DROVE OUT TO NEEL'S FARM TO GIVE HIM THE VIAL.

"Thanks, Lottie. Good work," Neel said. "I'll overnight this to Atlanta."

———•———

THE TIME WAS FOUR O'CLOCK. SEQ AND PIL WERE DRINKing Terrapin Beer at Bear Lodge.

"I appreciate your showing me Potter's Woods and Tayanita Village," Pil said. "I want to express my gratitude."

Pil reached into his jacket pocket and pulled out two small wrapped packages.

"One for you, and one for your girlfriend Annie."

Seq unwrapped a small otter.

"Wow. Thank you, Pilip. I really like it. I see river otters almost every day on Tayanita Creek. The Cherokee word for otter is *cheoah*."

"Unwrap Annie's if you like."

Seq did.

"What a cool walrus! Annie will love this. Did you carve them?"

"I did. During the long winters in my cabin in the Aleutian Islands I carve animals out of soapstone. It's an Inuit tradition. For Inuit men mostly, although now some women have taken it up."

"How did you learn?"

"My mother's father taught me."

"I paint feathers," Seq said. "I don't mean that I put paint on feathers. I collect feathers from birds around here and paint images of them. I have about thirty watercolors in my portfolio now."

"My Inuit grandmother was a painter. I paint some, mostly in oils, but I'm mainly a sculptor."

Pil called for another beer.

"Tell me about yourself, Seq. Why do you live here?"

"You tell me about yourself first, Pilip. How do you know so much about Witherston? How do you know so much about me? I know so little about you."

"I'll tell you. I got interested in my heritage, and I googled Witherston. I discovered your campaign to save Potter's Woods from development. That's why I came down here."

"You seem to know about Annie Jerden, Tabby Grammer, Lottie Byrd, my friends at Tayanita Village, a whole lot of us. Like you're God or somebody, seeing what we do down here."

Pil laughed. "Hardly God, Seq. I'm just a reader of OnlineWitherston. These days on the web you can find out everything you want to know about any place on earth."

"So I can visit the Aleutian Islands on the web? I can find you?"

"You can visit the Aleutian islands, but you'll probably not find me. I live off the grid. Now tell me about yourself. You're working to save Potter's Woods? Who is on our side?"

"Our side? Well, besides Annie Jerden, who is leading the protest, we had Tabby Grammer, my friend who died."

"I was sorry to read of Tabby Grammer's death. So she was Robin Hood?"

"She was not Robin Hood. She was not. She was a beautiful, caring, and intelligent woman. She was serene. She was not capable of threatening anybody's life."

"I'm relieved to hear that, Seq. Do you suspect anybody else in Witherston?"

"No. Some people suspect me, but I didn't send the extortion letter. No Cherokee would have sent the letter. The Cherokee people are spiritual. We treat others with respect."

"Who could have sent it then?"

"I don't know. Somebody angry. The FBI has closed the case. Maybe Robin Hood will never get caught."

"Well, Seq, the fifteen million dollars will go to a good cause, so no harm is done if the mystery is never solved."

Seq drank the rest of his beer and stood up.

"Thank you for our presents, Pilip. It's almost five o'clock. I want to give Annie her walrus before the Town Council meeting. Would you like me to take you to the Witherston Inn or to City Hall?"

"How about the Witherston Inn, Seq? I'm sixty-nine years old, and I'm tuckered out from a long day. I do thank you for all your attention."

——— • ———

NEEL KINGFISHER CALLED THE TOWN COUNCIL to order in the Mayor's Conference Room at six o'clock.

Seated at the table were Lydia Gray, Blanca Zamora, Trevor Bennington, Jr., and Ruth Griggs.

Seated in the chairs against the walls were Detective John Hicks, Amadahy Henderson, Annie Jerden, and Lottie Byrd.

The mayor was absent.

Outside the room's glass wall stood Seq and thirteen other Tayanita Villagers, all wearing green Deer Clan sweatshirts. They could see and hear the discussion.

"Where is Tom Tankard?" Trevor Bennington asked. "He was supposed to represent his project."

"He told me he was coming," Neel said. "I was expecting Tom, and I was expecting Pilip Pitka too, but we can't wait. So let us first observe a minute's silence to remember Tabby Grammer, our friend and colleague."

Neel allowed a minute to pass.

"I have one announcement," Neel said. "Mayor Rather has appointed me curator of the projected Witherston Museum of Material Culture."

"Good thing, Neel," Blanca said.

"Now I ask Lottie Byrd to present the revised proposal submitted originally by Tabby Grammer. I have divided it into three parts:

PROPOSED (by Tabby Grammer): That the Witherston Town Council allocate $1 million to buy back Potter's Woods from Thomas Tankard because of its value to the community as an old-growth forest.

PROPOSED (by Charlotte Byrd): That the Witherston Town Council assign it to Tayanita Village for safekeeping.

PROPOSED (by Charlotte Byrd): That the old-growth forest be renamed "Gaia's Woods."

Lottie rose to her feet. "If the Board does not buy back Potter's Woods, the Board is converting the health of the many into the wealth of a few. I can't imagine that our dear departed friend Tabby Grammer would tolerate that. On the other hand, if the Board does buy back Potter's Woods, then we have to ensure that it remain an old-growth forest for the foreseeable future. In that case I propose that Tayanita Village take charge of its preservation. I assume that Village Chief John Hicks would have the authority to accept the responsibility on behalf of the Villagers?"

"Of course, Lottie."

The Tayanita Villagers clapped.

"And if that part of the proposal passes, then I recommend that the Board give the name of 'Gaia's Woods' to the plot of land that has heretofore been called 'Potter's Woods.'"

Lottie sat down.

"How about 'Tayanita Forest'?" John Hicks asked. "Tayanita was the name of the village Hearty Withers buried when he founded Witherston."

The Tayanita Villagers cheered.

"I would certainly be amenable to that," Lottie said.

"The renaming of Potter's Woods will be discussed at the appropriate time," Neel said. "Now who would like to represent Thomas Tankard's interests?"

"May I?" Trevor Bennington asked.

"Certainly," Neel said. "You have the floor."

Trevor stood up. "I will forego a response to Ms. Byrd's inaccurate comment about our converting the health of the many into the wealth of a few. Instead, I ask the Board to consider the good that will result from our converting just thirty-nine acres of woods into living accommodations for a hundred and thirty-nine aging people."

"Who will be aging faster and faster without trees, Trevor," Blanca said.

Trevor took a breath and continued. "Witherston's population is getting older. Thirty percent of our population is over fifty-five. The young people are leaving to go to college or to make their living elsewhere. They won't be here to give full-time care to their elderly parents. Tom Tankard envisions a subdivision that will. Potter's Woods Retirement Community will provide not just houses and memory-care facilities for the elderly, but also togetherness in elderly-friendly activities and digestible daily meals. The elderly will find happiness there. Let me give you all our flyer."

Trevor distributed a glossy flyer titled "Potter's Woods Retirement Community, Where the Elderly Live, Laugh, and Love Again."

Lydia Gray raised her hand. "May I say something, Trevor?"

"Sure."

"Could you please stop calling us 'elderly.' I'm seventy years old. I won't be elderly for twenty more years. I want to move to the Retirement Community because I can't manage my farm alone. And I don't have children."

"How big is your farm, Mrs. Mallow?" Annie asked.

"Fifty acres. Mostly pasture."

"Is it for sale?"

"Yes, would you like to buy it?"

"No, ma'am. But I'd like to know how much you're asking."

"Nine hundred thousand dollars."

"If the Board bought Potter's Woods from Mr. Tankard for one million dollars, and Mr. Tankard bought your farm for nine hundred thousand dollars, Mr. Tankard would make a profit of a hundred thousand dollars which he could invest in his retirement community," Annie said.

"And build the retirement community on my pasture land. I like the idea," Lydia said.

"Would Tom Tankard like the idea, Trevor?"

"I hesitate to commit for Tom, but I can say that I like the idea, and I'm one of his partners in the project."

Seq tapped the glass partition. "I like the idea too," he said. "I will buy your animals."

"I will give them to you," Lydia said, "if you'll take all of them. Three cows, named Bossy, Bessie, and Betsy. Two goats, named Billy and Hillary. And a burro named Pepe. I'll keep my dogs and cats."

They heard a knock on the door.

"Come in, Officer Pete," Neel said. "We're happy to have you join us."

"I have terrible news," Pete said. "Mr. Tankard had a heart attack and crashed his car going down Withers Hill Road. He's dead."

"Oh my god!"

"Heavens!"

"He was on his way here!"

"Tom has never been sick."

"Does his son Albert know?"

"Not yet."

"I will contact him," Trevor said. "I've known him since he was a boy."

"What does Albert do? I haven't laid eyes on him in years," Blanca said.

"He's a developer in Atlanta. Considers himself eco-friendly. Very successful."

"Were there any witnesses?" Lottie asked.

"Apparently not," Pete said. "Someone going down Withers Road saw his car in the ditch and called nine-one-one. That was a few minutes before six. Mr. Tankard was dead by the time I got there. Withers Hill is still icy."

"In view of this tragedy, I move to table the Potter's

Woods proposal," Trevor said. "All three parts of it."

"Second," Lydia said.

"All in favor?"

The motion was unanimous.

"We will consider it at our January meeting."

"I'll invite Albert to join us," Trevor said. "He'll want to represent his father's interests."

"I move to allocate five hundred thousand dollars now to start the conversion of the Gertrude Withers School into the Witherston Museum of Material Culture," Lydia Gray said, "and to reconsider the motion in January."

"Second."

"Discussion?" Neel paused. "Hearing none, I ask all in favor of Lydia's motion to say "Aye."

All said "Aye."

"It's unanimous."

"I think we've concluded our business," Neel said. "The meeting is adjourned."

Seq opened the door and walked into the conference room.

"May I work with you, Dr. Kingfisher?" Seq asked. "I'd like to learn more about north Georgia culture."

"Certainly," Neel said. "You will be assistant curator. Come to the schoolhouse at ten o'clock on Monday morning."

Blanca Zamora approached Pete. "Officer Pete, don't you find the timing Tankard's death suspicious?"

"I can't say anything other than the police will investigate it, Blanca."

"I find it suspicious," Blanca said. "Very suspicious. And it happened the day after the mayor was run off the road. Robin Hood ran both off the road, for sure. Ruth, you'd better pay your five thousand dollars, or you'll be next."

CHAPTER TWENTY-TWO

Friday, December 27, 2019

After dinner, Jaime left the house to Big Yellow to visit Annie. Jorge, Paco and Mev lingered at the table enjoying a dessert of oranges and chocolates.

Mev answered the knock on the door. "Come in, Lottie," she said. "You're just in time for espresso."

"Do you think Tom Tankard really had a heart attack, Mev?" Lottie asked.

"I was just talking to Officer Pete Koslowsky about it. Officer Pete called me a few minutes ago."

"I think someone sideswiped Tom, the same person who sideswiped Rhonda," Lottie said.

"I agree," Paco said. "Too many catastrophes in one week. The Robin Hood letter, the Potter's Woods fire, Tabby Grammer's death, Rhonda's wreck, and Tom Tankard's death. There must be one person responsible."

"Or maybe one person triggered the sequence," Lottie said. "Tom Tankard got the building permit, which prompted Annie to move into Old Yellow and Tabby Grammer to publicize the threat to Potter's Woods. Since Tabby was on the Town Council, she was murdered. And since Annie was up in the tree, Potter's Woods was set afire."

"How does Robin Hood fit it?" Jorge asked.

"That's the puzzle," Lottie said. "Maybe there are multiple perps, multiple mysteries."

"Lottie, tell me about your date with Timothy Potter." Mev said.

"You mean, Pilip Pitka," Lottie said. "Pilip was a gentleman. Handsome, mannerly, soft-spoken, charming. I found myself wanting to know him better."

"What did you talk about?"

"My past. His past. Why I live here. Why he lives in the Aleutian Islands. Why I write. Why he carves."

"Pilip is an artist?"

"Yes. He carves little animals out of soapstone. He gave me a present."

Lottie opened her purse and withdrew the dancing bear.

"Astonishing," Mev said. "May I see it?"

"Sure." Lottie handed him the small carving. "Why are you surprised?"

Mev showed Lottie the dancing bear that Detective Hicks had brought back from Fairbanks. "John gave us this dancing bear as a Christmas present."

"The bears are identical!"

"Not perfectly," Jorge said, "but very much alike. Same color soapstone. They could be carved by the same artist."

"John bought ours at a gallery in Fairbanks," Mev said. "The Alaska Native Arts and Crafts Gallery."

"Well, that's possible. Pilip said that he sent his pieces to a gallery in Fairbanks."

"But the gallery owner told John that the artist lives in Nome. Where does Pilip live?"

"In the Aleutian Islands. At least that's what he told me."

Mev showed Lottie the signature of Oki Yukon on the bear's foot.

"Is your bear signed?"

Lottie look at her bear's foot. "No, nothing here. Maybe Pilip doesn't sign his bears until he's ready to ship them to Fairbanks."

"You're sure he said he lived in the Aleutian Islands, Lottie?"

"I'm sure. He said he lived off the grid on one of the islands. He said he was a hermit."

"A hermit?" Jorge asked. "Why would a hermit come all the way from the Aleutian Islands to visit Witherston? Real hermits don't put on a suit, board a plane, make themselves look handsome, and take a lady to a nice restaurant."

Mev set the two dancing bears on the table side by side.

"Cool," Jorge said. "So who carved them?"

"Either Pilip Pitka or Oki Yukon," Mev said.

"Or one did one and the other did the other," Lottie said.

"Seems to me that the same artist did both," Jorge said. "These carvings are alike down to the dancing bear's toenails."

"And both bears are perfectly balanced on one leg," Paco said. "That must be hard to do."

Jorge got out his phone. "I'm googling Aleutian Islands. Here's Aleutian Islands East Borough. Now I'll click on Aleutians East Borough Tax Collector. I'm typing in Pilip Pitka. What do you know? There's no Pilip Pitka in the tax records."

"So how do we find Pilip Pitka in Alaska?"

"I have another idea," Jorge said. "I'll take a picture of the two dancing bears and send them to the art gallery in Fairbanks for identification. What was the name of the art gallery, Mom?"

Mev looked at a card in the box. "Alaska Native Arts and Crafts, 215 Airport Circle, Fairbanks, Alaska, 99701."

"Mom, I don't use the US Postal Service. What about an email address or a website?"

"Here is the email address, and here is the website address." Mev wrote them down.

"Thanks, Mom. That helps."

Jorge took pictures of the dancing bears from several different angles, some together and others separately.

"Now I'm emailing these pictures to the gallery. I hope it's still open today."

"It's eight thirty here, so it's four thirty in Fairbanks," Lottie said.

"I'll check out the gallery's website. We'll use my tablet," Jorge said. "Ta da! Here we are! Let's see. There's a category of Inuit carvings. With lots of photos. Look, you all."

"Here's a list of the artists," Lottie said. "No Pilip Pitka."

"But here are two other Pitkas," Jorge said. "Anjij Pitka, who does these cool abstract paintings of owls and hawks. I'd like one of them. And here's Aput Pitka, who does soapstone carvings a bit like Pilip's."

"Oki Yukon is there. Click on Oki Yukon."

Jorge opened up Oki Yukon's web page.

"Oh, Lordy," Lottie said. "Here's a dancing bear just like ours, and an otter, and a walrus, and a seal."

"Does Oki Yukon have a photograph?" Mev asked.

"No. But other artists do."

Ding. Jorge got an email. "It's from Eska Tiktak. You all can read it." He put his phone on the table.

Re: INUIT SOAPSTONE CARVINGS
Dear Jorge Arroyo,
The two dancing bears you photographed were carved by one of our most popular artists, Oki Yukon

from Nome. Oki Yukon carves dancing bears, seals, walruses, and otters out of soapstone. He has won many awards.

Would you like to purchase another piece? I would be happy to work with you on the price.

Thank you for contacting me.

Respectfully yours,

Eska Tiktak

"Wow," Jorge said. "I think Eska Tiktak just proved that Oki Yukon is Pilip Pitka."

"Or that Pilip Pitka bought Oki Yukon's carvings and passed them off as his own," Mev said.

"But then they'd have Oki Yukon's signature," Paco said.

"I'll ask Ms. Tiktak if she's got a photograph of Oki Yukon, and I'll ask her how much Anjij Pitka's painting of the owl costs." Jorge sent Eska an email.

"Now google Nome Tax Collector, Jorge," Lottie said. "See if there's a record of Pilip Pitka."

Jorge did.

"No record of Pilip Pitka. I'll type in Oki Yukon. Yes! Oki Yukon lives at 22 Bering Sea Road in Nome."

Ding. Another email.

Re: PHOTO OF OKI YUKON

Dear Jorge,

I appreciate your interest in Oki Yukon. I am sorry we don't have a photo of him. I have asked him for one many times, but he says he wants to preserve his "hermit status." With his long white beard and long white hair he looks like a hermit, but he is also a well-educated gentleman.

Mr. Yukon comes into the gallery every few months with his cousin Toklo Aluki from Utqiagvik to deliver his sculptures. The sculptures, ranging from two inches in diameter to eight inches, depict arctic animals, mostly otters, walruses, seals, and bears.

I can sell you Anjij Pitka's "Owl Wheel" for $900. I can sell you her smaller "Bear Wheel" for $500. It is also a stunning piece. Check it out on our website.

The value of the art of Anjij and her husband Aput Pitka, has increased considerably since their deaths in 1968 and the more recent death of their daughter Akna, who was a fine quilter. Coincidentally, like Oki Yukon, the three of them were from Nome.

You must visit our gallery sometime, Jorge. I will show you a marvelous collection of Alaska Native art.

Respectfully yours,
Eska

"I'm gonna get the "Bear Wheel," Jorge said. "I'll write her back. Yay! I'm finally starting my art collection." Jorge confirmed the purchase.

"Let's pay attention to the information Eska just gave us, Jorge. She has unwittingly let us know that Pilip's mother was a quilter and his Inuit grandparents were the artists Anjij and Aput Pitka," Mev said.

"Preserve his 'hermit status.' Those are the exact words Pilip used with me. Pilip must be Oki Yukon," Lottie said.

"I'd guess that Pilip goes by both Oki Yukon and Pilip Pitka. For some reason he maintains two identities."

"The reason is probably financial," Paco said.

"The reason could be something else," Lottie said. "Pilip could be in hiding."

Jorge got a FaceTime call from Jaime.

"Hey, Jaime. You coming home tonight?"

"No. The good news is that I'm not. I'm staying here with Annie."

"Lottie is here. We've discovered that Pilip Pitka has another identity. He's also a sculptor named Oki Yukon of Nome, Alaska. Pilip Pitka gave Lottie a soapstone dancing bear just like the one John Hicks brought Mom from Fairbanks."

"Really? Well, guess what? Pilip Pitka gave Annie a little sculpture of a walrus. Do you want to see it?"

Jaime turned the phone to show Annie holding the small green soapstone carving.

"Actually, he gave two sculptures to Seq, one for Seq and the other for me," Annie said. "He gave Seq an otter."

"That walrus looks like an Oki Yukon sculpture," Jorge said, aiming his phone at Oki Yukon's webpage. "Does the otter look like this one?"

"Yes, exactly! The otter is playing on his back," Annie said.

Jaime's face returned to the FaceTime screen.

"Tomorrow I'll help Annie take down her campsite. Want to come over, Jorge?"

"Sure, I'll help. I'll see you mid-morning."

"Good night, son," Mev said.

"Mom," Jorge said. "I'd like to write a column about these little Inuit sculptures? Okay with you?"

"I guess so. Just don't mention Oki Yukon's name."

"So now we've got another mystery," Lottie said. "Why is Pilip Pitka dissembling?"

"Pilip Pitka has had several identities," Mev said. "He was born Timothy Philip Potter. Then he changed his name to

Pilip Pitka. And now he goes by Oki Yukon, except when he has to be Pilip Pitka again."

"I'll bet he gets his social security check as Pilip Pitka," Jorge said.

"Then he has a bank account somewhere," Lottie said. "Maybe in Fairbanks."

"Why did he come to Witherston?" Paco asked. "Was it just to see Potter's Woods? I don't think that was the reason."

"Mom, did you get Jaime's email with the characteristics we imagined for Robin Hood? I have it here."

Jorge read the list out loud.

"Lottie, could this be Pilip Pitka?"

"I think not. Pilip Pitka did not seem angry or bitter. He was charming, as I said. But he was concerned with justice."

"Maybe Jaime and I imagined Robin Hood all wrong," Jorge said, "or else Timothy Potter is good at changing identities and he has a fourth persona, Robin Hood."

"Timothy Potter, Pilip Pitka, Oki Yukon, Robin Hood," Lottie said.

"We've got to find him," Mev said. "If he's Robin Hood, he may be the individual who ran Mayor Rather off the road."

"So how do we find Pilip Pitka?" Jorge asked.

"We could send a picture of him to the U.S. Post Office in Nome, and to the financial institutions in Nome and Fairbanks," Lottie said. "Problem is, we don't have a picture of him."

"Amadahy has a picture of him," Jorge said. "I saw her take his picture last night when he stood up."

"I'll ask her to email it to me," Mev said. "But there's another problem. We can't arrest Pilip Pitka unless—or until—we have evidence that he has committed a crime."

"Extortion is a crime."

"Yes, it is a federal crime. If we could prove that Pilip Pitka, aka Oki Yukon, is Robin Hood, we could get him arrested in Alaska," Mev said.

"I think I'll write a letter to the editor about my date with him," Lottie said. "Let's see what he does after he reads it."

"Someone needs to go to Alaska," Mev said.

"May I go to Alaska, Mom?"

"I may send Detective Hicks again," Mev said. "But so far, all we know is that Pilip Pitka has another identity, Oki Yukon."

"And that Pilip Pitka was here Friday evening when Tom Tankard died," Lottie said. "And possibly Thursday morning when a black vehicle ran Rhonda off the road."

"I'll bet Detective Hicks could trace the anonymous email to Pilip's IP address," Jorge said.

"I'll ask him tomorrow."

"Oh! It's late. Time for me to go home to Doolittle," Lottie said. "Thank you for the delicious dinner."

"Before you go, Lottie, I need to make a list of people you know who drive a black SUV or pickup."

"Okay, Mev. I know that Arthur Hanley drives a black SUV."

"Trey Bennington drives a black pickup," Jorge said. "And Sequoyah Waters and Doug Hanley do too."

"And Billy Gardner," Lottie said. "Anybody else?"

"Mr. Farthy drives a pickup when he's hauling equipment," Jorge said. "But when he's not, he drives his big Cadillac."

"I wonder what vehicle Pilip Pitka is renting," Lottie said.

"I'll ask Detective Hicks to find out," Mev said.

CHAPTER TWENTY-THREE

Saturday, December 28, 2019

OnlineWitherston.com

NEWS

Thomas Tankard Dies of a Heart Attack

Real estate developer Thomas Tankard apparently suffered a fatal heart attack late yesterday afternoon while driving down Withers Hill Road toward town. The car veered into a steep embankment and hit a tree. Mr. Tankard was pronounced dead on the scene at 6:05 pm.

Tankard was driving a 2019 red Porsche Cayman. An autopsy will be performed on Monday.

Tankard's close friend and business partner Trevor Bennington, Jr., speculated that Tankard was hurrying to City Hall, where the Town Council was debating the purchase of Potter's Woods.

Tankard was divorced with one son. Albert Tankard drove up to Witherston from Atlanta last night.

—Amadahy Henderson, Editor

Town Council Tables Potter's Woods Proposal

At yesterday's meeting, in view of the death of Thomas Tankard, the Town Council tabled the three-part proposal to buy Potter's Woods from Mr. Tankard, to give Tayanita Village the responsibility for maintaining it as an old-growth forest, and to rename it. The Board will consider the proposal at its January meeting.

Annie Jerden offered the following suggestion: If the Board bought Potter's Woods from Mr. Tankard for one million dollars, and Mr. Tankard bought Lydia Gray's 50-acre farm for nine hundred thousand dollars, Mr. Tankard would make a profit of a hundred thousand dollars which he could invest in his Retirement Community.

Her suggestion was met with enthusiasm.

John Hicks, chief of Tayanita Village, proposed that the new name for Potter's Woods be "Tayanita Forest."

His suggestion was met with enthusiasm as well.

The Board unanimously approved the expenditure of $500,000 to begin conversion of the Gertrude Withers schoolhouse into the Witherston Museum of Material Culture.

The meeting was adjourned at 6:45.

—Amadahy Henderson, Editor

------•·•------

Tabby Grammer in Communication with Kallik Kootoo

Through an Open Records request for transcripts of the interviews FBI Special Agent Danzer conducted, I have learned the basis for Agent Danzer's conclusion that Tabby Grammer was Robin Hood.

In his interview, Sam Farthy offered evidence that Tabby Grammer was in email contact with Kallik Kootoo, director of the Indigenous Peoples Reparations Initiative. In her interview, Tabby Grammer acknowledged that she had been a regular contributor to IPRI for probably five years.

Over the phone Agent Danzer said that Tabby Grammer's publications, her confirmed relationship with IPRI, and her refusal to deny she was Robin Hood, in combination with the fact that she had motive and opportunity to extort money from Francis Hearty Withers's beneficiaries, convinced her that Tabby Grammer was indeed Robin Hood.

Many Witherston residents are not convinced.

—Amadahy Henderson, Editor

Fairbanks Has a Robin Hood

The Fairbanks Daily News-Miner received an anonymous letter to the editor yesterday signed "Robin Hood of Alaska" similar to the anonymous letter OnlineWitherston received a week ago.

Robin Hood of Alaska demands that all individuals who profit from drilling for oil in the Arctic National Wildlife Refuge (ANWR) give $5,000 each to The Grizzlies, an environmentalist organization headquartered in Fairbanks. Robin Hood of Alaska threatens to kill the CEOs of the oil companies if politicians in Washington DC do not halt drilling in the ANWR.

The letter ended: "The Grizzlies cannot repair Earth. Only time can repair Earth. But The Grizzlies can impose justice."

The Alaska Bureau of Investigation seeks to charge Robin Hood of Alaska with extortion.

Is Robin Hood of Alaska a copy-cat? Or is Robin Hood of Witherston striking in Alaska now?

—Amadahy Henderson, Editor

LETTERS TO THE EDITOR

To the Editor:

Yesterday I met the charming Pilip Pitka, formerly Timothy Philip Potter of Fairbanks. He gave me an exquisite soapstone carving of a dancing bear. Pilip also sculpts otters, walruses, and seals. Last night my neighbor Jorge Arroyo, who is an artist himself, discovered on the website of the Alaska Native Arts and Crafts Gallery that Pilip Pitka comes from a line of Inuit artists. Pilip Pitka's mother, Akna, grew up in Nome with parents who were prominent artists. Akna's mother, Anjij Pitka, was a painter, and Akna's father, Aput Pitka, was a sculptor. Aput left his mark on Nome's seacoast with a seven-foot-tall polar bear he had carved in white granite outside his home. Akna was a quilter.

I recommend that readers pay an online visit to the gallery to view the art of Anjij and Aput Pitka. Its website address is nativeartsandcrafts.fairbanks.com.

By the way, Pilip Pitka was happy to provide a DNA sample to help solve the mystery of his great-great-grandfather's disappearance in 1866.

I have given it to Chief Arroyo. The results of the DNA comparison will tell us whether it was Patrick Potter whom Harry Withers murdered.

—Charlotte Byrd

CHAPTER TWENTY-FOUR

Saturday, December 28, 2019

After breakfast Jaime took pictures of Annie inside her treehouse and outside her treehouse, pictures of her leaning over a branch pointing to the sign that said I am 300 years old. Don't kill me, and pictures of her standing on the ground beside Big Yellow pointing to the sheet that said Save Potter's Woods.

"I'm emailing you these photos so that you can show your children, Annie. They will be proud of you."

"In a few years, Jaime."

The last patches of snow at the base of Big Yellow were melting by ten o'clock when Jorge arrived.

"I can take pictures of you two together," he said. "Stand here and lean on Big Yellow."

Jorge snapped a couple of pictures. Then he approached the trunk and picked up a glittering rock. "What's this?"

"Hey! That's a gold nugget," Jaime said. "A real gold nugget! Like the ones they have in the Dahlonega Gold Museum."

"Why would it be here?" Jorge asked. "And why didn't you notice it when you and Seq put up the ladder, Annie?"

"Because it wasn't there," Annie said. "This must be the rock that my Christmas Eve stalker threw at the tree."

"So he wasn't planning to climb up and attack you," Jaime said.

"Why would he part with a valuable gold nugget?" Jorge asked.

"Because he wanted to frame me," Annie said. "He probably got the gold nugget from the chest in the schoolhouse. I bet my stalker was Trey."

"He wanted to discredit you, Annie."

"I'll call Mom," Jorge said.

———•———

Jaime and Jorge helped Annie dismantle her tree house in Big Yellow.

Chief Bracker picked up the fire station's ladder and took away the wood planks. "I can use these planks to make a treehouse for my kids," he said as he departed.

"Let's look at the burned schoolhouse before we leave the woods," Annie said.

The three of them trudged through the soggy blackened soil to the schoolyard.

"It's hard to believe that a week ago all this was green brush, Annie. Where will the does give birth to their fawns?" Jaime asked.

"By May there will be new bushes. And baby pine trees. The fire pops open the pine cones and releases the seeds. So in May the does will get their privacy."

"I'll write about forest fires sometime," Jorge said.

To their surprise, Sequoyah emerged from the basement to greet them.

"I was paying my respects to Tabby," Seq said. "I miss her."

"I miss her too, Seq," Jaime said.

"But you really miss her, Seq, don't you?"

"I do, Annie. So I came here to see what she saw in her last minutes of life. It's a way for me to walk in her moccasins. And I found something. I'll show you."

Annie, Jaime, and Jorge followed Seq down the steps. At the base of the stairway, under the last step, Seq slid open a hidden, very shallow drawer. It contained a rusty hunting knife.

"I didn't touch it. I think it has traces of dried blood on it."

"And it might have fingerprints," Annie said.

"But what would the prints tell us if we can't get a print from Harry Withers?" Jaime asked.

"Maybe his prints are on some of the tools."

"Good idea, Seq," Annie said. "If there are prints on the tools, they are probably his. His wife would not have used pliers or saws."

Jaime took a picture of the knife in the drawer. "I'm emailing this photo to Mom, and to Detective Hicks. I'm telling them where we found it."

"Copy Officer Pete," Seq said. "He could dust the knife for prints."

"Righto."

———

Detective John Hicks had done his research by the time Mev got to her office. It was eight thirty.

"Pilip Pitka, using a Fairbanks driver's license, rented a 2018 black Honda CRV at the Atlanta airport at one o'clock on the morning of December twenty-sixth and returned it at eight fifteen last night," John said. "The rental agency emailed me this photo of his driver's license." The driver's license showed a man with long white hair and a long white beard.

"Yes, that's the Pilip Pitka who visited us," Mev said. "It's interesting that he paid for two nights at the Witherston Inn but stayed only one night."

"I have more information, Chief. On Christmas day Pilip Pitka booked a Juneau-Atlanta round trip, leaving Juneau that afternoon and arriving in Atlanta at midnight, and then leaving Atlanta at eleven o'clock last night and arriving in Juneau at four in the morning today, Juneau time, just a half-hour ago. Pilip Pitka never intended to spend Friday night in Witherston."

"Fine work, John! Now can you get me just a little more information? Can you find out whether a man named Oki Yukon is a passenger on a Juneau-Nome flight today? He may be in the air now."

"Coming right up, Chief! You mean Oki Yukon the artist?"

"Yes. The dancing bear you and Patty brought my family from Fairbanks, which was signed by Oki Yukon, is almost identical to a bear Pilip Pitka claimed he carved. He gave it to Annie Jerden."

Mev explained.

"So Timothy Potter is Pilip Pitka who is Oki Yukon," John said.

"Who may be Robin Hood," Mev said.

Ding. Ding. Mev and John got Jaime's email at the same time.

"Hot dang," John exclaimed. "A long-blade hunting knife. With a deer-antler handle. This is an antique."

"I'll send Pete out to the schoolhouse to collect prints. I need you to do something else this afternoon."

"Sure, Chief."

"Would you be able to trace Robin Hood's anonymous email threat of last Friday to the IP address of the sender's tablet?"

"I don't know. Probably not. But I have a better idea. I could compare Robin Hood's anonymous email threat with Pilip Pitka's anonymous email invitation to Lottie. If they were sent through the same app, we've got our man. And we can arrest him."

"You, Detective Hicks, may be taking another trip to Alaska!" Mev said. "Would you like Jorge to go with you this time?"

"Sure."

"Now is the time for me to do fake interviews with the arsonist suspects and for you to listen to footsteps. Trey Bennington is first."

"Trust me, Chief. We'll catch our arsonist."

———•◦•———

"Thank you for coming in, Mr. Bennington."

"It's been a while, Chief Arroyo. I've stayed out of trouble. And you may call me Trey."

"May I record our conversation?"

"Sure. I've done nothing wrong."

"Thank you. I'm talking to a few people who have accused the late Tabby Grammer of being Robin Hood. You are one of her accusers. Why do you think that Mrs. Grammer was the extortionist?"

"I just thought she could have been. I didn't say I had proof."

"You wrote in a letter to the editor, which probably two thousand people read, that Mrs. Grammer and Sequoyah Waters might have concocted the extortion scheme together. Were you just speculating in front of two thousand readers? Words have consequences, you must realize."

"I was just speculating. I won't do it again."

"Were you trying to discredit Mrs. Grammer's campaign to save Potter's Woods? Your father has a stake in the retirement community, I hear."

"No, of course not."

"Why do you dislike Sequoyah Waters? Do you resent his attention to Annie Jerden?"

"I don't dislike him. I was just wondering whether he was involved in the extortion. He's Cherokee, or part Cherokee, you know."

"You were dining with your parents at Bear Lodge Monday night. Where did you go afterwards?"

"Home. I went home."

"Where were you the night of December twenty-fourth?"

"At my parents' house for dinner. Then in my apartment."

"And finally, what size boot do you wear?"

"Size nine. Why?"

"Just curious. Thank you, Mr. Bennington. You may leave now."

———◆———

Mev welcomed Doug Hanley next.

"Mr. Hanley, you wrote a letter to OnlineWitherston about Tabby Grammer. Were you trying to discredit her campaign to save Potter's Woods? Your father has invested in Thomas Tankard's retirement community."

"No. That's not why I wrote the letter."

"Why did you?"

"Tabby Grammer tried to impose her Gaia-centrism on all of Witherston. She tried to make us think like her. She was not aggressive in her personality, but she was aggressive in her writing. She pushed egalitarianism. She was a socialist. She threatened our way of life."

"Where were you on Monday night, Mr. Hanley?"

"I was at home in my apartment."

"Where were you on Tuesday night?"

"Christmas Eve? I had dinner with my parents. Then I went home."

"I notice you usually wear boots. What size, may I ask?

"Size nine and a half."

"Thank you, Mr. Hanley. You may go now."

———◆———

"Sit down, Mr. Farthy."

"Why are you interviewing me, Chief Arroyo? You already know that Robin Hood was Tabby Grammer."

"I have read the transcript of your interview with Agent Danzer. I have a question for you. How did you get the names of Tabby Grammer's charities?"

"What? Oh, you mean the Indigenous Peoples Reparations Initiative and those other Indian charities?"

"Yes. That's exactly what I mean. Where did you get the list?"

"Tabby Grammer showed me the list. I visited her Saturday afternoon to offer her a stake in the Potter's Woods Retirement Community, and I asked her about her interest in Native American paraphernalia. She showed me the list."

"Did she accept your offer?"

"No."

"So in anger you wrote the letter to the editor accusing her of being Robin Hood?"

"Not in anger. I was convinced that she was. I remain convinced."

"Where were you Monday night, Mr. Farthy? Where did you go after dinner at Bear Lodge?"

"Oh, I guess you know I had dinner with the Benningtons."

"Yes. What time did you leave Bear Lodge?"

"About nine o'clock."

"And did you leave the parking lot then?

"Yes."

"Where did you go after you left the parking lot?"

"I went home. Is there a problem?"

"Thank you, Mr. Farthy. That will be all."

———•—•———

Mev's interview with Trevor Bennington was short.

"Thank you for coming, Mr. Bennington. I have been interviewing many people today, including your son."

"What's the problem, Chief Arroyo?"

"I would like to know what you observed the evening of December twenty-third, when you and your wife and son were dining at Bear Lodge. What time did you leave?"

"I observed nothing unusual. That is, other than Tabby Grammer's date with Sequoyah Waters. We finished dinner about nine o'clock."

"And did you leave Bear Lodge then?"

"Of course."

"Did you go directly home"

"Yes."

"Did you see the Meltons at Bear Lodge?"

"Yes. But they left before we did."

"How long have you used a cane, Mr. Bennington?"

"Must be four or five years. Ever since I broke my ankle. It didn't heal properly."

"Thank you, Mr. Bennington. That will be all."

———•—•———

Mᴇᴠ's ɪɴᴛᴇʀᴠɪᴇᴡ ᴡɪᴛʜ Mɪᴛᴄʜ Mᴇʟᴛᴏɴ ᴡᴀs ᴇᴠᴇɴ sʜᴏʀᴛᴇʀ.

"I appreciate your coming in today, Mr. Melton. I have just a few questions."

"I'm happy to help out, if I can."

"You and your wife dined at Bear Lodge Monday night?"

"We eat at Bear Lodge every Monday night. We like the Monday wine special."

"Did you notice anything unusual?"

"I noticed that Tabby Grammer was eating with Sequoyah Waters, and that she had dressed up."

"What time did you all leave?"

"We left about eight thirty."

"Did you go directly home?"

"Yes."

"One last question. Do you always wear athletic shoes?"

"I'm afraid so. I have painful bunions."

"Thank you, Mr. Melton. That will be all."

———•———

"Tʜᴀɴᴋs ғᴏʀ ᴄᴏᴍɪɴɢ ɪɴ, ᴛᴏᴅᴀʏ, Mʀ. Wᴀᴛᴇʀs.

"You can call me Seq, Chief Arroyo. Everybody does."

"I have just one question for you. Where did you go after dining with Tabby Grammer Monday night?"

"I went home. To Tayanita Village."

"Did anybody see you?

"I don't know. But I have proof that I wasn't with Tabby."

Seq showed Mev on his phone the thank-you note he had emailed Tabby after he had returned home.

"This note is very personal," Seq said, "but it shows you that I didn't follow Tabby to the schoolhouse."

"Thanks, Seq. That will be all. I am sorry for you that Tabby died. You must have had a wonderful evening together."

"We did, Chief Arroyo."

"I see you're wearing running shoes today. Do you ever wear boots?"

"No. I wear high-topped running shoes in the winter. And moccasins when there's no snow on the ground. The Cherokees say: 'Walk lightly on the earth and live in balance and harmony.'"

"I see why you and Tabby got along. Thanks, Seq, for the interview and the wisdom."

———•———

A minute after Seq's departure, Detective Hicks entered Mev's office.

"We've got our killer," he said. "It's Sam Farthy."

"You could tell from the digital recordings?"

"Easily. Actually, I could tell with my own ears. Seq treads lightly, as I said he would. Trey and Doug walk with the carelessness of healthy young men. Trevor Bennington uses a cane. Mitch Melton wears rubber-soled shoes that don't make much noise. Farthy walks like the overweight, overconfident sixty-year-old that he is. Farthy set the fire in the schoolhouse."

"But we have to prove that Farthy knew Tabby was there," Mev said. "Her phone shows she called out to him, but it doesn't prove that he heard her."

"Farthy could have seen her cross the highway. He left Bear Lodge about the same time Seq and Mrs. Grammer did."

"Maybe he didn't intend to kill Tabby. Not at first. Maybe he simply wanted to see what she was doing at the schoolhouse."

"And then he found the kerosene and decided on the spot to set the building on fire?"

"He was a smoker. He would have had matches or a lighter on him."

"Maybe he did want to kill her. But Chief, why would he want to kill her?"

"She had threatened to accuse him of attempted blackmail."

"What will you do now?"

"I'll ask the district attorney whether digital recordings of footsteps will convince a jury. If she says yes, we'll arrest him for arson on Monday."

———•———

ON THE BASIS OF THE DISCOVERY OF THE GOLD NUGGET by Big Yellow, Mev got a warrant to search Trey's apartment. She sent Pete.

An hour later Pete reported that he'd found a plastic trash bag with approximately nine pounds of small gold nuggets, which he had confiscated, and a pair of muddy boots, size nine.

"Arrest him," Mev said.

CHAPTER TWENTY-FIVE

Saturday, December 28, 2019

A fter a hearty lunch, Pilip Pitka opened a can of beer and settled down in front of the fire to read the news of Witherston.

He liked the name "Tayanita Forest." And he liked Annie Jerden's suggestion that Tankard build his development on Lydia Gray's land. Good thinking.

He read the third item.

So it was Sam Farthy who identified Tabby Grammer as Robin Hood. The skunk. He killed her for money, to get her out of the way of the lucrative Retirement Community project. And he convicted her in public opinion. He must have known she was not Robin Hood.

How could Farthy have discovered that Tabby Grammer was associated with Kallik? She wouldn't have told him.

Tabby Grammer couldn't defend herself because she was dead. That was convenient for Robin Hood, and for Farthy. Could Farthy have killed her? If so, he deserved to die.

What was Sequoyah Waters thinking now? Seq might be ready to kill Farthy. Farthy had something on him. Farthy could be blackmailing him.

Using his anonymity app, Pil wrote Sequoyah an email.

THANK YOU
Hello, Sequoyah.

Thank you for showing me Potter's Woods and Tayanita Village on Friday. I enjoyed talking with you.

I saw in OnlineWitherston that Sam Farthy identified Tabby Grammer as Robin Hood. He's a skunk. Do you think he murdered Tabby? He should pay for his crimes.

I wish you well.

Yours truly,

Pilip Pitka

How would Sequoyah react? Pil wouldn't find out, since Sequoyah couldn't email him back. But maybe he'd find out in the news.

Then Pilip read Lottie's letter to the editor. Uh, oh. Why had he told her he sent his little sculptures to a Fairbanks gallery? Why had he taken some to Witherston as gifts in the first place? Would Chief Arroyo compare them with Oki Yukon's sculptures? Would they find Oki Yukon?

Maybe it was time to move to Utqiagvik.

— • —

Neel got a phone call from the lab in Atlanta in late afternoon.

"We have a match, Neel, or at least a partial match. The DNA you sent me and the DNA I extracted from the bones you uncovered show a familial relationship."

Neel conveyed the news to Lottie.

— • —

DING. DING. MEV GOT TWO EMAILS FROM OFFICER PETE. Pete had taken thumb prints off the hunting knife, the handsaw, and the rifle. They matched.

Pete had compared the sole prints of Trey Bennington's boots with the sole prints he had photographed in the snow. They matched.

———•·———

JAIME BROUGHT ANNIE HOME FOR DINNER. MEV SAU-tééd Rainbow trout. Paco poured the Argentine Malbec that Lottie had contributed to the meal.

Over dinner, with everybody's help, Mev laid out the results of the police investigation. "We've had two mysteries to solve," she said, "the identity of Robin Hood and the death of Tabby Grammer. How are they connected?"

"Three mysteries, Mom," Jorge said. "The third is the mystery of the Withers School skeleton. Who was the dead man, and who killed him?"

"Four mysteries," Jaime said. "The fourth is the mystery of Annie's stalker."

"The fourth mystery is solved," Mev said. "Officer Pete found a bag of gold nuggets in Trey Bennington's apartment and a pair of size-nine muddy boots. The print on the soles of the boots matches the prints that Pete photographed. Trey Bennington stole the gold nuggets from the chest, took them home in a garbage bag, and brought one to Big Yellow to frame Annie. I believe he intended to leave it quietly at the base of the tree, but Annie blew her siren and scared him away. So he hurled it at the tree."

"The mysteries are all connected with Potter's Woods," Paco said.

"And the visit from Timothy Potter," Jorge said.

"Who happens to be related to the bones you all uncovered at the Withers School," Mev said. Mev told them of the DNA analysis.

"So Timothy Potter and dem bones are kin," Jorge said. "Dem bones belonged to Patrick Potter, who must have been murdered by Harry Withers."

"Who was probably murdered," Mev said. "Probably. We don't have proof."

"Probably murdered," Jorge repeated. "Could be that Patrick Potter wandered into the schoolhouse basement and up and died right there under the stairs. And Harry Withers threw some dirt over the body, and then forgot to report the death to authorities."

"Annie and Seq and I found the murder weapon, we think," Jaime said.

"It was a hunting knife," Annie said.

Annie reported Seq's discovery of the hidden drawer on the bottom step. Jaime showed his photos.

"The knife seems to have traces of dried blood," Jaime said. "And maybe fingerprints."

"The knife does have a thumbprint," Mev said. "Officer Pete found a thumbprint and matched it with thumbprints on the saw and the rifle."

"No kidding! Well, I'll be dumficked!" Jorge said. "Who done it? Harry done it."

"If Harry didn't kill Patrick Potter, Harry hid the body and the knife," Lottie said.

"Maybe Harry's wife Gertrude killed him," Jorge said. "And Harry hid the body and the knife."

"Or Patrick's wife Eula killed him. She was Harry's sister," Jaime said. "And Harry hid the body and the knife."

Jorge and Jaime got the giggles.

"What's significant is that Patrick Potter's death turned the Potters into enemies of the Withers," Lottie said.

"Do you all think that Timothy Potter knows this family history?" Mev asked.

"Yes," Lottie said.

"If so, he may want revenge on the Withers," Jorge said.

"Or he may want revenge on the Withers beneficiaries," Paco said.

"He may be Robin Hood," Annie volunteered. "Seq didn't like him. Seq said that Pilip was too snoopy."

"How can we prove that the artist Pilip Pitka is the extortionist Robin Hood?"

Ping.

"Excuse me, folks," Mev said. "It's Saturday night and I seem still to be working. I've got a text from Pete."

> *Hello Chief.*
>
> *Farthy is dead.*
>
> *Fell down steps to his basement.*
>
> *Medical examiner says he was drunk.*
>
> *Do you believe that? I don't.*
>
> *Let's talk.*
>
> *Pete*

"You all will not believe this. Sam Farthy is dead! So he won't be arrested for Tabby's murder."

"Farthy murdered Tabby?"

Mev reported the results of the test she and Detective Hicks had conducted that morning. "We identified Tabby's killer by his footsteps. Her killer was Farthy."

"How did Farthy die?" Lottie asked.

"Apparently he was inebriated and fell down the steps to his basement," Mev said. "So the death looks accidental."

"Is Farthy an alcoholic?" Lottie asked. "I never heard that."

"He deserved to die," Jaime said. "He turned on Tabby Grammer."

"And he threatened to tell Seq's secret," Annie said. "He was a blackmailer."

"Maybe someone else decided he deserved to die," Jorge said. "Who could that be?"

"Me," Annie said. "He set Potter's Woods on fire."

"And possibly Seq," Jorge said. "Seq fell in love with Tabby."

"Seq must be sad," Annie said.

"Farthy might not have set the fire if he hadn't stumbled across the containers of kerosene, and then he might not have killed Tabby," Jaime said.

"Right. Farthy committed second-degree murder, the unpremeditated but intentional killing of a human being. I believe that Sam Farthy set the schoolhouse on fire knowing that Tabby was in the basement," Mev said.

"And the flames spread to the dry leaves outside, and then to the dry brush of the woods," Annie said.

"Could Farthy have committed suicide to avoid going to prison?"

"Nobody commits suicide by throwing himself down the stairs, Jaime."

"Could Farthy have been murdered?" Annie asked. "Maybe Robin Hood murdered him because he didn't pay his five thousand dollars."

"But if Robin Hood murdered him, then Pilip Pitka is not Robin Hood," Mev said. "Pilip Pitka turned in his rental car at the Atlanta airport at nine last night. He was booked on an eleven o'clock flight to Juneau."

Mev got a call from Detective John Hicks. She took it in the kitchen.

"Hey, Chief. Robin Hood and Pilip Pitka used the same anonymity app, which means they are the same person."

"Terrific work, John. Now we have enough to arrest Pitka."

"Does this mean that I can go to Alaska?"

"Yes. And you'll need a companion because you'll be bringing Pitka back to Georgia to stand trial. Jorge will be delighted to go."

"Great!"

"After I get a warrant for Pitka's arrest, I'll contact Nome police, who will pick him up. The Nome police will hand Pitka off to you and Jorge. Your job is to escort him back to Witherston to stand trial."

"We can fly from Atlanta to Fairbanks tomorrow, and then on Monday we can charter a small plane to Nome."

"Make your reservations and email Jorge."

"Will do. I have other news, Chief. Pil Pitka disappeared after landing in Juneau. He didn't board another flight. And neither did Oki Yukon."

"He couldn't drive anywhere from Juneau in the winter, so he must have had somebody fly him to Nome."

"Jorge and I can look into that."

"I assume you know that Sam Farthy is dead. He apparently fell down the stairs."

"Pete told me. I suspect Farthy was pushed. Tell Jorge to be ready at five in the morning. I'll pick him up."

Mev reported the news to his family.

"Thanks, Mom! I'll email Eska that Detective Hicks and I will be in Fairbanks Sunday night."

"Time for me to depart," Lottie said. "Goodnight, everybody."

"Time for me to figure out what to tell Amadahy," Mev said. "She's waiting for a story."

— • —

Jorge sent an email.

> *I AM COMING TO FAIRBANKS*
> *Dear Ms. Tiktak,*
>   *Detective Hicks and I will be in Fairbanks tomorrow night and Monday morning.*
>   *What time does your gallery open?*
>   *I would like to meet you and pick up my painting.*
>   *Thank you.*
>   *Best wishes,*
>   *Jorge*

Eska replied.

> *Re: I AM COMING TO FAIRBANKS*
> *Dear Jorge,*
>   *I look forward to meeting you. My gallery opens at 11:00 on Monday.*
>   *I will have your painting wrapped and ready to go.*
>   *I will give you a tour of my gallery, which is like a museum of Alaska Native art.*
>   *Respectfully yours,*
>   *Eska*

CHAPTER TWENTY-SIX

Sunday, December 29, 2019

OnlineWitherston.com

NEWS

Sam Farthy Is Dead

Sam Farthy, at 2280 East Creek Circle, died yesterday from an accident in his home.

Mr. Farthy's sister and brother-in-law, Don and Wanda Jarvis from Atlanta, arrived at 7:30 for their family holiday dinner to find the front door unlocked and Farthy dead at the foot of the stairs to the basement.

The medical examiner determined that Mr. Farthy had broken his neck in his fall. He pronounced the death an accident most likely caused by excessive alcohol consumption. He estimated time of death to be between 4:00 and 5:00 in the afternoon.

An empty bottle of scotch was found in the kitchen.

Mr. Farthy was the owner of Farthy Construction Company. He was a major investor in the Potter's Woods Retirement Community.

—Amadahy Henderson, Editor

Sam Farthy Is Identified as Arsonist

According to Police Chief Mev Arroyo, Sam Farthy intentionally started the Potter's Woods fire that burned the Withers School and killed Tabby Grammer, who was in the basement.

Tabby Grammer's phone told a story of murder. It recorded her inventory of the contents of the basement, her awareness that somebody was inside the building, her calling out to the person, and her screams as the building caught fire. It also recorded the footsteps of the arsonist, who apparently ignored her screams.

Detective John Hicks compared the phone's recording of the footsteps with the recording of Sam Farthy's footsteps when Farthy visited Chief Arroyo's office. The digital representation of the two recordings proved them to be identical.

If Mr. Farthy had not died, he would have been arrested for arson and second-degree murder, Chief Arroyo said.

—Amadahy Henderson, Editor

DNA Proves Schoolhouse Bones Belong to a Potter

The DNA collected from the bones discovered in the Gertrude Withers School basement shows kinship with Timothy Potter, the great-great-grandson of Patrick Potter, who disappeared in 1866.

Timothy Potter, now known as Pilip Pitka, provided a sample of his DNA during his visit to Witherston on Friday.

The 153-year-old mystery of Patrick Potter's disappearance may soon be solved. A thumbprint found on a hunting knife hidden near the bones matches a thumbprint found on a rifle that presumably belonged to Harry Withers.

The knife may have been used by Harry Withers to murder Patrick Potter.

Harry Withers was himself murdered shortly thereafter, possibly as a revenge killing by Patrick's son Mark.

—Amadahy Henderson, Editor

TREY BENNINGTON IS ARRESTED FOR BURGLARY

Trey Bennington was arrested late yesterday for burglary.

Bennington confessed to entering the basement of the Gertrude Withers School on Sunday, December 22, prying open the locked chest, and stealing its contents, $1,600 worth of small gold nuggets.

The gold nuggets were found in his apartment in his backpack and in the pockets of his jacket.

When asked if he had had an accomplice, Bennington said that he had acted alone.

—Amadahy Henderson, Editor

WHAT'S UP
BY JORGE ARROYO

I have been researching the art of the Inuit people of Alaska since Detective John Hicks brought my parents this dancing bear carved by an artist named Oki Yukon of Nome. It is signed.

The polar bear is in a rapture, dancing to her heart's delight. Fathom it. In a small piece of soapstone, the artist carved a joyful bear perfectly balanced on one foot. Inuit artists also carve otters, walruses, seals, owls, geese, and other Arctic animals, but they consider the dancing bear the most difficult.

The Inuits believe that all these animals—like all living things, like Earth itself—embody spirit. For the traditional Inuit, spirit is not separate from Earth. Spirit is not above them, not below them. There's no heaven, no hell.

Writer Annie Dillard told this story. An Inuit man asked a priest, "If I did not know about God and sin, would I go to hell?" The priest answered, "No, not if you did not know." The Inuit said, "So why did you tell me?"

NORTH GEORGIA IN HISTORY
BY CHARLOTTE BYRD

Historians base the narratives they create on the evidence they find. They use legal records, obituaries, property deeds, diaries, news accounts, and the like to piece together their stories. They don't get from the documents the whole of what happened. They can't. The whole of what happened disappears into the past. The sounds, the smells, the sights, the words exchanged, the thoughts and feelings and memories of the individuals whose bodies have returned to the ground—all of it disappears.

But we can imagine what happened.

I am a journalist with a lifelong commitment to the truth, but today I shall imagine what happened in Witherston in 1866 between Patrick Potter and Harry Withers.

In April of 1866, after the War Between the States, which Harry had dodged, Harry and Gertrude Withers made plans to build a school for their son and other children on an acre of wooded land that abutted Patrick Potter's lot.

When the judge denied Patrick's claim to the acre, Harry offered to buy Patrick's entire lot. Patrick refused. "Hell, no!" he said. "These are my woods. These are Potter's Woods."

Patrick returned to Dahlonega.

In September Harry Withers opened the Gertrude Withers School for Children.

Three months later, on Saturday, December 15th, Patrick made the twenty-mile trip from Dahlonega to Witherston on horseback to view his property. He spent Monday night at an inn, where he found out that the road to the Gertrude Withers School went right through the undisputed part of his woods.

So the next morning Patrick rode up the hill to the schoolhouse, where he found Harry in the yard skinning a deer. Patrick accused Harry of stealing his land. He threatened to shoot him. Harry was quicker. Harry stabbed Patrick in the heart.

Harry then dragged Patrick's body down the stairs—thud, thud, thud—to the basement, where he dug a shallow grave behind the stairs. He hid the bloody knife in a secret drawer under the bottom step. He took Patrick's horse Glory to his stable to join his three other horses. Harry was a rich man.

Eula reported her husband missing on December 18th, when she had expected him to come home.

On Saturday, December 22nd, Patrick's son Mark traveled from Dahlonega to Witherston in his mule-drawn wagon to search for his father. At the inn Mark learned that his father had gone to the Withers school and not returned. Mark reckoned that his father was gone for good. The next night, under the cover of darkness, Mark visited Harry's stable and recovered Glory. Harry was not around.

Mark returned to town, saw Harry leave Finney's Saloon, and shot the man dead.

Harry's death was not met with sorrow in Witherston.

"Good riddance," the saloonkeeper said.

Mark hitched Glory to his wagon and returned to Dahlonega. Shortly thereafter, he and his wife moved to Savannah.

Harry's descendants inherited and passed down wealth, eventually enormous wealth. Patrick's descendants did not. They inherited and passed down resentment.

— • —

LETTERS TO THE EDITOR

To the Editor:

My friend Trey Bennington has been jailed for stealing gold nuggets from the Gertrude Withers School. I should be jailed too.

I was with Trey Sunday night a week ago. We had a couple of beers at Bear Lodge, got to talking about

Tabby Grammer, and decided to look around where she died. We went into the basement and found the chest. I pried the lock open with my knife. The chest was filled with gold nuggets. Trey put as many nuggets as he could into his backpack and the pockets of his parka. I put the rest of them into my jacket pockets. I would like to return them.

I apologize.

—Doug Hanley

To the Editor:

Robin Hood of Sherwood Forest broke the law to do good. He became a hero for children everywhere.

When Robin Hood of Witherston is captured and sentenced to prison for extortion, should the judge take into consideration the good he did for Native Americans?

—Lottie Byrd

CHAPTER TWENTY-SEVEN

Sunday, December 29, 2019

J aime met Annie for lunch at Bear Lodge. Billy Gardner showed them to a table by the window.

"You look pretty as a peach, Miss Annie," Billy said. "And Jaime, you look happy as a pig in the sun. Is this a special occasion?"

"We're celebrating Annie's success," Jaime said. "If it weren't for Annie and Tabby Grammer, Potter's Woods would soon be logged."

"Miss Annie, you've got gumption. So to honor you both, I'm giving you the best lunch in the house free of charge. I hope you like catfish."

"We do. Thanks, Billy."

"Thanks, Billy."

Billy disappeared into the kitchen.

"Have you been thinking about coming with me to the University of Georgia, Annie?"

"I've been thinking about many things, Jaime. Like what I'm going do with the rest of my life."

"You're going to sing."

"I am."

"Will you sing with me?"

"I will."

"Do you mean you'll come live with me in Athens?"

"I mean I'll come sing with you in Athens, for now. And maybe at the end of the semester, I'll transfer to UGA. And then perhaps I'll move in with you."

"I'll break the news to Jorge that he may be leaving our apartment."

"And I'll break the news to Seq that I may be leaving Witherston."

"I love you, Annie Jerden."

"I love you, Jaime Arroyo."

———•·•———

"Hello, Chief. We have more work to do on the Farthy case."

Officer Pete was panting from his climb up the stairs to Mev's office.

"Sit down, Pete. Take off your jacket. Tell me what's going on."

"Farthy's neighbor, Ms. Jolene Call, said she saw a black pick-up parked in front of Farthy's house about four thirty or so yesterday afternoon. She said it was gone by five. She said she didn't think anything of it till she read about Farthy's death this morning."

"Did she come to your office, or call you?"

"She told Amadahy, who was interviewing Farthy's neighbors for a story. Amadahy told me. I went by to see Ms. Call."

"Can you give me her contact information?"

Pete looked at his notebook. "I'll email it to you. She's Jolene Call, twenty-two ninety East Creek Circle. The neighborhood is fancy. Folks there drive Cadillacs and Lincolns, not black pickups. That's why she noticed."

"Could she tell you what model pickup—new or old, big or small?"

"No. I asked her. She said she was having a martini and glanced out the window. She said she wasn't wearing her glasses. When I went by at noon today, she was halfway through a glass of wine. She lives alone, but with a cat or three."

"So she's an unreliable witness."

"I guess."

———•———

In front of his fire Pil Pitka drank his spiked coffee and read the Witherston news.

Well, well, well. So Farthy had died. And on Saturday, after he, Pil, had boarded the plane to Juneau.

Then Pil read Jorge Arroyo's column.

Oh hell. Why had he taken carvings to Witherston? He'd left traces. He would be found. He would be imprisoned.

He read Lottie Byrd's column. Did Lottie suspect him?

But what could he be accused of doing? He'd written a letter. Yes, it was extortion. Would he be suspected of causing Rhonda's accident? Or Thomas Tankard's death? They were accidents.

He could not be accused of Sam Farthy's death. When Sam Farthy died he was back in Alaska.

What could be proven? Only that Pil Pitka was Oki Yukon. But not even Kallik Kootoo knew that.

It was definitely time to move on, to get a new identity, to live with Toklo in Utqiagvik. Pil called his cousin. Toklo would would fabricate a new identity for him.

Pil packed his clothes and boots, his snowshoes, his carving tools, his paints, and his tablet. He wrapped his grandmother's paintings in his mother's quilt and stuffed them into a crate. He put eight hundred dollars in the inside zipped pocket of his parka.

First thing in the morning he would withdraw nine thousand dollars in cash from his Nome bank account. Then Toklo would fly him to Fairbanks, where he would withdraw another nine thousand from his Fairbanks bank account. By noon he would be at the gallery where he'd sell Eska his grandmother's paintings. He would tell Eska that he was moving to the Aleutian Islands.

Then Toklo would fly him to Utqiagvik, where he would become Yutu Aluki, Toklo Aluki's uncle. He would open a bank account there for Yutu Aluki.

He wrote a note for his landlord and placed it on the kitchen counter: "Here is my last month's rent payment. Keep the deposit. I have gone to the Aleutian Islands."

Before settling down to watch the news, Pil wrote Eska.

MOVING TO ALEUTIAN ISLANDS
Hello, Eska Tiktak.
 I am moving to the Aleutian Islands.
 Tomorrow I would like to sell you five large paintings by Anjij Pitka that I've collected. Would you give me $2,500 for the lot? You could sell them for $900–$1,000 each.
 Toklo and I will bring them to the gallery around noon.
 Best wishes,
 Oki Yukon

Eska wrote back.

Re: MOVING TO ALEUTIAN ISLANDS
Hello, Oki Yukon.
I will be happy to give you a check for $2,500.
Anjij Pitka's art sells well.
By the way, you may meet one of your fans when you arrive.
Eska Tiktak

———•·———

"What do you think of Aunt Lottie's letter to the editor, Detective Hicks?

Jorge and John had changed planes in Seattle and were now on the flight to Fairbanks. Night had fallen.

"What do I think of Lottie's plea for leniency for Robin Hood? I'm on the side of the law, Jorge. And our mission is to arrest Pil Pitka for breaking the law big time. Extortion is a major crime."

"I know. But the letter got me to thinking. Which is worse? Robin Hood's extorting Withers's beneficiaries to transfer their unearned wealth to Native Americans to whom it belongs, which the law doesn't allow? Or white settlers' stealing the Native Americans' land and gold two centuries ago, which the law allowed? You're half Cherokee, Detective Hicks. Don't you think Robin Hood had good intentions?"

"Robin Hood's stated intention was to murder our mayor and at least one other person. He threatened violence."

"Outside of bequests, I bet that every large transfer of land and gold in the history of the world involved violence. Extortion is less violent than war."

"You've got a point, Jorge."

It was well after midnight when Mev got the text she was awaiting.

> Hi, Mom.
> Detective Hicks and I are in the Fairbanks Airport Hotel now. It is 8:45 pm here.
> We've chartered a private plane to take us to Nome tomorrow afternoon.
> But tomorrow morning we will visit the Alaska Native Arts and Crafts Gallery, which is inside the hotel. Eska and I have been texting. The gallery opens at 11:00. I will pick up my painting!
> Jorge

CHAPTER TWENTY-EIGHT

Monday, December 30, 2019

OnlineWitherston.com

NEWS
Was Sam Farthy Pushed?

Sam Farthy's next-door neighbor, Ms. Jolene Call of 2290 East Creek Circle, observed a black pickup parked in front of Sam Farthy's home at approximately 4:30 Saturday afternoon.

Ms. Call said the pickup was gone by 5:00 when she went into her kitchen to refresh her drink.

Since Mr. Farthy died between 4:00 and 5:00 that afternoon, we may assume that the driver of the pickup was at least a witness to Mr. Farthy's fatal fall down the stairs.

Mr. Farthy's sister and brother-in-law, Wanda and Don Jarvis, said that Mr. Farthy seldom drank more than a scotch or two at a time, and that he would not have been drinking three hours before they were to have dinner together. He would have been in the kitchen cooking.

Officer Pete Koslowsky said that the police would investigate the death as a possible homicide.

Anybody with knowledge of the black pickup should contact the police.
  —Amadahy Henderson, Editor

—————•—•—————

NORTH GEORGIA IN HISTORY
By Charlotte Byrd

Dear Readers: For the next week I will devote this column to a marvelous craft of the southern Appalachian mountains: chainsaw carving.

What is chainsaw carving?

According to Nashville writer Rob Simbeck, "Chainsaw carving is the revved-up, sawdust-spitting segment of the art world, a place where the scent of pine and motor oil are as vital as the sculptor's hands and eyes in creating gorgeous works of art."

According to Billy Gardner, "Chainsaw carving is the release of the tree's inner bear."

Driving through north Georgia and western North Carolina we find carved bears, owls, hawks, raccoons, and wolves for sale along the roadside. My favorites are the bears.

More tomorrow!

—————•—•—————

LETTERS TO THE EDITOR

To the Editor:

I live around the corner from Sam Farthy on Azalea Avenue. Since I live alone I pay attention to what's going on in the neighborhood.

I saw a green pickup truck parked in front of Mr. Farthy's house from 4:25 to 4:40. I couldn't tell if it was a late model or not because I don't see well anymore, but I can say for sure it did not belong in our neighborhood.

—Pastor Ned Clement

CHAPTER TWENTY-NINE

Monday, December 30, 2019

A t eleven o'clock in the Alaska Native Arts and Crafts Gallery, Detective Hicks introduced Jorge to Eska Tiktak.

"Good morning to both of you," Eska said, giving them each a hug. "What brings you back to Fairbanks, Detective Hicks?"

"We're just passing through this time, Eska. Jorge wanted to see your gallery."

"I didn't realize you were so young, Jorge! Most of our buyers are middle-aged or older."

"I just had my nineteenth birthday, but I've already started acquiring art. I hope that when I'm middle-aged I'll have a good collection."

"Great to see you both. You will like the painting you just bought, Jorge." Eska extracted "Bear Wheel" from a cardboard tube and showed it to him.

"I do like it, Ms. Tiktak!" Jorge said. "I will frame it and send you a picture."

"Call me Eska, Jorge."

Eska showed them a dozen similar paintings by Anjij Pitka, which John liked. John bought one titled "Rabbit Wheel."

"Patty and I will hang 'Rabbit Wheel' in our baby's room. We're having a baby in May."

"Wonderful!" Eska said.

"Wonderful indeed," John said.

"Now let's look at the soapstone carvings," Eska said. "You won't believe the coincidence, but Oki Yukon and his pilot Toklo Aluki are coming in around noon."

Jorge and John looked at each other.

"That is a coincidence," John said. "Why is he coming in?"

"He's moving from Nome to the Aleutian Islands, and he wants to sell me five paintings he's collected. Matter of fact, the paintings are by Anjij Pitka."

"I'd love to see them," Jorge said.

John looked at his phone. "Oh, shucks. I have a text here saying that our pilot is ready to take off. He wants to be in the air by the time the snow comes in. We've got to leave now, Jorge."

"Really?" Jorge said, looking at John.

"Really, Jorge."

"Where are you going?" Eska asked.

"To the Aleutian Islands. And Eska, please don't mention our names to Oki Yukon. Just say that a couple of collectors were here admiring his work."

"Of course, John. I never reveal my clients' names."

"Thanks so much for your hospitality, Eska. My son will see "Rabbit Wheel" from his crib.

"Thanks so much, Eska. I will return," Jorge said.

After hugs, Jorge and John exited the gallery into the lobby of the Fairbanks Airport Hotel.

"Did you really get a text, Detective Hicks?"

"No, but we must avoid Pil Pitka. We can't let him know we're here or he'll flee."

"He's already fleeing."

"Right, and probably not to the Aleutians. Let's sit at the bar and see who enters the gallery. We'll recognize Pil Pitka from Tabby Grammer's memorial service."

John ordered sandwiches and cokes.

"There he is," Jorge whispered. "He's with a younger man who is carrying a large suitcase. That must be Toklo, his pilot."

"Toklo Aluki from Utqiagvik. I'll bet they're going to Utqiagvik. Now keep your hat on your head and your back to the gallery," John said, pulling on a red wool beanie and facing the bar. "And while we're giving them time, can you find a home address for Toklo Aluki?"

"I'm on it!"

A minute later Jorge reported the results of his search. "Toklo Aluki lives at eighty Chukchi Road close to the airport and very near the Chukchi Sea. Should I text Mom that we're going to Utqiagvik?"

"I'll text her and ask her to authorize the Utqiagvik police to bring Pil Pitka in."

Hey, Chief.

Change of plans.

We're following Pil Pitka to Utqiagvik (formerly Barrow, Alaska).

Please send Utqiagvik police an arrest warrant for Pilip Pitka, 80 Chukchi Road.

It is the home of Toklo Aluki, Pitka's cousin.

Ask police to pick up Pitka today after 4:00 on the charge of extortion.

Tell police that they can hand Pitka over to Jorge and me at the police station.

We will report back later.
Jorge says Hello.
John Hicks

Before long Pil Pitka and Toklo Aluki left the gallery and passed right behind John and Jorge.

"They're headed toward the airport," John said.

"Can we follow them?"

"No need. We know where they're going. Let's give them a twenty-minute head start."

———•———

PIL PITKA FIGURED OUT WHO THE COLLECTORS WERE. They were his pursuers. One of them was obviously John Hicks, making his second trip to Alaska. The other one could be Sequoyah Waters, or else one of the police chief's sons. It didn't matter. They had told Eska they were going to the Aleutian Islands. That was because he'd told Lottie he lived in the Aleutian Islands. He'd tricked them then, and he'd trick them again.

Pil and Toklo walked quickly to Toklo's plane.

"When you file your flight plan, Toklo, say that you're going to Amaknak Island in the Aleutians. That will jive with what I've told Eska."

"Will do, Oki. Or should I call you Uncle Yutu?"

"Call me Yutu. And we'll go to Utqiagvik. What's our flying time?"

"Two hours if we can get there before the snow. But don't worry. My new Cessna can fly in bad weather. "

Toklo had a late model Cessna 207, which he had acquired with drug money.

"What happens if you don't follow your flight plan?"

"No problem. I can change it when we're on our way. I've done it before."

"I'm sure you have, Toklo." Pil laughed.

By twelve thirty Toklo and Pil were off the ground.

———•———

"No way they're going to the Aleutians," John said to Jorge, after being told that Toklo Aluki had filed a flight plan to Amaknak Island. "They're going to Utqiagvik, and so are we. If that's not their destination, we'll wait in Utqiagvik for Toklo."

"When did Barrow, Alaska, become Utqiagvik?"

"In 2016 the citizens voted to change the city's name from Barrow to Utqiagvik, which was its original Native name. Let's go. I'm texting our pilot that we'll meet him at the plane at twelve forty-five."

Their pilot introduced himself as Panuk Brownbear from Fairbanks.

"Can you take us to Utqiagvik?" John asked him. "We no longer need to go to Nome."

"Sure," Panuk replied. "I can take you anywhere you like in Alaska and at top speed. My plane is a Beaver. And I'm instrument-rated so I can fly through snow, which is a good thing because we're going to have some."

They did indeed fly through snow. But the skies cleared as they approached Utqiagvik. Panuk pointed to a small plane circling for a landing. "That's a Cessna 207," he said. "Good plane for short landing strips."

"How about giving the Cessna a bit of space," John said to Panuk. "We prefer not be seen."

"You guys chasing somebody?"

"Let's say we're following somebody."

"I'll do some big circles."

"Thanks."

"I know the pilot of that plane," Panuk said. "He's Toklo Aluki. Good pilot. Makes more money than the rest of us bush pilots. Lots more, if you get what I mean."

"Can you wait and take us back to Fairbanks tonight, Panuk?"

"No problem."

———— • ————

PIL PITKA FOLLOWED TOKLO THROUGH THE BLOWING snow into his small modular home. It was two-thirty in the afternoon but as dark as midnight. The ice stung his face.

"Temperature outside is minus eleven," Toklo said, closing the door behind them. "The wind comes off the Chukchi Sea, which is mostly frozen now. Need a little whisky?"

"I do, thank you."

While Toklo lit the wood stove, Pil drank his whisky silently on the worn leather sofa.

"The place should be warm soon, Yutu."

Finally Pil spoke. "Toklo, You're a good man to get me a new identity and to give me a home. Thank you."

"You're kin, man. That's what kinfolk do for each other."

"If the authorities find me, they will arrest you for sheltering me," Pil said.

"No they won't, Yutu. I'm safe. The police chief is my sister's husband's brother. He won't arrest anybody related to him. I do for him, and he does for me. He keeps my secrets."

"And you've got some, Toklo."

"More than you know, Cousin. Now go unpack while I get us some food. The back room is yours. Lock the door behind me."

Through the small window Pil watched Toklo get into his Ford F-150 truck and disappear into the darkness.

Pil took his suitcase into the spare bedroom. He hung his parka in the closet and donned a heavy wool sweater he found there on top of a large safe. He connected his tablet to an outlet. He laid his carving tools, oil paints, and brushes on the dresser. Then he fell asleep under a fox fur blanket on the bed.

Some time later Pil Pitka awoke to loud knocking the door. He opened it.

"Mr. Pitka? I am Chief Amaruk Hanta of the Utqiagvik Police. Do you know why I am here?"

"I do," Pil Pitka said. "May I take my paints?"

———•———

JOHN AND JORGE TOOK CUSTODY OF PIL PITKA AT THE Utqiagvik police station at five thirty.

With Pil in handcuffs, they flew back to Fairbanks, spent the night at the Fairbanks Airport Hotel, and caught an early morning flight to Atlanta.

———•———

WHILE ON THE AIRPLANE PIL WROTE THREE EMAILS.

REGRETS
Dear Lottie:

I regret that I may not see you again. I regret that I chose extortion as the means to undo the consequences of a greater crime. And I regret that I shall be imprisoned for my actions.

However, I do not renounce my motivation: to give America's indigenous people the same opportunities to prosper that the beneficiaries of their conquerors enjoy.

I wish you well, and from my place of incarceration I will continue to read your marvelous column "North Georgia in History."

It was a pleasure meeting you.

Most sincerely,

Pilip

NO HARM INTENDED

Dear Mayor Rather:

Please forgive me for frightening you with my email letter of extortion. I never intended to murder you.

I thank you for your generous contributions to Native American charities over the years.

Most sincerely,

Pilip

NO MORE CARVINGS

Dear Eska:

You know me as Oki Yukon of Nome. I am actually Pilip Pitka, formerly of Fairbanks. I am the grandson of Anjij and Aput Pitka and the son of Akna Pitka.

Because of a crime I committed on behalf of the indigenous peoples of America, I shall be spending some time in prison.

I won't be allowed a knife to carve dancing bears, but I will probably be allowed my paints. So I will paint dancing bears and otters and walruses.

I hope you will continue to represent me as an artist.

I look forward to corresponding with you.
Thank you.
Most sincerely,
Pilip

Then Pil turned to Jorge, in the seat beside him.

"I thank you and your friends for not withdrawing your contributions to IPRI. I promise you that the Indigenous Peoples College will benefit not only its students but also our country."

"Tabby Grammer's essay about reparations persuaded me," Jorge said.

John, sitting on Pil's other side, leaned over. "It persuaded me too, and our friends."

A few minutes later Pil said, "You are fortunate to have friends."

Epilogue

Pilip Pitka was sentenced to ten years for extortion, during which time he taught Native American history to his fellow inmates and wrote a book titled *A Crime in Service of Justice*. It became a *New York Times* Best Seller in 2022.

Trey Bennington was sentenced to a year in prison for burglary. The gold nuggets found in his apartment were valued at sixteen hundred dollars. Douglas Hanley was sentenced to six months.

Sam Farthy's death was ruled an accident.

The Indigenous Peoples College was built in Seattle in 2022. Everett Sail served as the founding president. Wallace Scout served as Dean and professor of computer science. Eska Tiktak became its first professor of Native American art and culture.

About the Author

Photo by Laszlo Soti

Betty Jean Craige retired from the University of Georgia in 2011 as University Professor of Comparative Literature and Director of the Willson Center for Humanities and Arts.

In the course of four decades Betty Jean wrote numerous books of scholarship and non-fiction, among them an intellectual biography titled *Eugene Odum: Ecosystem Ecologist and Environmentalist*, a shorter biography of her beloved bird titled *Conversations with Cosmo: At Home with an African Grey Parrot*, and a recent collection of essays titled *Ruminations on a Parrot Named Cosmo*.

She co-created an award-winning documentary titled *Alvar: His Vision and His Art*, published a book titled *Alvar: Thirty Years of Lithography*, and curated two museum exhibitions of the Spanish artist's work.

She translated the poetry of Antonio Machado, Gabriel Celaya, Manuel Mantero, and Marjorie Agosín.

Death in Potter's Woods is the fifth book in her Witherston Murder Mysteries, which includes *Downstream, Fairfield's Auction, Dam Witherston,* and *Saxxons in Witherston.*

Betty Jean resides in Athens, Georgia.

See: www.bettyjeancraige.org